Praise for
SWAMPED!

"No surprise for a Wells novel, *SWAMPED!* is propelled by crisp, evocative writing, a delicious sense of place, and a tale that will keep you reading and break your hearts, in a good way. Read it now."

—Bryan Gruley, award-winning author of the *Starvation Lake Trilogy*

"An immersive, atmospheric ballad of the Great Atchafalaya, *SWAMPED!* is a mesmerizing tale of love and survival set in the most hazardous of stews—a story that deftly whispers the mysterious beauty in which nature gives and takes away. I happily drowned in this novel."

—J. C. Sasser, author of *Gradle Bird*

Swamped!
by Ken Wells with Hillary Wells
© Copyright 2023 Ken Wells with Hillary Wells

ISBN 978-1-64663-887-1

All rights reserved. No part of this publication may be reproduced,
stored in a retrieval system, or transmitted in any form or by any means—
electronic, mechanical, photocopy, recording, or any other—
except for brief quotations in printed reviews,
without the prior written permission of the author.

This is a work of fiction.
All the characters in this book are fictitious, and any resemblance to actual persons, living or dead, is purely coincidental. The names, incidents, dialogue, and opinions expressed are products of the author's imagination and are not to be construed as real.

Published by

◀ köehlerbooks™

3705 Shore Drive
Virginia Beach, VA 23455

800-435-4811

SWAMPED!

KEN WELLS WITH HILLARY WELLS

VIRGINIA BEACH
CAPE CHARLES

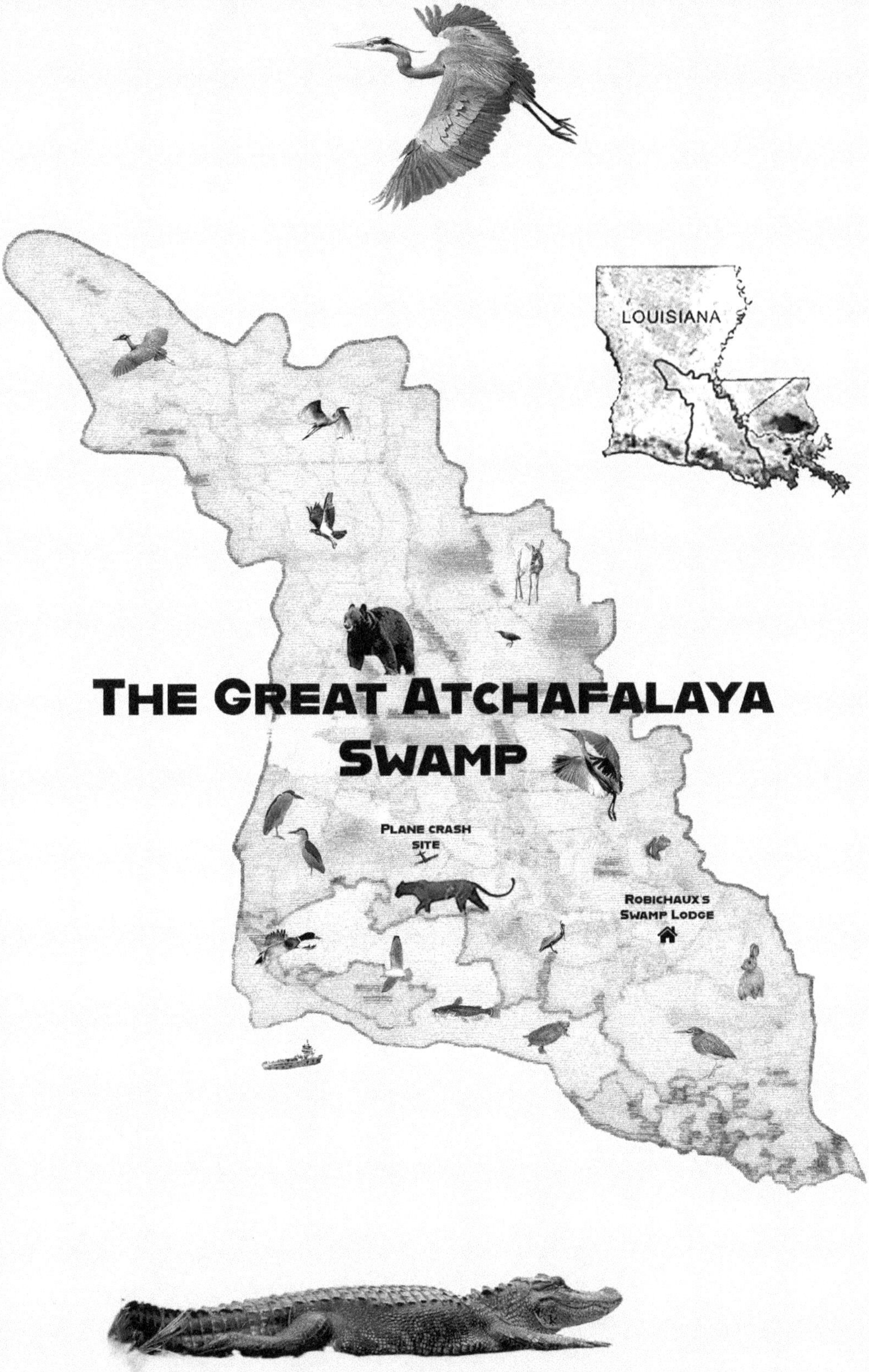

The Great Atchafalaya Swamp

LOUISIANA

Plane crash site

Robichaux's Swamp Lodge

*For Al Delahaye, my much-missed mentor
who steered me on a writer's course.
Rest you, my friend. ~ KW*

*To my parents, Bob and Mandy,
who taught me that not only could
I be anything I wanted to be,
but I could be everything
I wanted to be. ~HW*

This is a work of the imagination. While the Great Atchafalaya Swamp (also known as the Atchafalaya Basin) is a real place, the authors have taken some liberties in descriptions of flora, fauna, geography, and landscapes.

CHAPTER 1

JACK CANE LANDRY stirred awake from a deep and troubling fog, a bright sun warming his face.

Confused at first, he lifted an arm to block the golden orb stabbing at his eyes.

Where am I? he thought. *Is this a dream?*

Glancing to his right brought a shocking sight—and the horror of it cleared his head.

It *was* a nightmare—except the nightmare was real.

Olivia FitzGerald, motionless, eyes closed, sat slumped in the seat next to him, a smear of blood painting her left cheek. A jagged metal object separated them, something speared into the seat back with obvious violence.

Had it veered a few inches to either side, it could have severed limbs. Jack shuddered at the thought.

"Olivia?" he said. "Are you okay? Can you hear me?"

She didn't stir.

Was she alive?

A bolt of panic seared through Jack's fog. *God, the plane really went down. We crashed. We—*

Jack shook his head, trying to clear it.

The glaring sun made it obvious that the sheared-off rear of the aircraft that sheltered them faced east. He stared out at the gaping opening before him. The extended tail section of the Otter float plane sat on an apron of soft marsh, explaining, maybe, why they were alive. The spongy ground had cushioned their fall from the sky.

Across an expanse of dense marsh, Jack could make out the rest of the plane—the cockpit nose down, jabbing into the swamp bottom, wings bent and broken nearby. Debris lay all around.

A memory of terror filled his head—lightning, the violent explosion of thunder, the plane lurching crazily through the blackest clouds Jack had ever seen, Olivia clutching at his arm, screaming, "Oh, God! Oh, God! No, no, no!"

Joe Desmoreaux, the pilot, yelling, "C'mon, c'mon, gimme some speed!" as the plane coughed and sputtered and spun and then plummeted through the storm clouds.

Terrence FitzGerald, Olivia's father in the seat next to Joe, turning back and saying calmly, "It's okay. We'll be fine."

An opening in the clouds as the plane gained speed and tried to right itself, shuddering and rocking, its stall horn blaring. And then, just as suddenly, a shadowy line of trees appearing in the fading, eerie light, and a jarring *bang*, the shock rattling the cabin as the plane broke apart.

Jack could remember the blistering rain on his face; the slap of cool, wet air; the sickening, sideways roller-coaster gyrations as they spun around and hit the ground; objects flying around the cabin as they skidded upright across the marsh; Olivia's shriek; the scream that formed in his own head but that was swallowed by his terror.

A loud thump as they rolled across what might have been a log. And then, for a long while . . . nothing.

Until now.

How could they even be alive?

Cupping his hands to his mouth, Jack called out toward the wreckage of the cockpit. "Joe, are you there? Joe! Mr. FitzGerald, can you hear me? Anybody out there? If you can hear me, say something!"

He held his breath, waiting, but the swamp swallowed the fading echoes of his voice.

Silence.

The storm had clearly blown past, leaving behind a perfect autumn morning. The sky preened blue and calm. Layers of fog lazed in the nearby cypress tops.

A crow cawed in the distance, breaking the silence.

Jack forced himself to move. Unbuckling the three-point harness that had kept him in his seat and no doubt saved his life, he shifted gingerly at first, testing his arms and legs. Nothing seemed broken. A long, shallow gash on his right forearm still oozed blood. Something crowded the vision in his right eye. He reached up, his hand touching a large knot above his eyebrow.

It didn't hurt.

None of it hurt, though it should.

Shock? Jack wondered.

He shook his head. Swiveling in his seat, he looked into the compartment behind him. A pair of dirty work gloves sat atop a stack of life vests. How hadn't they been blown from the wreckage?

Everything else of value unsecured seemed to have been tossed into the void. Jack suddenly realized that their backpacks, which had been at their feet with bottles of water, energy bars, and their iPhones, were gone.

"Damn," he muttered under his breath.

Not that cellphones would work in the cover of the deep swamp. But Jack could see maybe getting a signal if he climbed to the top of a tall cypress tree. No use thinking of that now.

Jack pulled on the work gloves and tackled the jagged piece of metal between him and Olivia, clearly some torn-off part of the fuselage. He grabbed it top and bottom and, with a sawing motion, worked it back and forth until it broke free. He pitched it out of the gaping opening in front of him and heard it bounce, *sprong*, on the spongy ground below.

Tossing the gloves aside, he inched forward, hovering over Olivia. She was pale, almost colorless save for the thin track of dry blood on her left cheek and a bruise on the other.

It had been chilly in the plane. The heavy green sweatshirt she wore made it impossible to tell if she was still breathing. Steeling himself, he reached out to touch her forehead.

"Don't be dead," he whispered. "Please don't be dead."

He flinched as his hand touched her skin.

Warm.

Jack knelt awkwardly in front of Olivia, reaching for her hands. He knew some first aid basics. His town, probably still no more than seventy-five miles from them, was tiny; lots of high schoolers volunteered for the EMT crew.

He'd joined the crew the past two summers in a row. Why hadn't he paid more attention?

Fumbling a little, he felt Olivia's wrist. Her hands were icy but her pulse strong and steady.

He sat back in relief.

Now what? Stay with the plane? Hope someone finds us quickly?

The tail end of the plane was broken open, but it was still shelter. And it would be easier for rescuers to see that from the air than to see two people alone in the swamp. If they waited it out, they could—

Jack lurched backward as the plane suddenly shifted, leaning sharply left and throwing him off balance. He grabbed frantically for the handle on the seat back just in time to keep from being pitched to the marsh below.

They were sinking. He had a brief but terrifying vision of being trapped—swallowed up by a dark, marshy pit of muck and water.

Scrambling back into his seat, he did a quick inventory of the compartment behind him. Bleak. Even the five-gallon jug of emergency water was gone, gashed open by the piece of fuselage that had speared into the seat between them.

Hands shaking, he fought back the panic.

Jack stared at a stack of orange life vests, an idea forming in the back of his head. It wasn't a good idea, but it was all that he had.

Grabbing the life vests, he threw them one by one out of the opening and onto the mucky ground below. Beneath the sixth vest he got lucky—a white, waterproof, zippered nylon bag, about the size of a seat cushion, emblazoned with blocky red lettering.

"EMERGENCY KIT."

There wasn't time to look inside, but he tossed it out as well.

Scrambling back to Olivia, Jack undid the three-point seat harness. His first thought was to try to pick her up and lower her gently to the marsh bed. But, inching closer to the edge of the shattered opening for a look, he saw that the plane was cocked at a strange angle to the ground, probably lodged on a log. Metal shards of the fuselage bristled like knives below them.

There was only one thing to do.

Kneeling before Olivia, he heaved her unmoving body over his left shoulder, grunting with the effort.

Olivia was tall. When they had first met two days ago, it had taken him a minute to realize *how* tall; she bested him by at least a couple of inches. There'd been too many other things for him to notice about Olivia, like the fact that she was gorgeous, or how she had the greenest eyes he'd ever seen.

Jack was five-foot-seven-and-a-half (five-foot-eight to anyone who asked), but he'd dated girls taller than him. It had never been an issue. In fact, he'd hardly even noticed—until he met Olivia. It felt strange to be holding her like this. Breathing in the aroma of her hair, the smell of *her*, feeling her shallow breath as it rose and fell against him.

Reaching out with his left hand to grasp the seat back for balance, Jack rose slowly and inched his way to the edge of the opening, praying the plane wouldn't suddenly shift again. He stared down at the watery patch of marsh ten feet below them, now littered with life jackets.

Olivia was growing heavy in his arms.

Jack was fit. He was on his school's swim team, which he loved, and cross-country, not so much. An odd thought fluttered through Jack's mind. *What would Coach Galjour think?*

Galjour was his hard-assed cross-country coach, and Jack often groused with his teammates about Coach's insistence on a heavy regimen of weightlifting. What did that have to do with running?

Now, it was coming in handy. Jack mentally noted to thank Coach—if he survived.

He tightened his hold on Olivia, pulling her close to his chest. He took a deep breath, and then he jumped.

CHAPTER 2

THWUCK!

Jack hit hard, thankful that the ground was soft.

He pitched forward, ducking his shoulder as he rolled atop then over Olivia. He landed on his back, splattering Olivia with thick, wet mud.

So much for shielding her.

He picked himself up, shivering as a trickle of swamp water ran down the back of his collar. The warm, methane-drenched stench of disturbed marsh filled his nose.

Jack scrambled forward, dropping to his knees in the watery ooze to look Olivia over. Leopard-spot patches of mud covered her face, hair, clothes, and bare legs.

"Jesus," Jack said. "What a mess."

Olivia moaned but didn't open her eyes.

Jack rose, his sneakers sinking deeper into the disgusting ooze. Wiping a spray of mud from his forehead, he glanced around, trying to get his bearings, his mind racing.

What the hell are we supposed to do now?

Olivia was from New York City—the Upper East Side, just off Central Park—as she'd made a point of telling Jack. Her private high school was just blocks from her family's apartment. To Jack, who'd never been to New York—unless you counted the movies—it seemed an entirely different planet from the swamplands that edged Black Bayou, Louisiana.

Olivia wasn't like anyone Jack had ever met. Not that he knew her so well, but some things stood out. She was funny and interesting and, okay, yes, she was hot, but more than that she was . . . confident.

She had a way of carrying herself that made everyone else look like they were trying too hard. Everything about Olivia seemed almost effortless, from the tilt of her chin to her clothes.

Now, though, lying on the ground covered in mud, Olivia looked like a bedraggled swamp creature.

What's she going to think when she wakes up? That is, if she wakes up.

Panic stirred in Jack's chest.

Looking around again, Jack saw there was no obvious way out. The watery patch of muck holding them was what he and the other Cajun-French-speaking locals called *flotant*—basically a large, spongy clump of floating marsh. This one covered maybe a quarter of an acre, having broken off from some fixed stand to drift freely. It had cushioned the crash but also explained why the plane section was starting to sink. The marsh wasn't built to hold such weight for long.

Beyond this floating island was terrain that Jack knew all too well—Louisiana's Great Atchafalaya Swamp. In better times, it was the vast playground where, with family and friends, he hunted, fished, set out crawfish traps, and paddled about for miles and miles for the sheer sake of exploring. The Great Atchafalaya was a mix of ponds, bays, bayous, rivers, and lakes ringed by marshes and swamp decorated with stands of cypress and tupelo gum—a vast hardwood forest jutting from the water. Beautiful to look at but difficult to walk or swim, it was tricky to navigate without a compass or GPS.

It was a place Jack knew reasonably well, though he doubted any one person knew the swamp in its entirety. As a weekend swamp-tour guide, he had memorized the talking points. Stretching 125 miles north and south, and about one hundred miles east and west, the Atchafalaya, at about 1.4 million acres, was the largest contiguous hardwood swamp in North America. Alligators ruled the bayous, marshes, and lowlands; swamp bears, panthers, and bobcats the ridges. Snapping turtles, cottonmouths, and water snakes of all kinds prowled the dark waters shared with giant catfish, alligator gar, and ancient paddlefish. Hordes of mosquitoes invaded the warm-weather nights.

Knowing the list of things that could bite and sting made Jack not even want to go there. On the other hand, if you loved birds, it was paradise. Almost 300 species of indigenous and migratory birds filled its skies and foraged its bayous and wetlands. The Atchafalaya was also a key part of Louisiana's commercial crawfishing industry; locals annually harvested about fifteen million pounds of the crustaceans that were a staple of the Cajun diet and an icon of Cajun culture.

A few large upland ridges laced the interior of this watery wilderness, like giant pieces of a jigsaw puzzle, providing high ground for land-loving critters—but none of these ridges led in or out. People came to the Great Atchafalaya by boat, helicopter, or float plane, or they didn't come at all.

Even in a boat steered by locals, its vastness was a challenge. Still, Jack loved it. He'd thought about quitting school to become a full-time swamp guide, but his parents had quickly quashed that idea.

Now, to be stranded here, under these circumstances . . . no, there was nothing *great* about the Atchafalaya now.

Jack knew where their flight had started and had some idea of where it had ended. He was pretty sure they'd crashed in a corner of the swamp that was as remote and inaccessible as any place in North America—well, maybe outside of Alaska or some of the mountain ranges of the West.

It was Columbus Day weekend, and Joe Desmoreaux had flown the FitzGeralds into a base camp on the swamp's eastern fringe two days earlier. Jack was one of the guides hired for the FitzGerald's four-day tour.

Or at least, that had been the plan.

Oh, God! Could Joe and Olivia's dad actually be dead in the cockpit of the plane? The thought was too horrifying for Jack to process.

It didn't seem possible that Terrence FitzGerald could be dead. Like his daughter, Olivia's father had been . . . impressive. Tall, handsome, articulate. He oozed self-confidence. In his pressed khakis, safari shirt, and ankle-high leather boots, he'd reminded Jack of a swashbuckling general in some old war movie.

Jack stood, scanning the distance again for the other part of the plane. But though he'd been able to spot the cockpit from the higher vantage of the tail section, he couldn't see a thing now; it was as if the swamp had swallowed it up.

Should I leave Olivia and try to check on them?

What if he couldn't handle what he found when he got there? And what if he got stuck and couldn't get back? Olivia would have no chance then.

But maybe the smart thing to do *would* be to leave Olivia behind. He could move much faster by himself, maybe get to a spot where he could send help. Trying to drag her out would only slow him down.

An image came to him—both of them trapped in some Godforsaken marshy bog, him exhausted, Olivia unconscious, night falling, mosquitoes swarming. They might both die.

Jack Cane Landry had just turned seventeen in August. He was not prepared to die. And, anyway, he barely knew Olivia FitzGerald. Did he really owe her his life?

Another flutter of panic. *What the hell am I going to do?* Jack swallowed hard, trying to slow his racing thoughts. And then, an image of his grandfather popped into his head.

Paw-Paw Jack Landry, for whom Jack had been named, had grown up as a fur trapper in the salt marshes down by the Gulf of Mexico, about three hours south. Jack's dad called him Old

School—a man who seemed to belong to another century. He was one of the toughest men Jack had ever known and, as soon as Jack could walk, Paw-Paw had become his swamp mentor. He taught Jack fishing, hunting, and survival skills, but he made it fun and adventurous. Paw-Paw was not formally educated. Like many Cajuns of his generation who had grown up poor, he had dropped out of school by seventh grade to help work his father's traplines and support his parents and numerous siblings. But Jack felt his grandfather knew more about the intricate workings and life cycles of the swamp and its denizens than any college-bred ecologist he had ever met—knowledge gained through experience.

What would he do?

Jack could almost hear the gruff, thickly accented voice of his Cajun grandfather.

"*Git to high ground,*" the voice said. "*Ain't nuttin' but gators and muskrats can sleep happy in de marsh. As for dat pilot and dat girl's daddy, you'll never make it over dere, son. Only Gawd can help 'em now. You got to see to dis girl. You all she's got. And you cain't get caught out here in de open marsh after dark. Only bad tings can happen.*"

Jack rose to his feet and looked around. The section of plane he'd just jumped from was now visibly sinking. It would be gone in an hour, maybe less.

The voice in his head was right. Nightfall brought danger as well as mosquito hordes. If the temperatures dropped after sunset, they could die of exposure. Gators preferred to feed at night. So did prowling water moccasins.

Jack shook his head, trying to force himself to think. He needed a plan. But he could only feel himself shrinking in the vastness of the swamp surrounding him. He had never felt so alone.

But I'm not alone, he reminded himself. As soon as his father realized Jack was missing, he would come searching for him. His dad wouldn't give up, no matter how long it took. And Paw-Paw, old and slow as he was, would come with him. His mom and younger brothers, if they didn't come searching, would be praying for him. In the meantime, he just had to survive.

Jack glanced over his shoulder. The territory behind was most likely a lake or bay. Ahead lay a cattail marsh fronting a grove of cypresses.

Walking out through the cattail marsh trying to carry or drag Olivia simply wouldn't work. It would be like walking through a jungle set on quicksand.

"I'll swim us out—just until we find high ground," he muttered, as if saying the words aloud would somehow make it easier to do. They just had to get off this *flotant* island and into water deep enough to float them.

Those orange life jackets could be the ticket. Jack went to work, using their straps and snaps to tie the jackets into a makeshift raft. With some difficulty, lifting, tugging, and pulling, he positioned Olivia in the center of it. He placed one jacket in a collar around her neck to make sure her head stayed above water. Then, he put one on himself, cinching it tightly around his chest.

Grabbing the emergency kit, he rifled quickly through it. He pulled out the first useful thing—a length of sturdy yellow nylon rope, maybe a dozen feet long.

A tow rope!

Using a lifejacket strap, he tied the kit to the raft as well. He'd have plenty of time to examine the contents when—*if*—he was high and dry.

Glancing forward, he took a deep breath and plunged ahead.

CHAPTER 3

JACK HAD WALKED plenty of marsh, having duck hunted often enough with his dad, brothers, and Paw-Paw. But *flotant* was a different matter. Every step was a trial. Soon he was mired up to his knees, then up to his waist.

Trying to swim was like trying to kick his way through warm, honeyed oatmeal. Well, except for the stench. Mud, rotting marsh, methane gas.

Still, he had no choice but to plunge forward, battling for inches, not feet, all the time pulling Olivia behind him, battling, flailing, crying out in anger and frustration as the muck fought his progress.

Stopping, starting. Stopping, starting.

Had he ever sweated so much in his life? Had he ever felt so heavy, so wet and dirty, or unself-assured?

What if this is a mistake? What if I can't save Olivia?

But then another voice pushed its way into his head—Coach Galjour. The guy weighed 170 pounds at most, but he could bench press 240. At forty-five years old, he still turned in sub-eight-minute miles over a five-kilometer course.

Jack could hear Coach now, laughing his ass off at the thought of him surrendering. *"C'mon, Landry, suck it up! Don't be a candy-ass."*

Jack plunged on.

An hour, maybe two, later, he finally found himself at the edge of the *flotant* island. He fell forward, beyond exhaustion, into a cove of deep, tea-dark water.

Jack was a strong swimmer, in fact, a distance swimmer on his school's team. But right now, his life jacket was the only thing keeping him afloat.

He raised his feet and turned onto his back, trying not to waste energy, waiting for his breathing and heartbeat to slow to normal.

He stared up at the cloudless sky. High overhead, a line of white ibises winged slowly past his vision in a perfect V.

Jack was a big fan of birds. He'd made a study of them. He knew the names and nesting and feeding habits of pretty much every bird that inhabited this swamp.

But right now, the passing flock only reminded him of how lost they were.

Jack righted himself and recovered the tow rope, tugging on it until the makeshift raft holding Olivia floated as well. It rode higher than he thought it would, keeping Olivia's head above water.

Flipping onto his back, he managed to pull off his mud-soaked Nikes. Tying the laces together, he hung them off the raft as well. Jack would need them if—*when*—they reached a ridge.

God, he was thirsty. Theoretically, he could drink swamp water, but should he?

"Not yet," he told himself.

The water here was too still. It smelled of muck, and water bugs swam everywhere. It smelled *germy*. If he waited until they got to an open part of this lake or bay, where the water deepened, it would be fresher.

Of course, even then, drinking it could still make him sick. Diarrhea, vomiting, cramps, fever. But it wasn't like he had a choice.

His hunger gnawed at him as well, but there was no time to think about eating. Besides, there was nothing to eat.

Jack grabbed the tow rope and looped it through the shoulder of his life jacket, tying it off with a quick release knot his grandfather had taught him called the bank robber's hitch. Steeling himself, he began to kick his way forward, threading through the cypresses that stood in three to four feet of water toward what looked like a clearing in the distance.

At least the water was still warm; October in South Louisiana was usually the best time of the year, no longer sticky and hot, but not wet and wintry yet. A month later, they might have been battling hypothermia. Beneath her soaking sweatshirt, Olivia FitzGerald was in shorts and a T-shirt.

But warm October weather meant the gators were still around—they'd already seen a few this trip—plus alligator snapping turtles that could grow as big as wheelbarrows in these parts.

Jack was a seasoned gator hunter. He and Paw-Paw Landry took one or two a season, typically six- to eight-footers, selling the hides and meat for good money. Sometimes they kept an alligator tail. After Paw-Paw diced the meat into cubes, Jack's mom would fry it up in a spicy batter into what she called gator bites—delicious, in Jack's opinion. But hunting gators was undertaken from the safety of a boat, backed up by the barrel of a .22 caliber rifle loaded with lethal hollow-point bullets.

He would definitely have to be on the lookout. You didn't want to corner a gator by accident. Last year, hunters had taken a fourteen-foot monster from this very swamp. A gator that big could swallow you in two gulps.

At least alligator snapping turtles weren't aggressive. Unless you accidentally stepped on one as it prowled the mucky bottom.

In which case, it could bite off your foot.

Jack didn't even want to think about snakes. Water moccasins, also known as cottonmouths, *could* be aggressive. The bite of a big one, even this late in the season when they'd exhausted much of their venom, could easily kill a person unable to get quick treatment. Besides water moccasins, copperheads and cane brake rattlers roamed the ridges. Both were equally deadly.

Jack swallowed. He wasn't particularly afraid of snakes. He'd even kept king snakes and ribbon snakes for pets. But cottonmouths were something else. Most snakes, even the copperheads and rattlers, ran from people. But cottonmouths slithered *toward you*, curious and dangerous.

Jack shook his head, trying to push the thought of snakes out of his mind. He began to thread his way slowly through the watery cypress forest before him, Olivia in tow. Swimming slowly ahead with no certain destination gave him too much time to think.

They never should have taken off with that front approaching, carrying a line of thunderstorms. But Joe Desmoreaux thought they'd beat the front to their next destination. It was only forty-five minutes away, and Olivia's father wanted to stay on schedule.

Jack pushed forward through the neck-deep water, frog kicking, dodging logs and water lilies, trying to piece together what had happened before everything unraveled. Had the Otter started to cough and sputter before they entered the dark clouds as Joe slowed the plane for landing? Jack honestly couldn't remember.

Maybe I should have warned them about flying into the stormfront.

But to Joe, Jack was just a kid. The older pilot would've laughed at him.

Jack could hear him now. *"Relax, podnah, I got this. I've flown this plane through a doggone hurricane."*

Jack kicked harder through the water.

Surely Terrence FitzGerald couldn't *really* be dead in the mangled wreckage of that plane? Olivia's father hadn't just been vacationing. The quick bio that Jeff Robichaux had passed out to his crew had said he was both a philanthropist and a conservationist; part of the reason he was even in Louisiana was to see what he could do to help the stricken coast in the wake of Hurricane Katrina. It just didn't seem right.

And what about Joe? He was a local, and a nice guy, even if he did tell too many bad Cajun jokes. He had a large family, including a daughter Jack's age.

He and Olivia had survived, which got Jack thinking that maybe Joe and her dad had, too. Either way, there was nothing he could do about Mr. FitzGerald and Joe right now.

Jack swam and swam until his muscles ached past exhaustion and his fingers grew wrinkled beyond recognition. The pain that he hadn't felt when he came to in the plane had finally emerged. The gash on his forearm burned like a slow fire; the knot above his eye throbbed. Swelling began to obstruct his vision.

The clearing he had seen earlier was, in fact, the edge of a lake or bay—a vast stretch of water, judging by the line of cypresses Jack could see ringing the opposite shore. This lake or bay was miles wide. Trying to swim across it would be dangerous with still no guarantee of finding high ground. He had no choice but to stick to his course on this side of the bay and hope to find even a speck of dry land.

He'd been fooled twice by rafts of water hyacinths. The floating green lilies looked like grassy banks until he slogged his way toward them. Up close, he realized they were just large floating mats—dead ends.

Each mistake left him more exhausted.

He was on the verge of tears out of raw frustration when suddenly, in the far, far distance came the unmistakable throb of an outboard motor.

A commercial fisherman running crawfish traps? Sportsmen out for bass or catfish?

Jack frantically scanned the horizon, searching for the boat, but there was nothing but open water and the far-distant tree line. Still, he yelled—screamed—in the direction of the sound.

He screamed until he was breathless and his throat raw. When he stopped, he heard only the slow fade of the motor and the deepening silence of the swamp.

All the screaming did nothing to rouse the unconscious Olivia FitzGerald.

Jack was too exhausted to even swear. *But if there's one boat,* he thought, beginning to wearily kick again, *there could be others.*

CHAPTER 4

JACK FLOPPED ONTO his back and arm-paddled away from the shore toward a deeper part of the lake.

He couldn't ignore his thirst any longer.

Maybe fifty yards out, he slipped from his life jacket and tied it to the raft. Taking a deep breath, he pinched his nose, keeping his eyes open, and sank toward the bottom, a way of gauging the quality of the water.

It took maybe ten seconds before his feet touched soft muck. The water was definitely clearer here than under the cover of the swamp. After surfacing, he cupped water and drank deeply from the lake.

Bad, but not horrible.

Years ago, Paw-Paw had broken down in his beat-up skiff in this very swamp in the heat of summer. He'd been stranded for two days and was forced to drink swamp water. Jack remembered what he'd said. *"How could somethin' dat tastes dis bad taste so good, ehn?"*

It made more sense to Jack now. Desperate times make sense of desperate measures. If he became horribly sick, well, pick your poison. There was no pleasant way to die.

He kicked back to the raft to check on Olivia, noting the slow rise and fall of her breathing. She looked oddly peaceful.

Grabbing the raft's tow rope, Jack began swimming his way back toward the tree line, searching anxiously for high ground. Warm as the water was, he was beginning to feel chilled. He needed to get into the sun.

Ten minutes later, his head snapped up at the sight of a narrow, watery trail leading inward through the cypresses.

Several things could have made it—gators, maybe, but more

likely nutria. The South American rodent had been transplanted to South Louisiana in the 1950s by people hoping to give trappers another animal to harvest. It had worked too well. The beaver-sized nutria was now a pest, overrunning the swamps and marshes after chasing out the native muskrat.

It didn't matter *what* had made the trail, as long as it led to high ground.

Jack followed it warily, one eye out for gators, as it curved through the cypress forest. The canopy soon thickened. The trail narrowed, the water grew shallower, the bottom mucky and slippery, the going more difficult.

Cypress knees—the roots of cypresses that grow up out of the water, allowing the trees to breathe—poked up along the trail's edge, forming an eerie version of a picket fence. Twice, Jack had to stop and pull Olivia's raft through a blockade of them. It was exhausting work.

The day had grown warmer. He was just thinking about removing his damp, long-sleeved shirt when the low-volume buzzing of gnats in his ear made him stiffen.

"No!" he cried out as the buzzing grew louder.

On windless days, gnats out here could be more vicious than mosquitoes. As if on cue, they began to swarm his face. He looked back toward Olivia. A cloud of gnats hovered over her as well. Jack had only one choice—keep moving.

A thick green blanket of duckweed covered the water, making it nearly impossible to spot any dangerous reptiles that might be lurking beneath. Frogs seemed to spook from around every bend and tree as Jack forged ahead, half wading, half swimming through the narrow trail.

Jack was as jumpy as the frogs. If the trail was a dead end, they were screwed. He had no strength left to claw his way back out to the lake. And anyway, the gnats would eat them alive.

It was at that moment the snake appeared, side-winding its way from behind a cypress right into Jack's path.

Jack stopped breathing. The snake paused for a moment, and then waggled straight toward him.

There was too much duck weed; Jack couldn't be sure of its identity. But it was definitely big, dark, and round . . . like a cottonmouth.

The only other possibility for a snake this size was the beautiful but unpredictable diamondback water snake. It wasn't poisonous like the cottonmouth, but it wasn't exactly harmless, either. Jack had once tried to catch one and learned the hard way that a diamondback would bite you like a bad-tempered dog if you messed with it. He still had the scar on his forearm to prove it.

Jack looked around, searching for a fallen branch, or a stick, or anything he might be able to use to help ward off the snake. But there was nothing.

Jack froze.

Snakes hunted on motion. He was waist-deep in water. His only chance was to stand perfectly still and hope the snake wouldn't notice him. It quickly wound its way within arm's distance.

Icy fear trickled down Jack's back. The V-shaped head of the viper was unmistakable—a cottonmouth. A monster one.

Gnats buzzed louder in his ear. Clouds of them swirled above his head. He felt them landing on his cheeks, his forehead, ears, and eyelids. They were crawling and buzzing down the back of his shirt collar, attacking his neck. They bit ferociously, each bite stinging more than the last.

But to move invited death.

The moccasin slithered right at Jack, its tongue tasting the air. Its coal-black nose brushed against his shirt, the snake pausing a moment. Jack felt another jolt of raw fear.

The viper began to wind around him as if Jack were a tree stump in its way, and then headed directly for Olivia.

The itching, stinging agony of the gnat bites grew suddenly unbearable. But a jolt through his brain gave him clarity; he couldn't risk the snake reaching Olivia.

Jack moved in an involuntary twitch, snatching the cottonmouth by its tail and flinging it away with a frantic, desperate lassoing motion. He watched as if in slow motion as the snake rose from the water, twisting its body back toward him as it did.

Jack could feel the viper's rage. He could see its gaping white mouth and milky fangs.

Jack's grip gave way, and he saw the snake sailing through in the air, but too close to him, as if it were boomeranging back.

He recoiled in horror, throwing his hands up to shield his face, a yell scraping his throat as the moccasin helicoptered just above his head, fangs shimmering in the sunlight.

And then suddenly, it was gone, sailing out of his vision, and then a dull *clunk,* followed by a splash.

Jack tried to steady himself, his heart thudding. He looked toward the sound. It took a minute to realize that the commotion at the base of a small nearby cypress was the snake swimming in slow, erratic circles.

Jack had managed to slam it into the tree trunk, breaking its neck or back. Despite the horror of the moment, he couldn't help feeling a wave of sympathy for the snake. He hadn't come looking for trouble.

As his adrenaline ebbed, he suddenly realized that he was still being devoured by gnats.

"Ow, stop it! Bastards!" Jack yelled, swatting ferociously with his hands as he tried to shoo the swarm. He bent, violently sweeping away the duck weed and splashing water on his face, ears, and neck to try to calm the stinging bites. It didn't help; he was being eaten alive.

Just as he was starting to panic, Paw-Paw's voice once again silenced the screams in his head. *"Hey, now 'member what I showed you? Do what dem Choctaws did long ago."*

Jack immediately stooped and reached down to the water's mucky bottom, coming up with two handfuls of sticky, stinky mud.

He began plastering it on every exposed inch of skin, fighting back a sudden wave of nausea from the stench, until he was as sure as he could be that he'd completely covered every exposed surface. Long, long ago, Native Americans had showed the Cajuns this technique for surviving insect hordes if they were ever stranded away from shelter.

He sloshed back to Olivia; the sight horrified him. Feasting gnats swarmed her face and exposed legs in a seething fog. He frantically tried to swat them away. Olivia's cheeks were already bright red and beginning to swell.

"Oh, God. Please don't be allergic," he said under his breath.

Jack stooped again, hauling up more muck and frantically smearing Olivia with it. He tried his best not to clog her nostrils, covering every inch of exposed skin, including her long, pale legs.

Thank God for her sweatshirt.

Grabbing the tow line, he lurched forward, determined to make land even though fatigue burned like a raw fire in his bones. He moved cautiously past the cottonmouth, whose death circles had slowed. Jack could see it more clearly now. It was five feet long if it was an inch, and round as a softball at the middle. *A bite from that thing . . .* he couldn't even think about it.

In a while, the water grew shallower. The bottom seemed firmer. A breeze flared enough to fan away the gnats. And the solid bottom meant he could move faster.

The landscape began to shift, and finally, around a bend, he saw it—land!

A ridge. High ground. *Land!*

Jack plunged ahead, pausing in the deeper water just before the ridge to duck under and scrub the mud from his face, eyes, and hair. At last, his feet touched bottom on the other side. He stood, catching his breath as he looked around.

A towering cypress stood maybe fifty yards ashore, rising above a thin layer of late morning fog. A thicket of smaller, moss-draped oaks stood behind the larger tree, creating a sort of oval-shaped clearing.

What appeared to be a large log sat just in front of the cypress, practically begging for someone to sit on it.

Jack knew a good camping spot when he saw one.

He turned, gathering the tow rope in his hand, and pulled Olivia toward him. He stooped down to feel her forehead.

Warm? It was hard to tell through the plaster of mud that had begun to dry on her like a cast.

He'd need to figure out how he was somehow going to scrub the mud off of her. Their clothes needed washing, too. After that, they'd have to find a way to get dry.

His feet digging into the muck below, Jack waded ashore, towing the raft as far as he could. Then, looking around, he took stock.

The cypress meant shade, at least. The Spanish moss from the oaks could work as cushioning against the hard ground, and as a substitute for toilet paper, if it came to it.

The oaks were good for another reason, too—acorn season. They'd be bitter but edible unless he could figure out a way to boil them, in which case they would taste slightly less bitter, which isn't to say, good.

Maybe we won't starve, after all . . . at least not right away.

A brake of palmettos clustered to one side of the oaks. With their broad, dense fronds, the palm-like shrubs could be fashioned into some kind of lean-to against the weather, assuming Jack could harvest them. Best of all, they signaled high ground; palmettos only grew on ridges.

Shade, moss, acorns, palmettos . . . good but not enough.

He needed to open the emergency kit. What he found in it could determine whether they lived or died.

He looked down at Olivia for a long moment, trying to work up his energy. Kneeling, he removed the soggy life jacket from around her neck. Gathering her in his arms, he stood, carrying her toward the cypress.

The mud could wait.

Halfway there, Jack froze, suddenly realizing they weren't alone.

Oh, God!

What he'd thought was a log was actually an alligator, an eight-footer at least, basking in a bright patch of sunlight at the foot of the tall cypress tree. Most people didn't realize that, on land, a gator for a short distance could outrun a horse. Jack knew.

As Olivia grew heavier and heavier in his arms, Jack began to back away toward the water, peering desperately around as he moved.

He needed a weapon. A stick, a branch, a stump . . . anything that might fend off a charging alligator.

Jack's thoughts raced back to the moment he'd met Olivia FitzGerald and the dizzy anticipation he'd felt realizing he would be spending a few days with someone so exotic, so different . . . so . . . arresting.

Now?

Olivia was unconscious and looking like some half-dead, mud-caked swamp creature, and Jack had a brute of an alligator to confront.

He could imagine Paw-Paw saying, *"Son, dis is one helluva mess."*

CHAPTER 5

EIGHTEEN HOURS EARLIER...

"Hello, you must be Jack Landry. I'm Terrence FitzGerald. Pleased to finally meet you."

Jack, standing on the open front porch of Jeff Robichaux's Atchafalaya Swamp Lodge, looked up. Climbing the cypress steps that led up to the stilted cabin, FitzGerald smiled broadly as he held out his hand to shake Jack's.

His grip was firm. FitzGerald was a tall, intelligent-looking man with bright blue eyes and a shock of salt and pepper hair.

"I've read all about you," FitzGerald said. "Jeff sent me a link to the piece you wrote that got you your job here. You submitted it as a letter to the editor, but they gave you space for an Op-Ed, right?"

Jack blinked.

Terrence FitzGerald knows about my article?

"Yes, sir," he said aloud.

"Loved the title, 'Save the Cajun Glades.' And I liked your analogy to the Florida Everglades, about how the Louisiana wetlands are an ecosystem worthy of national-park status, too. Had you visited the Everglades before?"

Jack tried to process this. Terrence FitzGerald had actually *read* his article.

"Uh, no, sir," he said. "We don't get to travel much. But based on the research I did, the similarities seemed obvious."

FitzGerald nodded. "I sent your piece to a good friend who runs the research biology team in Everglades National Park. He said your observations were spot on, including the political ones. Down there, conservationists are trying to save the park from land developers and sugar cane barons trying to drain it. Here, I gather it's the oil companies?"

"Pretty much," Jack said, the conversation still feeling slightly surreal. "It's complicated. Remember that big oil spill in the Gulf of Mexico last year? Well, the 'fail-safe' gadget that was supposed to prevent a blowout failed. And then, the equipment that the oil company promised would be on hand to contain a spill was nowhere to be found. It took days instead of hours to respond, and by then, the damage had been done. It was a completely avoidable disaster. One of the local lakes that got really slimed is an ecologically important fish and shrimp hatchery. A lot of our commercial fishermen, and especially shrimpers, depend on it to make a living. They were devasted. Look, I drive a car and appreciate air-conditioning. I'm not, like, some anti-oil crazy person. And a lot of my friends' dads work on the rigs offshore. Oil's a big deal for our economy down here."

Jack shook his head, finding himself getting worked up. "Still, oil companies that behave recklessly and lie to the public need to be called into account and made to pay for their BS. They have no right to screw up our wetlands."

FitzGerald lifted an eyebrow. "Which is why you chained a six-foot alligator to your school's flagpole in protest?"

Jack shuffled his feet, forming a slightly embarrassed smile. "Oh. Uh, yeah. You heard about that, too, huh? How?"

FitzGerald smiled. "I have my sources. How did that go over, by the way? I loved your sign, 'Alligators not Oilygators.'"

Jack returned the grin. "Not so great. I got suspended for two days. But, to set the record straight, it was only a five-footer, and I'd taped its mouth shut. I didn't actually want it biting anyone."

"I see. Probably a good compromise."

FitzGerald glanced over his shoulder at the long, elevated boardwalk that threaded through a stand of cypress before ending at Robichaux's dock. The stretch of water before them was known as Lost Lake, one of the Great Atchafalaya's most scenic areas.

"Now where's my daughter, anyway?" FitzGerald asked, changing the subject. "Did Jeff tell you she was coming with me? Olivia? She's about your age, I think."

"Yes, sir. Mr. Robichaux briefed me . . . well, all of us."

The entire swamp-tour crew had received fact sheets on FitzGerald, along with a non-disclosure agreement that banned them from talking about any of the information included. According to the sheet, FitzGerald had gone to Harvard, graduated in both literature and law, and then taken a detour to study marine biology at some fancy institute on the West Coast. He'd sailed solo across the Atlantic, traveled widely in Africa, and had once organized an expedition to the more remote regions of the Amazon. He'd practiced law for a while but now made his money financing plays on Broadway. He gave lots of money to conservation organizations and causes.

The only mention of Olivia in the paperwork was that she was a senior at a private school in Manhattan. She played lacrosse and didn't eat red meat.

"I hope you like her," FitzGerald said. "Oh, and by the way, she speaks French. She did an immersion course last summer in France. I understand you speak French, too, your entire family, in fact. If I remember correctly from Jeff Robichaux, your Landry family descends from French-Canadian exiles who have been in coastal Louisiana for, what, six generations? They were originally known as Acadians, right?"

"Right," said Jack. "Cajuns, for short. And actually, the Landrys have been in Louisiana for seven generations. The French we speak is basically an antique version, more like the French that was spoken in rural France back in the 1600s and 1700s than the refined Parisian French your daughter's studied. I suppose you could compare it to hillbilly English. French Canadians who've been down here visiting understand it fairly well. People from Paris, not so much."

Jack shrugged and smiled. "But we're quite proud for having

kept it alive for so long even though fewer and fewer people speak Cajun French these days."

"Interesting," said FitzGerald. "Anyway, while we wait, do you know why I've come on this trip? Other than to see those white alligators Jeff promised me?"

Robichaux's fact sheet had been nothing if not informative. "Yes, sir. You're checking on recovery efforts since Hurricane Katrina last year."

FitzGerald nodded. "Exactly. And what about your family?" he asked. "You were spared a direct hit, right?"

"We got some wind and rain, but nothing like what happened in New Orleans and the fishing communities south and east of there. My dad's older brother had an oyster-sacking operation at a little place called Delacroix Island, and they were wiped out. Their house and store were on ten-foot stilts, but they got sixteen feet of water from the surge. When they came back from evacuating, the store was gone. They never found a single board. They found the house in the marsh . . . a mile away. It was broken in two."

"In *two*?"

"Yes, sir. Even Paw-Paw Landry, my grandfather, had never seen anything like it. And he stood through Hurricane Betsy in '65 and helped out after Camille wiped out part of the Mississippi coast in '69."

"And what's your uncle's family doing now?" FitzGerald asked.

Jack shrugged. "Rebuilding. That's what people down here do. Like my uncle says, you can't be an oyster buyer and live way up in Baton Rouge."

FitzGerald gave a thoughtful nod. "Do you think I might be able to meet your uncle while I'm here?"

"I'll call him," Jack said. "I'm sure he'd be honored. I'd go at suppertime if I were you. My aunt's seafood gumbo is awesome."

FitzGerald smiled. "In the van coming in from New Orleans, we stopped at a tiny roadside place . . . Hebert's Café, maybe? The driver insisted I have a crawfish dish served over rice *a-too*, something or other."

"*Étouffée*. It's basically a stew."

"Yes! Delicious. Amazing, in fact. Sadly, I couldn't talk Olivia into trying it. She had a salad."

At that moment, Jack heard voices. Joe Desmoreaux, the float plane pilot, was leading the way up the boardwalk, carrying bags and laughing loudly with a girl who obviously had to be Olivia FitzGerald.

Tall and willowy, her jet-black hair was pulled into a long ponytail. Even from this distance, Jack couldn't help staring. There was something about her that made it impossible to look away.

"So, what was that bug we saw scooting across the surface by the dock?" Olivia asked. "I don't think I've ever seen one that big. Well, outside of Africa and the Amazon."

"No idea," Desmoreaux said. "I can tell you the name of every duck that flies around down here 'cause I shoot 'em and put 'em in my gumbo pot. But I don't pay much mind to bugs 'cept when I swat 'em."

Desmoreaux looked up, catching sight of Jack. "Ah, there you are. *Comment ça vas*, podnah? Maybe you know. You pretty much live in the swamp. You the expert."

"Hey, Mr. Desmoreaux," Jack said, tearing his eyes away from Olivia. "What exactly did you see?"

Desmoreaux, one of two regular pilots for Robichaux's Swamp Excursions, held out his thumb and forefinger a couple of inches apart. "A big ass . . . uh . . . I mean, a big ole thing, 'bout yay long. Giant pincers. Nasty lookin."

"*Un gros cisseaux*," Jack said, using the Cajun term for the bug. "Or big scissors. Also known as the Giant Water Bug. It can grow up to, like, four or five inches long. Stalks minnows, little frogs, even people. We call 'em toe biters.'"

"Well, there you go," said Desmoreaux.

"Gross," Olivia said. "So much for swimming."

Her father laughed. "I think there are bigger things than water bugs to worry about in the swim holes of the Great Atchafalaya Swamp," he said. "Though maybe young Mr. Landry here isn't fazed."

Jack smiled awkwardly. "Well, true, I learned to swim in a lake not that far from here but, uh, it's what you grow up with. Nobody here thinks anything of it. I mean, we do have to watch for gators and snakes but, uh, I can see that an outsider might, uh . . ."

He trailed off, tongue-tied.

FitzGerald rescued him. "Jack, meet my daughter, Olivia. Olivia, this is Jack Landry. He'll be helping guide us this weekend."

Jack nodded.

"Hey," Olivia said, giving a perfunctory wave.

For a fleeting, wild moment, Jack wondered if he should greet her in French, then decided, *Duh, don't.*

"Hello," Jack replied. "Welcome to the Swampland."

She ignored him, turning to her father. "Is it okay if I go inside? You know how I am about small planes."

"Of course, sweetheart. Jack can show you to your room if you want to lie down."

"I'm fine with a couch," Olivia said.

"It's no problem," Jack said, kicking himself for sounding too eager. "Let me grab those bags, Joe."

Jack headed down the stairs, past Olivia. Up close, her eyes were the greenest he'd ever seen. He took the bags from Joe—two backpacks and two expensive-looking leather cases—and said, "Follow me."

Jeff Robichaux liked to call his place a "camp." It added to the sense of mystique and adventure he liked to cultivate, but it was really a large, four-bedroom cypress house built on fifteen-foot-high stilts above the swamp. It had walls of windows and skylights everywhere, as well as a broad deck on three sides that was perfect for dining and bird-watching in fair weather.

The view wasn't cheap; Robichaux charged $500 a night per person, though it did include meals and alcohol.

Jack's family's modest white clapboard farmhouse sat on stilts as well, and he loved the view of the banks of Black Bayou from their screened-in back porch.

But now, standing in Robichaux's swamp lodge, it paled in comparison.

After a short walk, Jack started to put the bags down so that he could open the screened front door, but Olivia pushed ahead of him. "Don't bother, I got it," she said, stepping into the wide, sunlit hall.

Like the rest of the house, the hall was designed to impress. An antique *pirogue*, the Cajun equivalent of a canoe, hung overhead, and the glossy pine walls held impressive taxidermy: a giant catfish, a huge snapping turtle, a bobcat, a mink, a bear head, deer heads, and an entire string of ducks frozen in flight.

"Ah, the Hall of Dead Animals," said Olivia. "Why does it feel like they're staring at me?"

Jack, who'd always found the hall mesmerizing, had never noticed the animals' stares.

"It is a little weird, I guess," he replied. "They're well done, though. Mr. Robichaux sent everything away to some place in Texas. Believe me, I've seen a lot of bad taxidermy."

Olivia looked at him. "Have you? Well, when I was little, my dad used to take me to the Museum of Natural History. We live pretty much across Central Park from it. There are these dioramas in the African exhibit—stuffed lions, gazelles, wart hogs, stuff like that—with these amazing painted backdrops. I'd pretended to like them because my father liked them, but I don't know," she said, shrugging. "I prefer my animals alive."

"Me, too," Jack said. "Well, except in my duck gumbo."

"Duck?" Olivia raised an eyebrow. "Seriously?"

"Duck and *andouille* sausage," Jack told her, grinning. "My mom's secret recipe. Way better than chicken and sausage."

"If you say so," Olivia replied.

"It would be worth trying at least once. The flavors are amazing. But I heard you passed on the *étouffée* at lunch for rabbit food."

Olivia raised the other eyebrow. "Rabbit food?"

"Uh, you know," said Jack, stammering. "Salad."

He was beginning to regret saying anything. "I mean, that's what my grandfather calls it. I just thought, you know, maybe you'd want to try some Cajun French cooking while you were down here in Cajun country. Because of how you studied in France and all . . . you know . . ."

Jack trailed off, breaking into an involuntary grin that gave away his growing embarrassment.

"So, wait. You know what I had for lunch?" Olivia asked. "And that I speak French?"

Oh, crap.

"Uh . . . yeah?" Jack stammered. "But it's not like I asked about you or anything. Your dad told me. We were just, I dunno, talking about, uh, stuff."

Olivia looked at him intently, her wide, green eyes impossible to read. She let him dangle for a while, then finally spoke. "For your information, I ate salad in France, too. So don't take it personally, okay?"

Jack gave an awkward nod. "Sure. I mean, no. Or . . . yeah."

Then she surprised him, breaking into a huge grin. "Relax, Swamp Boy. I know something about you, too. I've read your bio."

"My bio?" Jack repeated. "I didn't know I'd written one."

"You didn't. Jeff Robichaux did. My dad likes that kind of thing. 'The FitzGeralds must *always* be prepared,'" she quoted, rolling her eyes. "Knowledge is power, or whatever. Has he given you your quiz yet?"

"Who, Mr. Robichaux?"

"My father," Olivia said. "He's going to ask you, like, a thousand questions before this weekend is over. Literally. So get ready. Let me guess, he's already asked you about your famous editorial, right?"

Jack nodded. "Yeah, he did."

"And told you he loved it?"

"I guess so."

"Well, I read it. It was okay. You're a good writer. But I thought it was a little . . . uh, how can I put it . . . hmm . . . emotional."

"Emotional?" Jack stammered. "Well, it's about trying to save our way of life down here so, I uh . . ."

Olivia smiled. "It's okay, Jack. That's my opinion. My dad thought it was 'pitch perfect.' And Terrence FitzGerald doesn't call anything perfect, ever. Well, except me."

With that, she threw back her head and laughed.

Damn. Even her sarcastic laugh is charming.

Jack found himself unsure of what to say, a condition he hated. Jack was usually not tongue-tied, even in front of beautiful girls.

"You know what?" Olivia said, obviously changing the subject. "I *am* feeling a little out of it. I wasn't kidding about small planes. Would you mind showing me to my room?"

"Oh, yeah. No problem. You've got the best view of the swamp."

"Whatever's fine," Olivia said. "Thanks."

Jack led the way through the light-drenched living room, past an open kitchen, down a hall filled with yet more skylights. At the end of that hall, they came to a broad, planked door. Jack turned the antique brass handle and stepped inside.

Olivia strode past him.

Like the rest of the lodge, the bedroom was large, airy, and bright. A king-sized bed dominated the room, its headrest carved from antique cypress to look like the trunk of a tree.

"The blue backpack and the smaller leather bag are mine."

"Okay," Jack said. "The bathroom's through the door there."

"Good to know. See you later."

She was obviously ready for him to leave.

Still, Jack hesitated.

"So . . . you know the schedule?"

She nodded. "Maybe. There's, like, canoeing or something this afternoon?"

"Yeah. We're taking the pirogues out. They're these little boats like the one up on the wall. There should be a ton of gators, maybe even a white one. By the way, this is the only place in the world where they exist. We may see some bald eagles, too. And there's this grove of virgin cypress that we can paddle to if it doesn't get too late. They're awesome. Not so many of the old growth trees left out here."

Olivia seemed unimpressed. "If you say so," she said. "Knock on my door in forty-five minutes, okay? I might be napping."

He almost replied, *"Yes, ma'am"* but bit his tongue.

Instead, he said, "Sure. And I'm glad you're here. I mean, *we*. We're glad you're here. At camp. You're . . . going to like it. Really."

Oh, God. Idiot!

Olivia FitzGerald looked at him, her green eyes giving nothing away.

"We'll see," she said.

Forty-five minutes later on the dot, Jack knocked on Olivia's door.

A long minute went by, and then he heard footsteps.

Olivia appeared, her hair piled up high, sleep on her face, dressed only in a black T-shirt with the word *Paris* scrawled across it in large pink letters. It was basically a mini skirt.

Olivia FitzGerald would look good in a flour sack, which is what Paw-Paw's generation often used to make dresses, shirts, and pants. That's how poor they were.

"Already?" she asked, yawning. "Fine. I'll be right out."

She turned to go without closing the door, pulling her hair down as she went.

Jack stood frozen in the doorway, watching.

So beautiful. So well made. So self-assured. And I'm so stupid.

What was he *doing*? Gawking at her like this.

It was only when he heard the front door open and Joe Desmoreaux call out for him that Jack forced himself to move. He spun around and walked quickly down the hall, nodding hello to Joe as he passed.

Jesus, he told himself firmly as he walked away. *Get a grip.*

CHAPTER 6

TO JACK, NOW backing away from the massive alligator, Olivia unconscious in his arms, that afternoon back at the camp felt like forever ago.

The pirogue tour had gone well; Terrence FitzGerald, at least, had clearly enjoyed it. He'd been excited about the birds. They'd spotted the rare white alligators and, true to Olivia's predication, FitzGerald had asked Jack a million questions about both himself and the swamp.

Jack found himself surprisingly prepared.

Olivia, in cut-off jean shorts, a T-shirt, and a baseball cap pulled low over her eyes, had spent most of the afternoon looking bored and distracted. She'd barely spoken during the trip. Jack had pretended not to notice, doubling down on his conversation with her father instead.

But Olivia's disinterest had clearly bugged him. Well, deflated him. Which he knew was a stupid way to feel. *What did I expect? And why should I care?*

If someone had told him after that trip that Jack would soon have Olivia in his arms, he'd have laughed at them.

But here they were.

And, whatever else he knew, one thing was certain—he couldn't let the alligator have this ridge. There was no way in hell he could get back into the lake and start swimming again.

He needed a weapon, but first, a dry place to put Olivia down.

He looked left and right and finally spotted, near the edge of the deep pool they'd come out of, a tall tree stump that looked like it might have been hit by lightning long ago. He moved slowly toward it, keeping a wary eye on the gator.

At the stump, he knelt, lowering Olivia as gently as he could to the ground. Resting her back against the stump, he propped her up in a sitting position.

"Okay," he murmured aloud, realizing even as he said the words that she probably couldn't hear him. "Wait here. I'll be back . . . hopefully."

Jack had handled live gators before, but nothing close to this size. This thing was a monster. Goliath or not, Jack knew all gators have a weakness. If you could grab an alligator, even the biggest one that ever lived, by the snout before it tried to bite you, you could hold its jaws shut with one hand. A little kid could do it.

Their chomping power was something else altogether. A gator could strike with the speed of a snake and the bite force of a shark. If it considered you food, it probably wouldn't attempt to eat you on the spot. Instead, it would drag you off the bank in its steel-trap jaws and drown you, then swim down to some burrow where it would bury you until you became good and ripe.

The American alligator wasn't generally aggressive, nothing like its first cousin, the crocodile. And alligators spooked by hunting pressure grew extremely wary of people. But Jack and Olivia were stranded in the middle of the swamp, a place so remote that its alligators might never have been hunted. Or seen humans.

Which would explain why this gator hadn't spooked and run off at the sight of them.

He glanced back at the reptile, wondering if it was sleeping. On warm days like this, gators often lazed in a patch of sun like housecats, storing up the sun for energy. Most cold-blooded reptiles did.

Jack needed to wake it up. But how, exactly?

He'd required two things: something heavy to throw at the gator and a stick or branch that was both long enough and strong enough to fend off an attack.

There were no fallen branches nearby, but Jack thought he might have seen a knife in his hasty rummaging through the emergency kit.

He walked slowly to the life-jacket raft, which he'd pulled up on the bank, and unzipped the kit.

Jackpot! A decent sized Swiss Army knife with an array of tools. There was also a pen-sized flashlight and, best of all, a butane lighter.

A knife, a light, and a way to make fire. Jack almost couldn't believe his luck. Whatever else he found would be what the Cajuns called *lagniappe*—a bonus.

He removed the knife and opened it, running his right index finger over the three-inch blade. *Sharp enough.*

Farther up the bank past Olivia, Jack spied something else that buoyed him—a dense brake of bamboo cane growing at the water's edge. A lot of swamp bamboo was scraggly, but these stalks were giant, at least fifteen feet high. Probably because they'd never been harvested.

Jack went to work hacking at the base of the largest stalk he could find. Thirty sweaty minutes later, he'd trimmed off the shoots and leaves and shortened it into a seven-foot weapon, whittling the end into a spear point. Not perfect, but lethal.

But there was a drawback. Bamboo, while tough as wood, was also hollow. This meant that it was light and easy to throw. It also meant the gator could likely chomp it in two with a single snap of its jaws.

Hopefully, he wouldn't actually have to spear the reptile. He didn't care to kill it unless he planned to eat it. But the thought of skinning out a massive gator with a dull Swiss Army knife was daunting, never mind how he might cook it. Eating raw gator would be a challenge.

And, honestly, would Olivia even eat gator even if cooked? Well, maybe if desperate enough.

Jack put such thoughts out of his mind. The plan was to just poke the beast enough to scare it away.

Jack cut the remnants of the bamboo stalks into foot-long lengths. Then, taking a deep breath, he headed for the gator, spear in his left hand, bamboo sticks in his right.

When he got within throwing range, Jack dropped the spear. Taking another deep breath, he cocked back his right arm and threw the largest of the sticks, yelling as he did, "Get out of here! Go on, get! Get out!"

The stick crashed down on the gator, hitting its broad back just below its head.

It didn't even stir. *Is it dead?*

Jack took a couple of steps closer, shouting again as he let fly a second stick. This one hit the gator right between the eyes.

"C'mon, you bastard! Get going!"

Nothing.

Jack took another few steps forward. He was about to throw the third stick when the gator suddenly whirled toward him, jaws agape, hissing so loudly that it sounded like a giant diesel truck releasing an air brake.

Jack dropped the rest of sticks. He took an awkward step back, nervously glancing behind him for his spear. But as he stooped to pick it up, he stumbled, fell, and saw, horrified, the gator pushing itself up on all fours.

Jack scrambled backward, grabbing for his spear, keeping his eyes on the gator. His hand finally closed around the makeshift weapon, but at the wrong end; he was holding the sharpened point instead of the base. As he rose to his feet, shifting the sharpened point toward the gator, the beast charged.

Every inch of Jack's body was telling him to run, but he forced himself not to listen.

The gator would just grab him from behind, pulling him down, crushing bones before dragging him off into the swamp to die. There was only one other choice.

Jack screamed at the top of his lungs, shattering the stillness of the air. He charged forward, his bamboo spear thrust out in front of him like a knight's lance.

The gator kept coming, racing at him, mouth agape, another horrifying hiss filling the air.

But then, with only a few feet between them, the beast abruptly stopped, rearing up on its hind legs like some sort of modern-day dinosaur. Jack, skidding to a halt barely three feet away, stared up at the gator in disbelief.

He'd seen alligators launch themselves out of the water to snatch a meal off a low-hanging tree branch, but he'd never seen one stand on its tail and hind feet. He'd never even known it was possible.

But as this one loomed over him like a prehistoric monster, Jack saw his opening.

He flipped his lance end to end, choked up on the spear end, and swung it with all his might like a baseball bat.

The fat end caught the gator under its jaw—*thwack!*

The beast went down, twisting sideways, like a boxer running into a left hook. But as it fell, snapping at the air, its jaws managed to clamp on to the lance.

Jack heard it crack as the gator wrenched it violently out of his hands with a twisting of its jaws.

Forcing himself to stand his ground, Jack let out another cry as he watched what was left of his spear fall to the ground on the other side of the gator.

The reptile landed heavily on its belly, now facing away from him. Jack had no time to think. And then, as panic raced through him, a scene from some bizarre TV reality show he'd once seen about gator wrestlers flashed through his mind.

And so, somehow, suddenly, he was throwing himself on the gator's back, scrambling for a grip on the gator's neck and, realizing he had secured it, slamming his right fist into the gator's snout. He punched again, pushing down until he'd forced the beast's jaws closed and then, using both hands, he clamped them shut.

The gator went wild beneath him, thrashing like a rodeo bull. Jack closed his eyes, using every ounce of strength just to keep his grip. A disgusting, primal stench welled up from the beast, like something long dead.

Time passed, slowed down, sped up again. The gator writhed and thrashed. Jack couldn't let go the gator's jaws. His life depended on it.

At last, the reptile slowed and, finally, stopped moving.

Jack sat on top of it, just behind its head, beyond exhausted.

The gator-wrestling show he'd seen hadn't covered how to dismount an alligator. It took Jack awhile to come up with a plan. At all costs, he had to avoid the gator's tail. On a gator, it was a weapon; a hunter friend of Jack's family had been whacked out of a boat by the tail of a gator presumed dead. It almost cost him his life.

Fortunately, the remains of Jack's spear lay a couple of feet away. He swung his left leg over the gator, keeping both hands on its jaws. Kneeling beside it, he muttered a silent prayer and then let go of the jaws with his right hand, holding them closed with just his left.

He pivoted to face the reptile. "Okay, buddy," he said aloud, "time for you to go."

Raising his right hand, he jabbed his thumb sharply into the gator's eye, following his grandfather's advice that this was maybe the only lifesaving maneuver for anyone being dragged underwater by a gator.

The beast writhed, almost breaking free, but Jack grabbed the snout with both hands and held on. When the gator settled down, Jack abruptly let go, dashing backward as he scooped up what was left of his spear.

"Now, get of here!" Jack yelled. "Get!"

He leapt forward, using the spear remnants to rap the gator sharply on the snout.

The reptile hissed, baring its dangerous teeth, but Jack could tell it was done.

It turned and retreated toward the swamp, its tail bushwhacking through the undergrowth. Jack ran after it, yelling as he went, bringing the end of his makeshift club down on its tail as it fled.

The gator sped up, slithering toward a thicket. Jack gave it one more hard whack as insurance. The last thing he needed was for the beast to crawl back up on the bank in the middle of the night, looking for a meal.

The gator thrashed noisily through the tangle of brush ahead. And then it was gone.

Silence fell over the swamp once more, and Jack turned back toward the clearing, his heart rate finally beginning to slow. His best guess, based on the angle of the sun, was that it was still early afternoon.

He sniffed the air, realizing that the disgusting smell of sweat and alligator was coming from him. Glancing at Olivia to make sure she was okay, he walked to the edge of the bank and stepped into the deep pool. Wading out chest high, he began to scrub himself with both hands, trying to rinse away the stench.

When he'd done the best he could, he waded back out and began peeling off layers of clothing, stripping down to his boxers. He wrung as much water as he could from his long-sleeve shirt, soggy khakis, T-shirt, and baseball cap, spreading them out on a grassy patch to dry in the sunlight. Then he stood for a long time, eyes closed, letting the sun warm him.

The adrenaline that had fueled him through the alligator fight was gone. The knot above his right eye had begun to throb again, the gash in his forearm itched angrily, and the back of his throat burned with thirst.

With the gator vanquished, reality returned with a vengeance. He opened his eyes, looking at Olivia.

He forced himself to concentrate. Remembering the emergency

kit, he grabbed it from the bank, planning to look through everything this time. But as his hand closed around the kit, he heard a sudden cry. Olivia was awake.

Pushing herself to her feet, she began to weave forward, her feet unsteady beneath her. Caked in dried mud, her hair matted to her head, she looked like some sort of swamp zombie.

"Help!" she called out, stumbling forward. "I can't see anything! What's happening to me? Help!"

CHAPTER 7

JACK SPRINTED FORWARD, catching Olivia as she pitched toward the ground. She stiffened in his arms, trying to twist away.

"Hey, it's okay," he said. "Olivia, it's me. It's Jack Landry. It's okay, I've got you."

Olivia paused, her body rigid.

Silence, and then . . . "Jack?"

Olivia sagged against his chest, sobbing in great gasps.

Unable to think of what else to do, he wrapped her awkwardly in his arms, pressing her mud-crusted cheek against his chest. Minutes passed, but at last, her sobs began to slow. She drew back, clearing her throat.

"Where am I?" she demanded. "Why can't I see anything? What's happening?"

Jack stepped back, examining Olivia more closely. He might have been a little overenthusiastic with the gnat prevention. Dried mud caked her eyelids, sealing them shut.

Of course, she can't see.

"You just need to wash the mud off your face. Here, there's a pond right over here. If you take my hand, I can lead you in."

"Mud?" Olivia repeated. "Why the hell do I have mud on me? Where *are* we?"

"Um, you don't remember?"

"Remember *what*?"

Damn.

"Um. Okay. So . . . there's kind of a lot I need to tell you. But why don't we take care of the mud first?"

"Tell me!" Olivia said sharply. "Now!"

"Okay, well, see, our plane crashed in the swamp. We survived, but you were unconscious. But I was able to pull you to high ground. Which is where we are now. And, uh . . ."

"A crash?" Olivia asked, an edge to her voice. "What are you saying? I don't . . . I, uh, don't, uh . . ."

She paused and then said, "And where's my father . . . and . . ." She trailed off, her voice exhausted.

"Just, walk with me, okay?" Jack said. "We need you cleaned up. You've been out for quite a while. But just stay calm and follow me. Then I'll fill you in."

"Out? What do you mean *out*? And where's my dad? Why isn't he here?"

Her voice grew shrill and thin again.

"Olivia, please," Jack said, tension edging into his voice. "Just do as I ask. Then we can talk. Here, come this way. But first, let's lose the sweatshirt."

Jack helped Olivia out of the damp sweatshirt, reaching gingerly for her hand, and guided her to the edge of the pool. They waded slowly forward until they were about waist-deep.

"If you kneel down, you can get your face in the water," Jack said. "You should be able to scrub the mud off."

Olivia didn't move. "Why does it smell so bad?"

"It's the swamp," Jack said. "You're covered in dried muck. It kept you from being devoured by gnats but, well . . ."

She grimaced. "Hold on to me," she said finally, sticking out one of her hands.

Jack held on as she slowly lowered herself to her knees. She tentatively ducked her face into the water and began to scrub with her free hand.

As the caked-on mud began to loosen and melt away, she rubbed harder, letting go of Jack's hand to use both on her own. Finishing her face, she scrubbed her neck and arms clean and then, standing abruptly, her legs.

Finally, she looked up, peering intently at Jack for the first time. "It really is you."

Jack didn't know what to say. "Yeah. I mean, who else would it be?"

Olivia looked away. Catching sight of her reflection in the water, she stared down at herself for a long moment.

And then, as Jack watched in disbelief, she stripped off her T-shirt, tossing it toward the bank. Ducking down into the water, she pulled off her shorts, tossing them toward shore as well. Her sneakers came next.

She was in her bra and panties. Jack looked down at his own bare chest.

Duh. He'd forgotten that he was down to his boxer shorts.

Olivia paid him no mind. Plunging ahead, she began swimming awkwardly toward the center of the pool.

What the hell is she doing?

"Are you sure that's a good idea?" Jack called out. "You've just come to. Maybe you should be careful."

Olivia ignored him. Looking up at the sky, she took a deep breath and then—back arched, legs together and rising straight up, toes pointed skyward—she dove. She disappeared below the surface with barely a ripple.

Jack, though he admired the athleticism of her dive, watched in disbelief. She was clearly running on adrenalin. The seconds stretched on, but Olivia didn't reappear.

He was a heartbeat away from diving after her when she broke the surface, arms raised. She flipped onto her back, visibly winded.

For a long moment, she floated, unmoving. But then, as Jack watched, she jerked suddenly in surprise, beginning to sputter.

"Oh, God! I swallowed some of this horrible water!" she yelled. "Christ! It . . . it's . . ."

She broke into another coughing fit, her arms flailing wildly, sinking as she thrashed.

Jack dove in, reaching her in four quick strokes. He grabbed for her arm, trying to calm her, but she struggled against him, pulling him down with her.

His head went under, and he swallowed water, too.

As he coughed violently, he knew he'd made a mistake; he should've dived deeper and grabbed her from behind. Lifeguarding 101.

He tried to wrench free, but Olivia was holding onto him now, her panicked grip too tight. She was pulling them down to the bottom.

Jack had no choice; kick her away or they'd both drown. His foot found her stomach, and he kicked hard. Her grip loosened, and he fought to the surface, spitting water. Taking a quick breath, he plunged back down, grabbing for anything he could reach. His hand closed around her ponytail.

Latching on, his feet found bottom. He pushed up violently for the surface.

Breaking into the air, he pulled Olivia to him, treading water while he held the back of her head afloat.

"Olivia?" he said frantically. "Are you okay?"

No response.

An involuntary curse formed on his lips. "Shit!"

Jack looped an arm around her chest, kicking hard for the bank. His feet slid in the mud as he pulled Olivia ashore, laying her flat on the ground. Her body was limp and deathly pale; she clearly wasn't breathing.

Jack breathed deeply, trying to remember his CPR training.

Head back to relax the jaws and lips. Sweep the throat for blockages. Pinch the nostrils, cover their mouth with yours, and blow in three quick breaths. Repeat, repeat, repeat, and if no response, place two fingers just below the sternum and give a sharp rap on the chest before beginning chest massage.

Okay, he could do this.

Pressing his thumb down on Olivia's chin to open her mouth, he covered her mouth with his, blowing in three quick breaths.

Olivia didn't move.

He tried again, and this time, during the second breath, Olivia's limp body came to life. Her eyes flew open, and she pushed him wildly away, sitting up as she did.

"I'm going to be—"

She vomited, water shooting from her mouth so violently that Jack stumbled back in horror. She puked again and again, until there was nothing left.

Easing herself down to her elbows, Olivia dropped back on the ground.

"I'm sorry," she said. "That was, uh, beyond gross..."

"It's fine," Jack said. "Really. Don't worry about it. Good Lord, I thought you were, well... uh..."

She nodded. Closing her eyes, she lay still for a long, silent moment.

Then she spoke. "You thought I was dead?"

"Hmm, I dunno. Maybe."

"Sorry, I panicked. It's not like me. I just..."

"Right. Everyone panics now and then."

"That water is disgusting."

"I could see how you'd say that. There's worse, though."

"Well, I think I'd rather die of thirst than try to drink that stuff."

"If we boil the water—well, if we could find a way to boil the water—it might taste better."

"If you say so. By the way, has anyone ever told you that you need to work on your kissing technique?"

"What?"

Olivia offered a wan smile. "That was a joke, Jack. But I could feel what you were trying to do. I guess I was sort of dead but not totally dead."

Jack shook his head. *This girl is too much.* He couldn't think of what to say. Not too much about this seemed funny to him. Actually, nothing about it.

Olivia spoke again.

"I appreciate what you did, getting me here. But where's my father? The pilot?"

Jack dreaded this moment, but it was unavoidable.

"The plane broke apart in a storm. We were both knocked out. When I came to, it was morning. I thought I could see the front section in the distance, but then the part we were in began to sink. So, I had to get us out and find high ground. At that point, I couldn't see the nose section anymore, so there was no way to even check on anyone."

"So you *didn't* check on them?"

"I couldn't. But look, we survived, and they could've, too. Joe Desmoreaux is an old swamp rat. He'll know what to do. The plane has a radio. Maybe they've already called for help."

Olivia looked at him, eyes widening.

"But what if they didn't make it?" she said, her voice quavering. "What if . . ."

She broke off in mid-sentence, choking sobs, swallowing her voice.

Jack leaned forward, taking her gently into his arms.

"It's okay, it's okay," he said. "Again, we made it. We're here. Your dad and Joe could've easily survived, too."

Olivia looked up at him, tears in her sad eyes.

"Yes, right," she said. "Thank you for getting us here. I just wish . . . I just wish you could've checked on Dad."

With that, her eyes began to droop.

"Sorry, Jack," she said, almost in a whisper. "I'm exhausted. All this almost-dying stuff, you know."

A second later, she was out, her head slumped to one side.

Jack hovered over her, more than a little anxious. He hoped she was simply sleeping and not falling into some deep swoon. *What if she has a serious concussion? What if she doesn't wake up?*

An awful thought surged through him. Though he hardly knew

Olivia FitzGerald, he now knew that he would be devastated if she died. Having gotten her this far, he'd invested some strange part of his heart and soul in her.

"This sucks," he said under his breath.

Finally, he stood. He should recover her clothes, wring them out and spread them in the sun to dry. Maybe, once they dried, he could dress her.

Something told him she wasn't going to be happy if she woke up, half-naked, on the ground. Would she think Jack had been staring at her the whole time? *Well, it's hard not to stare.*

He snapped out of this useless reverie. Olivia's feelings were the least of his problems.

Jack still had no idea how they were going to get food, or drinking water, or shelter.

He scanned the sky above the clearing, looking for some sort of sign. But there was only the blue and empty heavens and the sighing of the deep swamp all around them.

CHAPTER 8

DUSK CAME QUICKLY.

Crickets and tree frogs chirped from the palmetto brakes surrounding the clearing and, in the distance, the deep bass of a bullfrog echoed across the marsh. A nutria brayed nearby, its bleat sounding almost like a sheep.

Jack was just thankful that he couldn't hear the buzz of mosquitos. Of course, it was still early.

Just before sunset, a small flock of great egrets, maybe a dozen or so, swooped in, noisily winging into the circle of oaks nearby. They flapped so low across the clearing that Jack could have reached out and almost touched their fluttering white wings. Squawking noisily, they'd settled in for the night and went silent as dark sealed its grip on the swamp.

Jack was strangely comforted by their presence; if a person or anything dangerous approached, they would squawk, alerting him.

He was also happy about the emergency kit, in which he'd found a ten-by-ten-foot space blanket—one of those shiny, silver-colored ultralight polyethylene sheets that reflected back body heat.

It made a decent substitute for an actual blanket and, even better, it had grommets at the corners—brass-rimmed holes that you could run a rope through.

Jack had taken his braided yellow tow rope from the raft and, using his knife, unraveled it into four separate thin ropes. Then he rigged the blanket into an open-ended tent by running one of the ropes from a convenient broken-off branch up six feet on the cypress tree to a tripod of bamboo stakes he'd driven into the spongy ground, then draping the blanket over the rope. He'd anchored the sides by driving small bamboo stakes into the ground through the grommets.

He doubted his contraption would endure high winds or a big thunderstorm, but for now, it was at least a roof over their heads. The soaking life jackets from the raft had dried more quickly than Jack had expected thanks to the warm October sun. So, he'd dragged them into the tent, covering them with Spanish moss from nearby trees.

Jack had carried Olivia to the lean-to from her resting spot on the bank. She hadn't even stirred in his arms. She now slept fitfully on the makeshift mattress, calling out every so often in her sleep. Her clothes were dry as well, and Jack had somehow managed to pull them back on her without waking her. Her low moans were at least reassuring.

He'd managed to keep his eyes averted as much as possible, which hadn't exactly been easy. Not easy at all. But, oh, well. His mother would've been proud of him.

His own wet clothes had dried, too, except for his damp sneakers. Jack hated wet feet.

Jack took the last bite of half an energy bar, the only one left in the broken-open package he'd found at the very bottom of the emergency kit. There were supposed to be six.

The bar tasted like dried sawdust, probably because its "best consumed by date" was a year ago.

Jack was saving the other half for Olivia. He'd already gathered a pile of acorns to boil into a mush—assuming he found something to boil them in. He couldn't believe the kit hadn't contained some sort of pot, not even one of those Boy Scout mess kits in which you could boil water.

And where are the lines tied with fishhooks?

He could have rooted under rotting logs for grubs and earthworms that the catfish, bream, and crappie around here would have loved. Not including fishing lines in a survival kit for a plane that routinely flew over this swamp? *Pretty stupid.*

Actually criminal. He made a note to complain to Robichaux about that. If he ever saw Jeff again.

He found a few other useful things in the kit: some basic first aid supplies, including a tube of antibiotic salve and gauze bandages. He rubbed salve on his open cuts and the small gash on Olivia's cheek. He also found two empty, one-liter plastic water bottles, and a bottle of water purification tablets. He'd filled both bottles with pond water and put in the right dosage of the tablets, but a swig of the tepid water almost made him gag. It tasted like swamp water taken from the bottom of an over-chlorinated swimming pool.

Still, it was better than drinking untreated swamp water, or worse, dying from dehydration.

The water bottles were the last useful things in the kit. Short of a pot miraculously appearing out of thin air, they'd have to cook everything on spits over an open fire. Assuming they could catch anything to cook.

There *was* game everywhere, and Jack had crafted two new weapons—another seven-foot-long bamboo spear and a *death star*, which was really just two twelve-inch pieces of bamboo tied tightly together with a strand of his tow rope to form an *X*. Jack had whittled the ends into arrow-sharp points.

The idea was to hold it like a hammer and throw it hard end-over-end, hoping one of the sharpened ends buried itself in the intended prey. Paw-Paw Landry had taught him how to make them, but Jack had never thrown one at anything besides a cardboard target in his backyard.

The list of game that might be actually catchable *and* taste good was depressingly short—bullfrogs, turtles, and crawfish. Rabbits, squirrels, and birds (ducks, coots, dove, and quail) would be good, too, but a lot harder to catch.

He'd also made an easier-to-catch-but-gross list. Possum and nutria were both slow and made decent-sized targets for the death star. But Jack had eaten both before and already decided that once was enough. Raccoons were somewhere in the middle. Cooked properly, they were okay. Kind of. But raccoons were wary. Once spotted, they wouldn't sit still for long.

Hunting would have to wait till daylight. Their pen-sized flashlight was too weak for a hunting light and, anyway, they needed to save it for emergencies.

Jack had also made a small fire with the butane lighter he'd found in the emergency kit. He wasn't cold, but it warded off mosquitos. Plus, there was something comforting about a fire. And besides, maybe a low-flying rescue plane would spot it.

Although, he hadn't seen or heard a single plane fly over in the entire time he'd been here. If rescue planes were searching, they were looking in the wrong place.

The Great Atchafalaya was home to quite a few oil and gas wells, which meant there were a fair number of boats and planes dedicated to their upkeep. The fact that he hadn't heard any meant they really *were* in the middle of nowhere.

"Jack? Are you here?"

Jack turned at the sound of Olivia's voice, switching on the penlight and pointing it in her direction. She raised a hand to ward off the beam.

"Oh, sorry," he said, lowering the light. "Yeah, right here. You're awake? Are you okay?"

"Yes on the awake," Olivia said. "I'm not sure about the okay part. Can you help me sit up?"

"Sure."

Jack scooted over, holding out his hand. Olivia grabbed his arm at the elbow with both hands and pulled herself upright.

She looked around, blinking in the dim glow of the flashlight.

"Where are we, exactly?"

"Exactly? I don't know," Jack admitted. "Somewhere in the southern quadrant of the Great Atchafalaya Swamp."

"I meant, is this a tent?"

"Yeah, kind of. I found a tarp in the emergency kit. It should keep the dew off. And maybe rain. If the rain's not too heavy."

Olivia pointed outside the tent. "And we have a fire?"

"I was worried about mosquitoes. But they haven't shown up yet."

"Good," Olivia said, offering him a ghost of a smile. "I'm not a big fan of insects."

Jack didn't say anything as she stared into the fire for a moment, unmoving. Finally, she spoke. "I thought this might be a bad dream. But it's not, is it? Our plane went down."

Jack gave a cautious nod. "You remember it?"

"Starting to," Olivia said, still staring at the fire. "It was stormy. The plane was all over the place. I remember screaming. But after that..."

She shrugged. "Nothing. Well, until I woke up caked in dried mud. Oh, and then almost drowned."

Jack nodded.

"Geez," she said. "*You* must be exhausted. It's hard work saving me."

"Well, you would've done the same for me."

Olivia managed a wan smile. "Let's not get ahead of ourselves. But tell me again. Maybe you saw the front of the plane?"

Jack hesitated, still uncertain as to what to say. He didn't want to alarm Olivia, but he didn't want to give her false hope, either.

Finally, he said, "When I first came to and our section was sitting up high, yes, I thought I could see something in the distance. I called out a couple of times, but no one answered. Which doesn't mean anything. They could've been knocked out, too. Or maybe it wasn't even the plane."

"And then what happened?"

"Well, we must've been propped up on a log or something because suddenly, everything shifted, and it was clear we were sinking. I had to get us out—or else."

"Sinking?" Olivia repeated.

"Yeah, we must've lodged on a log that kept our part of the plane tilted up out of the marsh. But the patch we landed on was basically like quicksand. We call it *flotant*. By the time I got us away, the tail section of the plane was totally swallowed. Had we stayed . . . well."

Olivia stared at him. "But I'm still confused as to how you got me all the way here."

Jack reached up to scratch his neck, feeling awkward. "Um, I made a raft for you from life jackets from the plane. I tied them together. You're sleeping on them right now. And then I just sort of . . . swam, towing you along. Well, I crawled some of it. But mostly I swam. And swam. And swam."

"How long?"

"I don't know," Jack admitted. "Miles? It took hours to find high ground. I kind of lost track of time."

"But how are we going to find them again?" she asked. "I mean, my dad and Joe? What if they're hurt and need help?"

She trailed off, then said, "Shouldn't we have stayed closer to them?"

"We couldn't. As I said, the plane was sinking. And, trust me, you don't want to be out in the open marsh after dark." A note of defensiveness crept into his voice. "I mean, I did my best, okay?"

Olivia shook her head. "I get that. It's just . . ." She swallowed. "My dad can't be dead, he just can't be. I couldn't handle it. And my mom . . . she couldn't live without him."

She looked away, wiping tears from her cheeks with the back of her hand.

"Hey," Jack said awkwardly. "It's going to be okay. Again, we made it, right? They probably did, too."

"We have to go back," Olivia said, tension rising in her voice. "We could try to find them . . . help them if they're hurt."

Jack searched for a way to tell her no without sounding like a jerk. Finally, he said, "The truth is, even if I knew where the plane was—and I don't from this location—I don't think either of us could make it right now. It was crazy exhausting just to get here."

He shrugged. "Look, I think our best shot is to wait until morning. We can try to get somebody flying overhead to notice us. Start a bigger fire, or use the tent cover like a mirror to signal them. This clearing isn't that big, but it should be visible to anyone looking for us."

Olivia turned away, wiping more tears from her cheeks. Her voice turned suddenly cold. "I *never* should have come here. I didn't want to. My dad is obsessed with these father-daughter trips. But I hate them. *Hate* them."

Jack fought against a flicker of annoyance. "I'd say you're lucky," he said. "If my parents had money, I'd go anywhere with them. Seriously, anywhere. No question."

Olivia shot him a withering look. "You don't know anything about my life," she said. "So, no offense, why don't you keep your opinions to yourself?"

Jack's annoyance flared to anger.

"You're right," he said. "I *don't* know anything about your big, fancy life. And you know what? I don't *care*. I didn't make you come here. I didn't make the plane crash. I could have just swum away and left you. I don't even know why I . . ."

He trailed off, taking a deep breath.

Stupid! he self-admonished. *Arguing right now is stupid.*

After a long, strained silence, he spoke up again.

"Look, I'm really sorry. If I'd seen your dad, or Joe, I would have gone after them. But I didn't. So, I decided to save you—*us*."

Jack wondered if she was ever going to speak to him again, but she did, this time in a quiet, halting voice.

"I'm sorry. I'm not a jerk, really. I just . . . I need to find my dad. My mom is . . . not good. She hasn't been good in a long time. MS. The worst possible form of it. My father's brought in every specialist in the world, but nothing ever helps. She's in one of those long-term care places. If he's gone, it'll destroy her. And then I'll just have . . . nothing."

Jack stiffened as she leaned forward, resting her head on his shoulder.

"I'm sorry," she whispered. "Really. I'm just . . . scared."

Jack could feel tears soaking his shirt.

"I'm sorry, too," he said. "I had no idea about your mom."

Olivia pushed herself back up, running her fingers through her long, black hair. "Okay," she said, obviously trying to pull herself together. "You know what? I'm just going to believe he's alive. Otherwise, I'm going to be useless. And a FitzGerald, as Terrence says, can *never* be useless."

Jack managed a weak smile. "Never," he agreed. "Anyway, it's been a rough day. We should try to get some rest."

Olivia yawned. "It seems like all I've been doing is resting."

"Being unconscious might not quite be the same thing."

"True. How's *your* head?"

"Fuzzy. But mostly okay, I think."

"That's good. "

Olivia glanced at her wrinkled clothes.

"Hmm. How did I get dressed?"

"Oh, so you remember your striptease in the pond?"

"Vaguely."

"Well, uh, I fetched your wet things from the pond and dried them out. And then I figured, uh, you might prefer to wake up this way than half naked. I mean, I was mostly worried about bugs. You know."

"I see. Well, I guess I should thank you."

"Oh, no, you don't have to. It was my pleasure, uh . . . I mean . . . uh. I didn't mean to say it that way. That it was a pleasure to dress you. I meant . . . aw, forget it."

Jack couldn't hide a sheepish grin.

Olivia managed a hint of a smile. "It's okay, Swamp Boy. I

appreciate all your effort. How is it that *you* aren't exhausted?"

Jack smiled, relieved for reasons that eluded him. He realized his exhaustion was mostly mental.

"I dunno. I don't feel that tired. I guess I'm still running on adrenaline."

Olivia nodded. "By the way, we don't have any food, do we?"

"Oh, we have food," Jack said.

"Really?"

"Well, if you expand the definition of food. Ta-da!" he said, holding up the leftover half of the energy bar. "Best sawdust you'll ever eat."

Olivia stared at the wrapper. "Yay," she said flatly. "I love sawdust. What about water?"

"We have that, too. Doesn't taste good, but it's safe to drink. There were some water purification pills in the emergency kit, and a couple of plastic bottles."

"The same water I swallowed?"

"Afraid so."

"Yuck."

"I agree. But it'll keep us hydrated."

Olivia nodded again. "If you say so. But first, I've got to go . . . you know. Any ideas?"

Jack had already thought about it. "Here," he said. "Take the flashlight and turn left outside the tent. There's a fallen log about fifty feet away that's pretty level. I marked the smoothest spot with a life jacket."

"Fancy," Olivia said. "This is embarrassing, but do you mind going with me? Not all the way," she added quickly. "Just a little. Not close enough to, you know, *hear* anything."

"No problem," Jack said. "You won't even know I'm there."

"But you *will* be there, right?"

Jack grinned. "Yeah."

"Okay," Olivia said, nodding. She tried to stand, but didn't quite make it.

"Here," Jack said, holding out his hand and helping pull her to her feet. She looped her right arm around his.

"Lead the way."

Using the penlight, Jack guided Olivia toward the log. He aimed the flashlight at it, pointing it out to her in the distance.

Then, handing the penlight to her, he turned away.

"I'll be thinking about football," he said. "LSU's playing Alabama next weekend. Game of the season for the Tigers."

Olivia grinned. "Good to know."

A long silent minute passed in which Jack *really did* try to think about football. But Olivia's voice suddenly cut through the silence.

"Um, Jack? I'm not going to scream, but can you come here? Like, *now*? Because there's something crawling in my hair. Something big."

Jack turned. Olivia was looking down, the flashlight beaming into the ground between her feet.

Jack walked quickly over. "Hand me the light."

He found the culprit almost immediately. "Okay, nothing to worry about. Just hold still for a second."

"What is it?" Olivia asked, an edge to her voice.

"I'll explain in a second. Just . . . don't move."

"Do you *see* me moving?"

Jack held the light between his teeth, freeing up his hands. The black and gold banana spider which, legs outstretched, could reach four-inches long, making it by far the largest spider in the swamp, froze as the light pinned its eyes.

It was a female; all the big ones were.

Jack placed one outstretched hand in front of the spider, gently prodding it from behind with a finger from his other hand, hoping to guide it onto his open palm.

Instead, the spider leapt, scrambling up his arm. Jack flinched, deftly flicking it away with his finger. It sailed noiselessly off into the darkness.

"Sorry, girl," he said.

"What girl?" Olivia demanded. "Me?"

"Just a spider."

"A *spider*?"

"Nothing to worry about," Jack told her. "Not poisonous to humans. Their jaws are too small to inflict a bite. But they kill a ton of bugs."

"Uh-huh," Olivia said. "That's probably all I need to know."

"They have really good sex lives, too."

She stared at him, her bemused look apparent even in the dim glow of the flashlight. "What are you *talking* about?"

"Female banana spiders rule the web. The guys are tiny, maybe a tenth their size, and basically their only job is to have sex with the female. And then, when they're done, she eats them."

There was a long silence, then Olivia asked, "Where do you get this stuff?"

"It's all true. Mr. Delaune, my tenth-grade biology teacher, told us. He was spider crazy. We had a banana spider field trip once. You should see their webs. They can get, like, ten feet across."

Olivia shook her head. "Tempting but maybe that's a pleasure I'll pass on," she said. "And I'll keep that in mind when I'm trying to go to sleep tonight. In the meantime, can I have a minute here?"

Jack handed her the flashlight. "Oh, right. I'll wait where I was, okay?"

"Fine."

He thought about football again until Olivia joined him.

"Let me guess, no toothbrush?"

"I wish."

Back at the tent, Olivia picked up the leftover half of the energy bar. She was about to take a bite when she turned to Jack. "Here, you take it," she said. "All I've done today is sleep."

"I'm fine," Jack lied, his stomach growling. "Besides, you need food. Don't worry, I have breakfast plans."

"Oh, yeah? Bacon and eggs for you? Organic yogurt for me?"

"I'm thinking spit-roasted rabbit rubbed in a little sassafras."

"I'm sorry, but I'm a little behind on my sassafras education. What are you talking about?"

"It's basically a wild herb," he said, laughing. "I saw a sassafras tree down by the water. You dry the leaves and grind them up into a powder. Cajuns call it *file* and use it as a flavoring in gumbo. The Native Americans who lived in this swamp long ago also used it as traditional medicine. It supposedly works on toothaches and headaches, that kind of stuff."

Olivia nodded. "Well, maybe, given the starvation option, I would eat a sassafras rabbit. And the rabbit is where, exactly?"

"In my dreams," Jack admitted. "But maybe we can get lucky with the death star."

"Okay, c'mon. Stop joking. Did you just say *death star*?"

Once again, Jack was grateful it was dark.

"Um . . . yeah. I'll show it to you tomorrow. It's a crude weapon my Paw-Paw Landry showed me how to make."

"I see. And if we *can't* kill a rabbit with a death star, then what?"

"Well, we have acorns," he said. "Kind of like peanuts. Only . . . worse. Or we can find muscadines—wild grapes. They grow around here, and it's the season. They're tart but good. Anyway, you eat the rest of the bar. You'll need your strength."

"Are you sure?" she asked. "I feel bad eating in front of you."

"Don't worry about it."

Olivia unwrapped the cellophane covering, taking a bite.

"Delicious," she said. "It reminds me of being back in France."

"I can only imagine."

Jack sat and stared out at the dying embers of the fire as she ate. He wasn't going to stoke it; he just didn't feel like scrounging for more wood.

When she was done with the bar, Olivia lay back on her life-jacket mattress, tucking her hands behind her head.

Jack turned on the flashlight to check that everything he wanted was by his side—the bamboo club, spear, the death star, the two water bottles, the butane lighter. Satisfied, he switched off the light, stretching out on the moss bed he'd made for himself, not too close to Olivia—but not too far.

The glow of a rising full moon settled over the clearing. Something about it cheered Jack.

"Goodnight," he said to Olivia. "I hope you sleep okay."

There was a long silence that made Jack wonder if she were already asleep. And then she spoke.

"I'm kind of cold. Would you mind getting a little closer?"

Jack was chilly, as well. The temperature had dropped several degrees since sunset. And, if he was being honest with himself, it wasn't like he hadn't already run the scenario in his head. Trapped in the wilderness, forced to huddle with a beautiful girl for warmth... *I mean, come on.* He'd seen movies before. Still, he felt creepy suggesting it in real life.

"Are you suggesting we snuggle?" he asked, trying to make a joke out of it.

"Did you just use the word *snuggle*?"

"Yeah, why? Is that a forbidden word?"

"It's just so corny."

"I see. How about if I scooch up to you?"

Olivia laughed. "Is that even a word at all?"

"I think so."

Olivia lay silent for a while, then said, "Just come here already. And don't get too carried away."

"But being *simply* carried away is okay?"

Olivia shook her head. She laughed again. "You are *so* lame, Jack Landry."

"Right. Okay, I'm coming over."

Jack rolled over and pulled himself into a spoon position besides Olivia FitzGerald, his right hand resting on her shoulder. "How's that?" he whispered.

After a long silence, she said, "A little closer, please."

She reached out and grabbed his hand, pulling his arm around the warmth of her waist.

"Better," she said. "Goodnight, Jack."

Jack closed his eyes, resting his cheek on her shoulder. "Sleep tight, Olivia."

It took him a long time to fall asleep.

CHAPTER 9

ON THE SECOND morning since the crash, daylight crept in on a chilly fog.

Jack stirred awake, confused at first as to where he was. He hadn't slept well, his dreams flicking between disturbing and confusing.

A replay of the plane falling out of the sky; Jack's mother calling to him from a dark corner and Jack unable to answer; Paw-Paw Landry telling him he couldn't come home until he had learned the secret only the egrets knew.

"What secret? I don't even speak egret," he'd said in the dream.

His grandfather had smiled, his lips creasing like a horseshoe. *"Don't worry, you'll figger it out, Jack."*

His brothers Jake and Jerry throwing flowers on his grave.

Olivia crying.

Except Olivia's cries were real. He'd woken up twice in the night, hearing her whimpering in her sleep. He'd draped his arm around her, pulling her closer. "I'm sorry," he'd whispered. "I'm so sorry."

Olivia hadn't replied.

Anxiety gnawed at his stomach.

Terrence FitzGerald had to be dead in the wreckage. Joe, too. What's Olivia going to do when she realizes it?

Jack thought about his parents, his brothers, and Paw-Paw, and how worried they must be. A strange feeling of guilt surged through him. *This is all my fault.*

But just as quickly, Jack flicked the thought away like the spider from his arm last night. He couldn't go there. It wouldn't do anyone any good.

Pushing himself up on one elbow, he reluctantly rolled away

from the warmth of Olivia, who stirred in her sleep. He stared out at another perfect Indian summer day in the swamp. At least the weather was *something.*

Weak sunlight had begun to pierce the fog. Dew sparkled off the grass in the clearing. Not far away, a red-winged blackbird creedled unseen from a thicket of cattails. Jack heard the *phlit, phlit, phlit* of acorn cuttings falling from oaks to the soft, leaf-littered ground. Squirrels were feeding in the oak tops beyond the cypress.

If he had a shotgun, breakfast would be solved. Jack liked squirrel crispy-fried in his mother's Tabasco-cornmeal-and-egg batter. Delicious. Of course, cooked on a spit on an open fire with no seasoning, maybe not so great. But food was food.

Olivia had said desperation might lead her to eating sassafras rabbit. Maybe she'd feel the same about squirrel.

But the squirrels only reminded him of his empty stomach. Hunger gnawed at him like some primitive, unseen animal. The half of the energy bar seemed like a week ago. He felt vaguely nauseous.

He took stock of the rest of his body. The knot over his eye had receded, but not entirely. The gash on his arm still burned, but not as much. Maybe the salve he'd found in the emergency kit was working.

An infection out here could be deadly.

God, he thought, *I'd kill for a cup of coffee.*

Yawning, Jack glanced back at Olivia. He wished he could pretend that none of this was happening. All he wanted to do was curl up against her and go back to sleep.

He was just about to give in to that temptation when the sound of gunfire jolted him to his feet. It was distant, coming from an unexplored direction of the ridge beyond the big cypress, but Jack knew the sound. It was unmistakably the muffled report of a shotgun.

Blam, blam, blam. Three shots in a row.

Hunters! Could they actually be here, on the same ridge?

Jack grabbed for his sneakers, cramming them on without tying them and bolting from the lean-to toward the direction of the shots, only to skid to a halt.

Olivia was still sleeping. He couldn't leave her to wake up alone.

He turned, scrambling back into the lean-to, dropping quickly to her side.

"Olivia, Olivia!" he said, shaking her gently. "I've heard something . . . gunshots. There could be hunters on this ridge. I'm gonna run and see if I can find them. Just . . . stay here and I'll be back as soon as I can. You'll be fine."

"Wait, what?" she asked, opening her eyes, sleep and confusion on her face. "What's happening? Where are you going?"

"Gunshots . . . I heard gunshots. Far away, but somebody's out there. If they're on our ridge, maybe I can get to 'em. We'll be found! Rescued!"

As Jack spoke, another gunshot echoed across the swamp, maybe even closer.

"Hear that? Definitely a shotgun," Jack said.

Olivia turned toward the sound. She nodded, the reality of it sinking in.

"Oh, my God," she said. "Yeah, okay. Go. Hurry! Or wait, should I come with you?"

"I don't think you're up to it," Jack said. "Let me just try to go quick."

Olivia frowned. "For your information, I'm faster than I look. I play—"

"Lacrosse," Jack finished. "I read it on the FitzGerald fact sheet Mr. Robichaux passed out. And I'm sure you're fast . . . when you haven't just spent the day unconscious from a plane crash."

"Hey, you were knocked out, too."

Jack nodded. "Look, I get that you're not, like, helpless. You could probably take me in a sprint. But those hunters could be miles away and I run cross-country. I'm not bragging, but I'm fast over long distances. What if you fall behind and we get separated? I'd feel guilty about leaving you behind, but we can't afford to miss this chance."

Olivia shook her head in exasperation. "Fine, go. But don't get lost out there. I'm not up for a solo camping trip."

"I'm thinking the ridge can't be that wide. There's no way to get turned around."

"Famous last words."

"I'll be fine. Back soon, with help, I hope."

Jack turned to go, stopping at the tent's entrance to tie his sneakers. Then he had another quick thought and pivoted to pick up the bamboo club.

"In case I run across some food," he said.

"Your dream rabbit?"

"Exactly," he grinned. But even as he said the word, he heard another muffled gunshot in the distance. With a backward wave, he sprinted from the tent.

Maybe a half mile from their clearing, Jack skidded to a stop. Just ahead lay a brake of palmettos as dense as any he'd ever seen.

"Are you kidding me?" he muttered.

Despite the cool temperatures, his sprint had left him sweaty and breathless. He stripped off his long-sleeved shirt, wiping his forehead before tying the shirt around his waist.

Catching his breath and gazing at the tangled thickets, he realized he was just going to have to batter his way through. At least he'd brought the club.

Palmetto brakes were full of all kinds of spiders, and red wasps liked to build giant nests on the undersides of them. They attacked in huge swarms.

Snakes like them, too. Especially canebrake rattlers.

Steeling himself, Jack used the club to probe first, rapping hard on the chest-high fronds before pushing and stomping them aside with his hands and feet.

Foot by foot, he battled his way through, cursing under his breath as the fronds resisted, clawing at him at every turn. More than once, they scraped against the gouge on his arm, making him cry out in pain.

A tangled web of sinewy jackvines ran along the ground in places, catching at his sneakers and slowing him even more. Twice, he tripped, crashing loudly into palmetto thickets in front of him.

Only the thought of rescue pushed him onward.

When Jack finally made his way through, swiping at the thin, sweat-covered scratches on his arms, hands, and face, he was relieved to hear another round of distant gunfire. Even better, he saw a very obvious animal trail that ran snake-like ahead of him through a glade of dwarf oaks. Clearly, he wasn't the first to make his way along the narrow, turtle-backed ridge.

Wishing suddenly that he'd brought a bottle of that overchlorinated water, he began to run at a slightly slower pace, not knowing how far he'd have to go. Gauging how far the sound of a gunshot had traveled was tricky. Over water, with the wind blowing in the right direction, it could be miles.

Through the swamp, though? Under a canopy of cypress, gum, and oak trees? Probably not more than a mile, maybe less.

The going was surprisingly easy now, the ground flat and relatively smooth, free of mudholes and covered with a soft leaf-litter that cushioned his step. With the morning still cool and a soft breeze beginning to blow in his face, he realized it was a perfect day for a run—or at least it would have been if he'd had a good night's sleep, drunk a cup of coffee, and wasn't lost and more or less starving in America's biggest swamp.

Long minutes passed with no sound except for his footfalls and the catch of his breath. The wind was growing stronger. When Jack finally heard another muffled shotgun blast, he picked up his pace and began to call out, hoping that whoever was firing the shotgun might hear him.

The ridge grew narrower. The dwarf oaks cloaking the high ground gave way to cypress and tupelo gum in a watery expanse on both sides. Glancing right, he spied a clearing ablaze in bright yellow swamp sunflowers that stretched as far as the eye could see. Normally, he would have stopped to look at the huge expanse of swamp painted yellow.

As he glanced ahead, Jack saw something else—an animal slowly crossing the trail. A few steps later, he realized it was a decent-sized snapping turtle.

His first thought: *Dinner!*

He didn't have time to deal with the turtle now. Still, he found himself speeding up, pulling alongside the snapper before it even realized he was on it. Jack shoved his club out in front of the turtle. It did exactly what Jack thought it would do; hissing, it struck the club.

As the turtle latched on to the length of bamboo, Jack grabbed the snapper by the tail, yanking it up and flipping it over on its back before it had time to whirl around and bite him. It was at least twenty pounds.

The enraged snapper hissed and squirmed as its jaws released the club and snapped wildly, lunging for Jack.

Too late.

The turtle was now helplessly on its back, its legs bicycling in the air. It wouldn't be able to right itself without help.

"Just stay here, buddy. I'll come back for you," Jack said. Glancing at his club, he saw an impressive dent. Had it been his finger, it would've been gone.

He wasn't exactly sure how he was going to kill and clean an enraged reptile with only a Swiss Army knife, then cook it without a pot, but he'd figure it out later.

Unless they were about to be rescued, in which case he wouldn't need to. He could flip the turtle over again and send it on its way when he went back for Olivia.

Jack pushed forward, quickening his pace. The wind had picked up even more and was pushing against him. The day was growing warmer, even with the breeze. He hadn't heard a shot in a while.

Still, he kept going. The next gust of wind carried a new sound, but this time, not a gunshot.

Jack slowed to a stop, straining to listen. Maybe it was in his head. Or the wind, gusting through the trees. But then he heard it again.

Voices!

He couldn't make out the words, but it was clearly people talking.

Jack yelled out again—louder than he'd ever yelled in his life—then stood waiting eagerly for a response. But none came.

He could hear the voices, the way you could hear the muffled sound of the TV playing two rooms away.

Damn!

He knew what was wrong. *I'm downwind.*

Their voices were being picked up and blown as randomly as leaves toward him, the same wind that swallowed his yells.

Jack began sprinting. Fifty yards down the trail, he spotted three cast-off, red plastic shotgun-shell casings. He stopped and scooped one up, examining it closely and sniffing the opening. The casing was faded and the smell of gunpowder faint. Still, it was proof that hunters used this ridge, however remote.

Jack raced ahead, calling out as he went, straining to pick up any sound ahead of him. A sharp bend welled up and, as he rounded it, he skidded to a stop.

A bayou or slough blocked his path. It was at least thirty feet wide, the water shallow and weedy with steeply-pitched muddy banks. Too shallow to swim, too muddy to wade.

A makeshift footbridge spanned the water, two moldering cypress logs that looked like they could be a hundred years old. Green moss and white lichens carpeted their tops, which meant they weren't exactly high traffic. Still, someone had nailed flat two-by-four crossties every few feet to hold the logs together and form a path across. At some point, people had clearly used this bridge.

Jack hesitated until he heard a more complicated noise—the unmistakable roar of a motor cranking up. The roar grew louder, filling the swamp around him.

Airboat. Has to be!

Airboats were popular among a certain type of Atchafalaya hunter, particularly deer hunters who needed to penetrate the swamp's interior ridges unreachable by other boats. Essentially, it was a heavy, flat aluminum skiff with an airplane engine and propeller mounted on the stern. It could run in inches of water and even on dry land for short distances.

Jack could feel it in his gut; whoever was cranking up the airboat was leaving.

He yelled again, realizing it was useless against the roar of the engine and the stiffening wind. He had no choice; he needed to sprint across the log bridge and try to catch whoever it was before they got away.

Halfway across, he realized he should have thought it over first. He heard the cracking sound of the right log beginning to splinter about the same time he felt his left shoe slide on the slick moss.

Before he knew it, Jack was airborne, swallowing his horror as he tumbled backward, toward the bayou, part of the log tumbling after him.

He couldn't even scream.

CHAPTER 10

JACK HIT HARD on his back, feeling the weight of the log pounding him into the shallow bottom just above his knees. He cried out in pain as his head went under, sucking in a mouthful of mucky water, the worst he'd ever tasted.

He gagged, on the verge of panic, feeling the broken-off log like a giant anchor across his legs.

He pushed up violently with his arms, hands digging into the slippery bottom, trying to regain the surface. His head popped up, covered in water grass that cloaked even his eyes. He coughed and spit, raking the grass from his face. He could breathe again, but he had a serious problem—he was pinned to the bottom, more or less in a sitting position, in about two-and-a-half feet of water.

Jack squirmed, trying frantically to free himself, but his legs wouldn't budge. He could wiggle his toes and rotate his feet side to side, so he was fairly sure nothing was broken. But at his angle, he couldn't push the log away with his hands and keep his head above water at the same time.

The fall had distracted him from the roar of the airboat, but he heard it gaining in volume. He wondered for a second if the boat was headed his way, but suddenly, the sound shifted. He could hear the engine accelerate, clearly traveling away from him.

"No!" he screamed. "No! No! Not fair! You can't leave! No!"

Jack screamed until his throat was hoarse and tears were running down his cheeks. He screamed and screamed with frustration and rage until he screamed himself out. And then he stopped abruptly, wiping the tears and mud from his face.

Get it together, he told himself. There had to be something he could do.

He breathed deeply, waiting for his heart rate to return to normal. Looking around, he surveyed his situation. *Not good.* The wind had finally dropped, barely whispering through the treetops above. An eerie quiet had returned to the swamp.

Jack tested his legs again and got the same results. The log had him pinned like a moth in a display case.

At least his bamboo club floated on the weedy surface within grabbing distance. He wrapped both hands around the large end, jabbing it into the soft, muddy bottom. Pulling it close to his chest, he realized he could use it as a kind of leaning post. Something, at least.

Out of the corner of his right eye, Jack caught a flash of movement on the bank. A gator was slipping slowly into the water. He suddenly thought of another purpose for the club. *Weapon.*

It wasn't a big gator, at least not like the eight-footer he'd chased off earlier. Jack was guessing four, maybe five feet, max. On the other hand, he wasn't exactly in the best defensive position. Plus, he was completely blind to anything sneaking up on him from behind.

The gator stopped, eyeing him with only its snout, eyes and part of its tail above water. After a long minute, it began a slow swim toward Jack.

Jack rescanned the water around him, catching sight of another possibility. A chunk of log about the size of a softball floated just out of arm's reach. Pulling the club from the bottom, he used it to rake the chunk of wood toward him. Then, clutching it in his right hand, he swiveled toward the gator.

He'd only have one chance to make an impression.

As the gator continued his slow approach, Jack waited until it was six or so feet away. Then, yelling at the top of his lungs, he flung the piece of log with all his strength.

Thwack. It caught the gator right between the eyes. He'd never made a luckier throw in his life.

Surprised and stung, the gator boiled at the top the water, its tail thrashing the surface as it pivoted back toward the bank.

"Take that!" Jack yelled as the gator gave the surface one last violent beating with its tale before diving under.

It was gone, or at least Jack hoped so.

Of course, there could be—no doubt *were*—more. Not to mention other things.

Jack jammed his club back down into the bottom, silently cursing himself for rushing across the footbridge. He looked down at his watch, a digital Timex sports model that somehow, miraculously, still worked. It was still early, not even nine yet. He glanced up through the canopy of trees. Pockets of blue sky painted openings in the branches. It felt like the weather was taunting him.

An hour passed, then two, then three, then four. As the day grew warmer, Jack grew incredibly tired. A sense of doom descended like a dark cloud. And if he was doomed, so was Olivia.

Way to go, Landry. I've killed us both.

Thirst and hunger burned at his core. He could still move his toes, but his legs had grown numb.

Time blurred, faded, fled. Twice he dozed, only to be awakened when he lost his grip on his club and his head slipped beneath the surface. He came up sputtering and choking, spitting water each time.

Then, as the sun moved lower in the trees, a cloud of deerflies swarmed him.

He'd never seen so many before. He swatted and swiped them from his arms and his head, but still they bit and stung, relentlessly attacking. On the verge of losing it, Jack could only hold his breath and slip beneath the disgusting water to escape them.

Past exhaustion, Jack found himself on the verge of surrender. Surely it was better to let himself drown than be bitten to death by flies. He honestly tried to hold his breath till he lost consciousness. But he couldn't do it. He bolted to the surface, gasping for breath, batting at the air involuntarily, expecting the onslaught to continue.

But something had changed. The flies were gone. The sunny day had turned eerily dark. Clouds scudded low above the treetops, and the wind had changed directions. The temperature was dropping. A low-grade moaning filled the swamp.

In the distance, Jack heard what he first thought were more gunshots. After a minute, he realized it was something else—thunder.

Great. Why not? Might as well pile it on.

Seconds later, the swamp grew even darker and the wind began to whipsaw the branches. He glanced at his watch again. Probably an hour before sunset.

Trapped like an animal in a giant, muddy ditch. Clearly another front moving in, which meant rain, lightning, probably dropping temperatures.

He wondered if hypothermia was a better way to die than a lightning strike. Or being mauled by a gator. Or bitten by a snake or a poisonous spider. Or just sitting here, slowly dying from hunger, thirst, and exposure.

With that thought, Jack began to struggle again, trying to arch his legs, jamming his club deeper into the bottom to try to give his body leverage over the log. As he strained and groaned and cried out in deepening frustration, the club snapped, sending his head under water again.

He had broken his leaning post, the one thing that had provided any comfort.

Jack, pushing himself upright again with his hands, came up sputtering, wondered why he'd bothered.

The day was growing darker still, the wind quickening, more peals of thunder rattling through the distant swamp. The storm was clearly edging closer.

Jack began to sob. Not out of fear but out of the rawest frustration and rage he had ever felt.

He tossed away the broken end of the club. "I give up!" he shouted. "Okay? I give up!"

Jack listed backward, exhausted, dizzy, no longer caring about anything. Maybe he would go to sleep. *Sleep would be good.*

He was seconds away from slipping under the water again when a thin beam of light struck his eyes.

"You asshole!" Olivia yelled. "*There* you are! What *happened* to you? I thought you left me! What are you *doing* down there?"

Jack rubbed his eyes, wondering if he was hallucinating.

But Olivia, standing on the edge of the log bridge, was real.

Before he could answer, she spoke again. "I'm coming down, Jack. And don't you dare give up!"

CHAPTER 11

"IT'S GROSS DOWN here," said Jack. "Slippery, too. So go slow."

Jack wondered if he should tell her about the gator he'd chased off.

He decided "no" was probably the right answer. Anyway, if Olivia couldn't rescue him, he doubted she could save herself out here alone. They were in this together.

"What happened?" she said.

"I was stupid. There *were* people here. I heard them talking. They took off in a boat. I yelled, but they couldn't hear me. The wind was too strong and the engine was too loud. So, I tried to chase them down."

He described the disastrous fall from the log bridge and the fallen log that had him pinned in the muck.

"Jesus," Olivia said. "Are you hurt?"

"My pride, mostly, I think," Jack replied.

"I thought you weren't coming back. I thought you *left* me."

"Sorry," Jack said. "But, seriously, I would never leave you. I promise."

Olivia nodded. "Fine. But when we get you out of this mudhole, we're sticking together. No more you-going-off-alone-to-be-a-hero crap. I mean it."

Jack raised his hands in mock surrender. "Deal."

Olivia shook her head, a crease forming on her brow. "Hey, what were those bushes I had to go through, by the way? Because I *hate* them. If I hadn't found your path, I wouldn't have made it. You'd have totally died here."

"Palmettos. They're the worst."

As he spoke, thunder pealed in the distance.

"Awesome," he said. "Because that's just what we need right now... a thunderstorm."

"What should I do?" Olivia asked, glancing toward the sky.

"Before you come down, see if you can find a long stick or something. A broken branch, or anything like that. We need something to use as leverage, so we can try to roll this log off my legs."

"Will your spear work?"

Jack shook his head. "You brought it?"

"Well, I wasn't going to come after you unarmed," she said. "I'm not stupid."

Jack grinned. "Have I told you how amazing you are? Because seriously, you're *amazing*. You'll just have to make sure not to snap it. If you do, we're screwed."

"So no pressure, right?"

"Right. Just our lives, hanging in the balance."

"Great. I knew I shouldn't have let you go off alone."

"It seemed like a good idea at the time."

"Well, Swamp Boy, this is a major disappointment. You'll owe me big-time when we get out of here."

"You mean *if*."

Olivia literally growled at him as more thunder pealed in the distance. "Stop with the pessimism! Man up! I'm coming down."

"Okay, okay, I'm sorry."

"You should be. So exactly how gross *is it* down there?"

"On your scale, probably worse than gross," Jack said.

Olivia looked up and away for a second as if plotting strategy. "Shoes on or off?"

"On. There might be sharp stuff down here."

"Excellent," Olivia said. "I love having perpetually wet feet. Oh, wait, one sec, let me grab the spear."

Olivia disappeared from view for a moment and reappeared,

holding the length of sharpened bamboo aloft in her right hand. She held up the left hand, showing him the flashlight.

"Here, catch this," she said, gently tossing him the spear.

Jack caught it deftly with his free hand. She put the flashlight between her teeth. He watched intently as Olivia edged down the muddy bank, skidding at one point but managing to keep her balance. She waded slowly in, sinking past her knees after only a few steps. She kept slogging forward and soon stood, thigh deep, at Jack's side.

She pulled the flashlight from her mouth. "Gross," she said. "Here, hold this."

Jack took the light from her.

"So what's the plan?" she asked.

"Wait, you think I have a plan?"

Olivia narrowed her gaze. "Wrong answer."

"Just kidding," he said, pointing at the log. "There. Jab the big end of the spear down under the log at an angle, then pry up slowly. Once I feel it lift, I should be able to move forward and help you roll it off."

"Okay," Olivia said. "Let's do it."

She moved into place, jabbing the butt end of the spear into the gap between the log and bottom that had been created by Jack's leg. She strained to pry it up, but the spear began to bend. The log wasn't budging.

"It's not working," she said, panting.

"Maybe move it farther in?"

Olivia tried, but it didn't help. Frustrated, she twirled the spear around and jabbed the sharp end into the muddy bottom.

"This is ridiculous. I'm going down there."

"Are you sure?" Jack asked.

"You have a better idea?" He shook his head. "I wish."

"I'm going to try to get my arms under it and lift it, and then push up with my legs. As soon as you feel it move, feel free to help."

"Got it."

Jack watched as Olivia took a deep breath, closed her eyes, and plunged down. He could feel her brushing his knee. The water began to churn as she wrestled with the log.

At first, nothing happened. Jack began to count the seconds, dreading the moment Olivia would quit, but then he felt the log lift slightly.

Jack rose, awkwardly at first, and began to push, too, harder than he'd ever pushed in his life. And then suddenly, he was on his feet, knocking into Olivia, who had come up sputtering. She fell backward again into the mud and slush.

She pulled herself up, shuddering.

"God, sorry," Jack said.

She waved him off. "Are you okay?"

"I feel, uh, weird," Jack replied. "I can feel my feet and ankles, but I can't feel my knees. It's like I'm standing on stumps."

"At least you're standing. Let's get out of here. It's getting chillier by the minute."

As Olivia spoke, thunder cracked overhead and a flash of lightning lit the treetops. A wind gust rattled branches above them, and then the sound of pelting rain suddenly filled the swamp. Giant drops exploded in the water around them.

There was another crack of thunder, this one so loud that it rattled their eardrums.

"Which way?" Olivia asked, pulling her arms around herself.

Jack hesitated. "I don't know," he admitted. "It's at least a couple of miles back to the tent. We need somewhere closer, some place to wait out this storm."

Olivia peered around. "Where?"

The wind picked up as the rain began to literally roar from the sky. Another flash of lightning gave Jack an idea.

"Up that bank!" he shouted, pointing to the opposite side of the slough. "The hunters were down that path. There might be something there, a campsite or a duck blind or something."

Jack tried to take a step forward, but his legs were unsteady. Olivia grabbed his hand as he pitched back into the muck, almost bringing her down with him.

"What's wrong?" she yelled.

"My legs aren't working right," he called back. "It's like they're asleep. Here, help me."

Olivia pulled Jack up into a standing position again. He shook his legs up and down, trying to get some feeling into them.

"Okay," he said. "Let's go!"

Another streak of lightning gashed the sky, illuminating the swamp like the pop of a giant flashbulb. A cannon shot of thunder followed.

"Run!" Jack yelled above the din. "Up the bank!"

They lurched forward, hand in hand, scrambling through the knee-deep mud and water. They reached the bank, churning and clawing their way up the slippery incline. Jack's legs tingled painfully, but at least he could feel them again.

Olivia reached the top first, panting loudly, yanking on Jack's arm as she pulled him to level ground.

"That way!" Jack yelled, pointing toward what seemed to be path through a clutch of oaks.

They sprinted ahead, Jack gasping for breath, too, as the full fury of the storm descended. As they reached a clearing in the path, rain pelted them like dull needles. Jack hit a puddle and slipped, dragging Olivia down with him. As they slid headlong through a slick of mud, lighting struck a large branch in a tree behind them. They looked back in horror to see it splinter from the trunk in a haze of gray smoke, dragging down other branches with it.

"Stop falling!" Olivia yelled.

They scrambled up, trying desperately to gain traction on a trail that was becoming a quagmire. The path took another short bend, and as they rounded it, coming up on a straightaway, another bolt of lightning struck the treetops right above them. More branches crashed noisily to the ground.

Jack felt the hair rise on the back of his neck. "Keep running!" he yelled to Olivia over the crash of the storm. "We've got to keep running!"

They sped ahead in the failing light, the rain blasting them forward, the wind pushing them back, the mud-slick path trying to knock them off their feet.

Jack slowed first, clutching his stomach. "I can't go anymore. I think I'm going to puke."

"No!" Olivia screamed. "Come on! No puking allowed!"

She yanked violently on Jack's arm, pulling him forward. He tried his best to follow, stumbling behind and thinking at any moment he would collapse.

He might've, too, but as they reached the end of the straightaway, Olivia suddenly stopped, pulling Jack up short and pointing.

"Holy shit! Do you see that?"

Jack peered ahead in confusion, weaving on his unsteady feet.

Maybe fifty yards away, barely visible through the blowing rain and fading light, stood a small wooden hunting camp set on stilts maybe six feet off the ground. Steps led up to a small porch and a door.

When another blast of lightning speared the path behind them, sending an electrical charge along the ground that sizzled up their legs, they sprinted for their lives. The charge somehow cleared Jack's muddled brain, and he suddenly realized there was a good chance the camp would be locked. They couldn't stand around in this, trying to get it open.

"Underneath!" he shouted as they neared the cabin.

As two back-to-back bolts of lightning jolted the ground behind them, seeming almost to set the very air on fire, they dove on their stomachs between an opening in the stilts, sliding on the slick mud beneath the cabin.

Feeling dry ground in front of them, they scrambled back from the edge as far as they could, bumping into what felt like a wall.

By this time, it was close to pitch dark. Jack, who could barely see Olivia to his left, clutched for her arm. Just then, they heard a low growl in the darkness beyond Olivia.

"Uh, Jack," she said. "I don't suppose you have that flashlight?"

Jack frantically patted his pockets, searching for the penlight.

"Shit," he said. "I must've lost it. But wait, wait . . . I have something."

He dug into his filthy right pants pocket and came out with the butane lighter. "It's sealed, I think, so maybe it doesn't matter if it got wet."

Jack gave it a flick, then two, then three. On the fourth, it flared.

The underside of the cabin was enclosed by wooden walls on three sides.

In a far corner to their left, illuminated by the flickering light, was the biggest animal Jack had ever seen in the wild.

"What *is* that?" Olivia whispered, clutching for Jack's arm.

Jack stared for a long moment.

And then, his voice barely above a whisper, he said, "I'm pretty sure it's a panther."

CHAPTER 12

ANOTHER GASH OF lightning lit up the rain-swept darkness, framing the giant black cat in all its awful glory. It was coiled, maybe thirty feet away, in the corner, as if ready to pounce, ears pinned back, fangs bared, eyes glowing cold and red, its snarl even louder than the thunder.

Icy fear raced down Jack's back.

In all his years traveling the Atchafalaya, he'd never encountered a panther, and though hunters claimed to have occasionally seen one, most people believed they didn't exist this far north. Jack knew that, technically, the cat was the Florida panther and technically panthers were brown, not black. But there were extremely rare instances of a genetic mutation that produced a black cat.

Jack would've loved to have met this panther from the safety of a boat. But this way? He shuddered.

Olivia whispered again, "Are we going to die?"

Jack, gazing at the cat in the flickering glow of the lighter, didn't have an answer.

"The storm must have driven it in here," Jack whispered. "It's got to be scared, too. We just need to stay calm."

"Easy for you to say," Olivia murmured. "I'm closer."

"I have an idea," Jack whispered. "You're never supposed to run from a big cat. You're supposed to talk to it in a firm voice and make yourself look bigger. Make it think it'll get a fight if it attacks."

"How do you know this?"

"I saw it online."

"Oh, great. That's terribly reassuring. And we're supposed to do this how, exactly?"

"We'll stand up, really slowly. I'll hold the lighter up. Our shadows will make us look huge. And then we'll just tell it to . . . go away."

"Oh, I see. Do panthers speak English, Jack? I doubt it. Why don't *we* go away?"

"Where? Back out into the storm? Be my guest."

"We could break into the cabin," she whispered.

"We *are* going to break into the cabin. But if we try to leave, he might think we're running away and attack. That would be a very bad outcome. These things are the first cousin to the mountain lion. They can bring down a full-grown deer. Easily."

Olivia drew in a deep breath. "I didn't go through all this to become cat food."

"We're not going to be. We just need to stand up. *Slowly.*"

"Are you positive about this?"

"Not really," he said grimly, pushing himself unsteadily to his feet.

Olivia set her jaw, following his lead.

Jack spoke in a calm but firm voice. "Okay. Time for you to go," he told the giant cat. "Got it, big guy?" He raised his voice a notch. "Come on, let's go. Get out of here!"

As Jack spoke, he slowly rotated the flaming butane lighter. It began to cast slow-moving shadows on the walls.

The panther stiffened, swiveling its head back and forth toward the shadows. Then it turned his gaze back toward Jack and Olivia.

"Okay," whispered Jack. "Raise your hands as high as you can. Start waving them back and forth. But slow. Real slow."

Olivia complied. The cat glanced away from them, clearly curious about the shadows now dancing on the wall behind it. He threw his head back and let out another snarl.

"Okay, Swamp Boy," Olivia said. "I'm not sure this is working."

"Here," Jack told her. "Switch positions. Get behind me. But, again, slow. Real slow."

Olivia rotated slowly to the other side of Jack. He pushed the lighter directly out in front him, raising his voice again. "You need to get out of here," Jack said, dropping his voice as deep as it would go. "Get out!"

The panther rose. But instead of heading for the exit, it shook itself and began inching toward Jack, looking past him at Olivia.

She tightened her grip on his arm. "Jack?"

"Hold on," he said. "Just . . . wait."

And, before he could think about what he was doing, he threw back his head and barked the loudest, fiercest snarl he could summon. Olivia jumped back in alarm, letting go of Jack's arm as she did.

Jack barked again, even louder, letting out a burst of menacing howls. He rotated the butane lighter in a widening circle, finally thrusting it directly at the cat.

And just like that, the panther vanished into the night so quickly that Jack didn't even see it happen.

He peered toward the opening, wondering if the flickering light had tricked him.

But no, the giant cat was gone.

Jack turned toward Olivia, who was gazing toward the opening in disbelief.

"It's really gone?" she asked.

"Yeah. I mean, uh, I think so. Yeah."

She shook her head. "Where on earth did you learn to do that?"

"You mean howl like a mad dog?"

He gave a shaky laugh, feeling the adrenaline flood through his body.

"I don't know," he said. "I've always been able to do it. My dogs hate it. They never know where it's coming from. They think a strange dog has invaded the farm."

"That's insane."

"Yeah, well, I didn't actually think it was going to work."

At that moment, Jack rocked unsteadily on his feet. He suddenly clutched at his stomach.

"Here," he said to Olivia, his voice quavering. "Hold the lighter. We need the fuel, but keep it on for a few more minutes. Just to make sure the panther's really gone."

Olivia took the lighter from him. "Sure," she said. "But what you are going to do?"

"I'm going to throw up."

And, with that, he turned away and vomited.

A second later, he crumpled to the soft dirt.

CHAPTER 13

"JACK, COME ON, get up. Get up. I can't get you up there by myself!"

Jack could feel someone shaking him. He felt like he was in a deep, cold fog. He didn't want to get up. He just wanted to lie in the dark. Let go of everything and just sleep.

"Leave me alone," he mumbled.

The voice grew louder. "Jack, listen to me. The cabin door wasn't even locked. There's running water and a sleeping bag. There's a bed! But we have to get you up there. You could have hypothermia, okay? And I can't carry you."

Jack tried to open his eyes but couldn't. He felt a hand on his forehead and weakly tried to push it away.

"No," he mumbled again. "Just let me sleep."

A second later, he felt a hand smack across his cheek. "Stop it, Landry!" Olivia yelled. "Just get the hell *up*, okay? I'm not going to let you die down here!"

She slapped him again, harder this time.

Jack forced open his eyes. Olivia's hand loomed in front of his face, ready to strike again.

"Hey," he said, glaring up at her. "Stop that!"

"I will if you get up!" Olivia said. "Come on, there's a break in the storm. We need to go, *now*."

Jack shook his head, trying to clear it. "How long have I been sleeping?"

"I don't know," Olivia said, her voice agitated. "An hour, maybe? I couldn't get upstairs right away. It was still lightning, and I wanted to make sure that . . . *thing* . . . was gone. I spent forever trying to pull the stupid door open, but then I finally just pushed on it, and it opened. There are kerosene lamps and a bunk bed and an old sleeping bag. I don't even know what else. So come on, let's go."

"I'm so cold," he said, shivering. "Why am I so cold?"

"That front's moved through," said Olivia, urgency in her voice. "It feels like the temperature has dropped at least twenty degrees. It's chilly and getting colder. Come on, up. Grab my hands."

He nodded, reaching for her with shaking arms. With her help, he pulled himself unsteadily to his feet, immediately slumping against her. She staggered beneath his weight.

"Work with me here, okay?" she said.

"I can't," he panted.

"You *can* . . . you *have* to," she said firmly. "Now come on."

She half-carried, half-dragged him out from beneath the cabin, pausing at the base of the steps to catch her breath. Jack looked up; the soft glow of the kerosene lamps lit up the open doorway and two windows on either side.

"Twelve steps," Olivia said. "You've got this."

Jack nodded, shivering so violently that he could feel his teeth slam together. "Okay. Yeah."

Somehow, they made it to the top of the stairs. Jack felt like he'd never worked so hard in his life. He stumbled through the door, beyond exhaustion.

"No falling down," Olivia warned him. "Here, hold this." She led him over to the bunk bed, transferring his hands to the railing.

"Just for a sec."

Jack focused on staying upright. He heard the door close, then the click of a latch, and then Olivia was back at his side.

"Okay, we need to get you out of your wet clothes and into the sleeping bag. Which, for the record, looks like it's never been washed . . . but whatever. You get in first, and then I'll climb in."

"What do you mean?" Jack asked, clenching his jaw to try to stop it from shaking.

"Jack, you're *hypo*thermic," she explained, over-annunciating each syllable. "We can't exactly make a fire in here. So body heat it is."

"I'm getting naked?" he asked, shivering.

"Yes," she said. "Come on."

He looked down at himself. "I'm pretty gross."

Olivia rolled her eyes. "Because that's our biggest problem right now. Body odor. C'mon, you're the Swamp Rat. Get over it!"

She snapped her fingers in front of his face. "Jack, *focus*. You're in trouble, here. Do you understand?"

Jack nodded. His brain was having trouble wrapping itself around her words. Olivia untied the filthy long-sleeve shirt that was somehow still tied around Jack's waist, helping him shrug out of his T-shirt.

"Okay, sit down," she said.

Jack slumped obediently on the edge of the lower bunk. He was wracked by another violent shiver.

Olivia pulled off his wet, muddy sneakers and filthy socks. "Belt, let's go."

Jack tried, but his hands were shaking too hard.

"Never mind," Olivia said. "I got it."

With quick movements, she pulled his belt free, then tugged at the bottom of his green swamp-tour khakis, tossing them aside.

"Underwear," she said matter-of-factly. "Off now."

Jack managed to struggle out of his boxers by himself, which felt like a small victory.

"Sleeping bag," Olivia ordered him. She leaned over him, unzipping the cheap, green sleeping bag, exposing its standard lumberjack-check lining.

Jack crawled in, still shaking, and turned over on his side. As he wrapped his arms close to his chest, Olivia pulled the sleeping bag up around his neck.

"One sec," she said.

Jack closed his eyes. He heard Olivia walk across the floor, followed by a quiet rustling noise as she undressed.

The room suddenly went dark as Olivia blew out the kerosene lamps. A second later, she was slipping in beside Jack, zipping the bag shut and pressing her warm body against his, draping an arm over his chest.

"Don't get any ideas," she said.

"About what?" Jack replied, teeth chattering. "I'm too cold to have ideas about anything. Anyway, I've never heard of a snowman having sex."

Olivia snorted with laughter. "Funny. But, oh, my God," she said. "You're *so cold*. I don't know if this is going to work. Here, roll over on your stomach."

"Why?"

"Plan B."

Jack did as Olivia told him. The next thing he knew, she was easing on top of him, covering his body from head to toe.

"Tell me if I'm crushing you," she said. "But I think this is probably the best way."

Jack was too exhausted to do anything other than nod. He closed his eyes and lay perfectly still, absorbing Olivia's warmth.

Slowly, ever so slowly, his chills faded.

He dozed on and off. An hour passed, maybe two; his sense of time had disappeared. Finally, he drifted into a deep, warm sleep filled with Technicolor dreams.

He woke to a warm hand on his forehead.

"Hey," Olivia said. "You in there?"

Jack opened his eyes a tiny crack, blinking at the soft light above him. Sleep tugged at him, but so did Olivia's voice.

He felt like a fish rising in slow circles from the bottom of a warm, clear lake toward a patch of golden sun on the surface.

Is the night over?

Olivia spoke again, her hand moving to his cheek. "Jack, you awake?"

"Getting there," he mumbled. "But I'm definitely alive."

"I was kind of counting on that," she said.

Jack's eyes finally focused. Olivia was sitting on the edge of the bunk bed, wrapped in a tattered green blanket.

"Nice outfit," he said.

"Thanks," she said. "I went shopping." She pointed at the small closet in the corner. "If you play your cards right, there's a brown one in there, too. I think it'd look good on you."

Jack nodded. He let his head fall back against the bunk. "So . . . last night. Was I dying from hypothermia?"

Olivia nodded. "Seemed that way."

He stared up at her. "I don't remember it all. Except the getting naked part."

She grinned. "Shocking."

"How'd you know to do that, anyway?" he asked.

"The body-to-body thing?" Olivia asked. "It was part of my training. We got super lucky with the sleeping bag. Who knows what would have happened if we hadn't been able to get in here?"

"Training," Jack repeated. His brain still felt a little foggy. "Like . . . Red Cross?"

She raised an eyebrow. "Ever heard of Outward Bound?"

"What, survival school?"

Olivia shrugged. "Basically."

Jack was impressed. "You never said."

"Well, it's not like we've had a lot of time to get to know each other," she jabbed. "You know, what, with trying desperately to stay alive and all that stuff."

Jack smiled. "You're funny. You know that?"

"Yeah, right. I'm hilarious," Olivia said, pushing her hair back. "I should do stand-up."

He stretched inside the sleeping bag, starting to slowly revive. It felt good to talk. "So where'd you do Outward Bound?"

"Up in Maine," she told him. "The summer before last."

"I've never been. Well, I've never been most places. Did you see a moose?"

"A few. Not on my solo overnight campout, luckily. They're *huge*. And dangerous in the wrong circumstances."

"I'm impressed," he said. "Solo camping trips aren't exactly my favorite thing."

"Really? You? *Mister I Kill Alligators and Chase Black Panthers Away?* I took you for someone who would be out here alone for days communing with nature."

"Yeah, well, sure, I've come out here fishing and hunting alone from time to time. But I actually prefer sharing this place with people. Family, friends. It makes it more interesting."

Jack paused. "Anyway, you don't know me that well."

Olivia smiled. "True. But I did just spend the night with you, totally naked. I think that counts for something."

Jack blushed. "Unfair," he said. "If I'm going to spend the night naked with a hot girl, I should at least be able to remember some of it. But it's a blank. Well, mostly. Could I get a do-over?"

Olivia punched Jack on the arm. It seemed a little hard to be playful, though a promise of a smile creased her lips.

"In your dreams. And, uh, excuse me, Jack Landry. Did you just call me hot?"

"Please," Jack said. "You know you are."

"I dunno. But anyway, is that relevant?"

Jack shrugged. "It's not irrelevant. Like my grandpa says, 'Jack, beauty ain't everything, but doggone, it is *somethin'*.'"

She laughed. "Your grandfather actually says that? Seriously?"

"All the time," Jack replied.

"Hmm, okay," she said, readjusting her blankets as she found a more comfortable position. "So that's me? Hot? That's it?"

"I didn't say just hot. I could add a few other things."

"I'm waiting."

"You're a lot like the swamp."

"What?"

"You know . . . beautiful, mysterious, but an easy place to get lost."

Olivia shook her head. "Okay, that might be the weirdest comment I've ever been paid. It's actually a compliment."

"It is. And it's poetic, yes?"

"Maybe. Anything else weird you want to add?"

Jack stroked his chin in an exaggerated way, looking up at the ceiling.

Finally, he said, "You're smart, obviously. Brave. Determined. Feisty. Sophisticated. And funny. But I already told you that. Now it's your turn."

"Who says I want a turn? Are you fishing for compliments?"

Jack smiled. "Of course!"

Olivia nodded. "Well, don't get too carried away, but it's possible that you're nothing like I expected you to be."

"You mean like a hick from the sticks?"

"No, not that at all. I'm not *really* a snob, even though we all have our stereotypes. No, the real problem is that my dad wouldn't shut up about you. 'Oh, Olivia, that boy down in the bayou, isn't he something? Did you read this great thing he wrote? It's so insightful.' On and on. I guess I was . . . jealous. I didn't think I was going to like you. I actually didn't *want* to like you. But, okay, don't let it go to your head, but you might be alright."

"Maybe?"

"Well, you still have time to prove me wrong."

"Hah!"

Olivia's face turned serious. "Look, I hate being here. I feel like I'm always a minute from a complete meltdown. But if I had to crash, I'm glad it was with you. You stayed with me and looked after me and risked your life even getting us here, even though you didn't have to. That basically explains why I'm alive."

Jack smiled. "Well, rescuing me from that ditch and saving me from hypothermia kind of makes us even. And that's nice of you to say, but anybody would've stayed with you."

"Duh, yeah, because they would've had no choice. Who else would've known how to get to high ground in the first place? Not anybody that I know. Well, my father, maybe, but my city friends? No way. I'd probably be alligator food by this time."

"Possibly. But I'm sure you'd be tasty."

Olivia punched him on the arm again.

"Gross! That's not funny."

"Right. But why are you smiling?"

"I'm not smiling."

"You are too smiling."

Olivia surrendered. "Oh, whatever, Jack! But just remember we're a team now. We stick together no matter what."

"Like, Swamp Boy and Swamp Girl? If only we had capes."

Olivia laughed hard.

"We do have these really ugly blankets," she said when she recovered. "In fact, I should get yours for you."

"Sounds good,'" Jack replied. "Speaking of what we may not have, I don't suppose you found any food last night?"

Olivia frowned. "No. But there's water. Or at least there's a tap. The water comes out kind of yellow, so I don't know if it's good or not. And there's another closet with a padlock on it. Maybe that's where they stash their supplies."

"Really? A locked closet? That's promising."

"Yeah," said Olivia. "Why, do you know how to pick locks?"

He shrugged. "I know how to break them."

"Great. Our clothes are still wet, so let me get you that blanket. Let's get to work."

Olivia returned with the bedraggled brown cover. Jack dragged it into the sleeping bag, wrapping it around his waist like a towel before emerging. "Coming out," he said. "No laughing."

"I like what you've done with it," Olivia said, looking him over.

"Very stylish."

"I try," Jack said, looking around the cabin for the first time.

※

It was basically a one-room shack. Besides the bunk bed, there was small wooden table shoved under one window, flanked by two scuffed-up wooden chairs.

A ratty green armchair sat against one wall. Opposite it was a small couch, so faded that Jack couldn't tell what its original color had been. A wire rectangular crab trap with a piece of plywood on top of it sat between them, serving as a coffee table.

Still, compared to their makeshift tent, it was luxurious.

"The closet's there, by the sink," Olivia said, pointing.

Jack walked first to the sink, which was flanked by white wooden cabinets. The doors were warped and hung partially open. He turned on the tap. Olivia was right, the water ran yellowish. It could just be rust in the pipes. He twisted the spigot full open and stood there until the water ran clear.

He cupped some in his hand, sniffed it, and took a tentative sip.

"It's cistern water!"

Olivia raised her eyebrows. "Is that a good thing?"

"It's rainwater! The yellow stuff was just gunk in the pipes. It's running clear now."

He bent forward, mouth level with the faucet, cupping both hands and drinking deeply for a long minute. Considering the circumstances, it was the best thing he'd ever tasted.

"Come on," he told Olivia. "You need to drink, too. You're probably dehydrated."

She hesitated. "Are you sure it's okay?"

"Positive. There might even be a cup or something. Did you check the cabinets?"

"Yeah. Not a lot to work with," Olivia said.

Jack bent down, pulling the doors open. Olivia was right. On one side, there were two dime-store plastic glasses decorated with apples and oranges and one chipped white coffee mug featuring a cartoonish red crawfish. On the other side, Jack found two tin pie plates and a fire-blackened skillet with half a handle.

"These people are either cheap bastards or they don't come here very often."

He turned and handed one of the glasses to Olivia. "I'd rinse it out first."

"You think?"

Jack checked the drawers on either side of the sink. They contained one spoon and a bent fork.

"These people officially suck."

Olivia laughed. Edging past Jack to the sink, she rinsed out the glass, filled it, and drank.

"Oh, my God," she said.

"Told you so." He rummaged through the other drawers, finally hitting pay dirt—a rusty hammer and a screwdriver with a paint-spattered handle. "Now we're talking," he said.

"What?" Olivia asked.

Jack held up the tools in triumph.

She looked unimpressed. "Yay?"

"Just wait," Jack said. He walked to the closet, fingering the padlock and eyeing it carefully. He placed the head of the screwdriver expertly where the shackle met the locking chamber and then rapped sharply on the butt of the screwdriver handle with the hammer once, twice, three times. The lock sprung open.

"Thank you, Jesus!" Jack declared, pumping a fist into the air.

He removed the lock and tossed it aside, along with his tools.

"Impressive," she admitted, refilling her water glass. "How'd you know how to do that?"

"Paw-Paw. He was in the Marine Corps long ago. It was part of his survival training. He thought it could come in handy one day."

"Good thing. You just earned another brownie point."

"Good to know. Now, let's see what we've got here," Jack said, flinging the closet door open.

It took a couple of seconds for his eyes to adjust to the dimness inside.

"Ah, better than gold. This is so freaking awesome!"

Jack began to count, rummaging as he went. "One, two, three, four, five, six, seven, eight."

He turned to Olivia. "I hope you like beans."

CHAPTER 14

ON THE THIRD morning since their crash, Jack and Olivia sat in their blankets on the shack's small porch, soaking in the morning sun. Olivia had showed Jack how to tie his blanket like a toga, like hers.

"The benefits of a private-school education," she told him.

The view from the porch overlooked a pretty marsh through which a narrow bayou carved a dark, curved ribbon. Swamp sunflowers flanked both banks, framing the ribbon in bright yellow.

A golden haze hung over the water. The sky beamed crystal blue, as if the storm had somehow purified the air—a perfect day, maybe seventy degrees with temperatures definitely rising. A chalky day moon hung up in one corner of the sky like a fingernail.

Jack didn't let himself get too excited. The weather had been a fickle friend. As they'd seen yesterday, it could turn on them in a minute.

Jack had been forced to hack two cans of beans open with the Swiss Army knife, going painfully slow so he didn't bend or break its blade. That would be a disaster. It was inelegant, but it worked. They'd dragged the two rickety chairs outside and were now feasting on lukewarm Campbell's Pork & Beans. At least they were the twenty-eight-ounce cans.

They still bore their barely legible Walmart price stickers. So did the two other items Jack had found behind the bean cans—a box of salt and box of a popular seafood spice called Zatarain's. Cajuns boiled crawfish, shrimp, and crabs in it.

Jack felt like he could eat all eight cans of beans in one sitting. Instead, he was thinking about the best way to ration them. Very slowly, he scooped another spoonful into his mouth with the bent fork. He'd given Olivia the spoon.

Which, for the record, was also bent.

He decided they should each eat one can now, to replenish their energy, and then split a can for supper. They could forage something for lunch or skip it altogether.

Jack had been a little worried that Olivia would be squeamish about the pork flavoring in the beans, but she was eating just as ravenously as he.

Food, check.

Water, check.

Shelter, check.

Now, they just needed to come up with a plan to get rescued. A glimmer of one began to form in Jack's mind.

He spooned up another mouthful of cheap, cold beans, savoring the taste.

He looked at Olivia, smiling. "Just curious," he said. "Have you ever been to Walmart?"

She returned his smile. "Now, why would I ever go to Walmart?"

"It's fun," said Jack. "And they've got everything."

"I don't think we even have a Walmart in Manhattan," she replied.

"Well, you're missing out."

"Am I? Somehow, it's not on my fun-places-to-visit-before-I-die list."

"Really? Now, for people like Paw-Paw, who grew up in a place where they didn't even have a grocery store, Walmart is, like, crazy exciting. For him, it's like going to the circus. Plus, they'll take anything back. I have a crazy uncle, my mom's youngest brother, who brought back his used underwear because they still pinched after the first washing. And they gave him a refund and put the stuff right back on the rack . . . I'm serious."

Oliva nearly spit her beans, she laughed so hard. "That can't be true, and if it is, it's a great reason *never* to go to Walmart."

Jack smiled. "Well, that's what my uncle said."

"Though I hate to change from this riveting subject," she said, taking another bite of the cold Walmart beans, "what about dinner?"

Jack nodded. "I've thought about it. We can split a can of beans. And I forgot about my turtle, too."

"Your what?"

"A big snapping turtle. I'm surprised you didn't see it when you came looking for me."

"Wait, *that* thing?" Olivia paused with her spoon halfway to her mouth. "Yeah, I saw it. It was huge. I thought maybe it was sick or something. It was on its back and kept waving its feet around in the air."

"I saw it crossing the path, so I grabbed it by the tail and flipped it over so it couldn't crawl away. Turtle meat's delicious. My mom makes this amazing turtle *sauce piquant*."

Olivia scrunched up her nose. "Hmm. If you say so. But the poor turtle."

"Right. I see that point. If I'd found our rescuers, I planned to set it free on my way back to you. But we need more food. Eight cans of beans—six, now—isn't going to last long. Plus, now we have a frying pan. And we still have the lighter. We can set up an outdoor kitchen."

"Do I want to know how you're planning on killing the turtle?"

"The preferred way involves a .22 caliber rifle shot to the head. But I guess I'll have to use the knife. Or the hammer, maybe?"

"Ugh."

"I know," Jack said. "And those things are mean and tough. It's not going to be pretty."

"How are you even going to get the meat back?"

Jack hadn't thought of that; survival was complicated.

"I guess I could butcher it back here."

"Really?" Olivia asked skeptically. "You're going to lug that thing over the log bridge? Maybe you should try for a rabbit. Or a fish!

Ooh, I could definitely eat fish right now."

Jack nodded. The thought of fish brought sudden memories of his mom's batter-fried Cajun catfish. He forced himself to flick the thought away.

"We should make a trip back to the tent," said Jack. "Bring everything back here and get the turtle, too."

"Seriously? You really want to cross that bridge again?" asked Olivia. "Because I'm just warning you, I'm not going muck diving to save you again."

Jack nodded. "We'll just go slow. If it looks sketchy, we'll turn back."

Olivia sighed. "When do you want to go?"

"Unless you want to run naked through the swamp, not until after our clothes dry," Jack said.

"Yeah, that's a pleasure I think I'll forgo," Olivia said.

"Right," Jack replied, grinning. "Being naked in the swamp isn't usually a good idea."

Their clothes and the sleeping bag were spread out all over the porch. The sun would definitely speed the drying process.

Finishing their beans, they headed back inside to dunk their cans and utensils in the sink and open the windows to air the cabin out.

"Why don't you check all the drawers and closets again?" Jack asked. "Maybe we missed something."

"What are you going to do?" Olivia asked.

"I'll go down and take a quick look around. Maybe they have a boat stashed in the bushes somewhere. If they had a pirogue hidden someplace and we could find it, we could paddle our way out of here."

"Okay," said Olivia, "Just don't, like, wander off."

"I'll stay within yelling distance," Jack promised.

Jack reluctantly slipped back into his still-damp sneakers—was there anything worse than wet feet?—and headed down the wooden steps, a little surprised at his sudden burst of energy. At the bottom, he turned left to circle the camp. Behind the cabin, he found the tall wooden cistern that held their water supply, as well as something else that surprised him—an outdoor shower plumbed to the cistern.

Jack would give anything for a bar of soap right now.

He looked around, finding a well-worn trail that snaked from the camp through a thicket of middle-sized cypresses and tupelo gum. It led to a faded wooden building that he immediately recognized as an outhouse.

Jack wondered what Olivia would think of it. At least it was private; the door was fastened with a crude wooden latch that turned on a rusty nail. Jack opened the door expecting the worst.

He couldn't believe what he saw. The outhouse was reasonably clean and neat, mostly devoid of spiderwebs and wasp nests. It smelled bad, of course, but not as bad as it could have. Best of all, it held a real toilet seat and two rolls of toilet paper, a huge discovery.

Of course, there could still be a black widow spider or worse, a brown recluse, lurking in one of the corners. He'd need to scout it out before showing Olivia.

Jack shut the door and latched it. Looking around, he saw that the trail continued beyond the outhouse. Luckily, it didn't lead far.

After a sharp bend, the trail ended at the apron of a sprawling pond ringed by a cattail marsh checkered with brakes of roseau cane. Two small diving ducks—hell divers—spooked from the bank and disappeared with hardly a splash. Just a little up the bank, a great blue heron rose, long legs trailing, and flapped across the water.

Right now, Jack didn't care about the pond's obvious beauty. He was too busy staring at a rickety wooden dock in front of him that extended maybe a dozen feet out into the water. A cane pole sat at the end of the dock, the kind locals used for fishing. If equipped with a line and hook, it could be a lifesaver.

Jack sprinted to the end of the dock, scooping up the pole and staring in wonder. It was fully rigged—line, bobber, sinker, tiny hook. All it lacked was bait, which should be easy enough to procure out here. Grubs, worms, a grasshopper, anything like that would work.

He was already dreaming about fresh fish—bream, bass, catfish, and crappie—when Olivia's shrieks suddenly filled the air.

CHAPTER 15

JACK DROPPED THE pole and bolted for the camp.

He made the steps in no time. Bounding up them, he found Olivia on the porch, her blanket toga sleeve pulled down like a strapless gown.

"God, what are they? What *are* they?"

She peered anxiously over her shoulder, turning to show Jack. "I was checking the closets again like you said. And I found this old mirror in the corner, and I dragged it out because my back was itching, and then I looked and . . . oh, God, get them *off*!"

Leeches. Jack recognized them immediately.

In the dark, with everything else that was happening, they'd gone unnoticed. He'd need to check himself, as well. Clearly, they'd come from their time in the mucky slough.

"Okay, so it's not a crisis," he told Olivia, trying to sound reassuring. "They're just, uh, leeches."

"*Leeches?*"

"But it's not a problem," Jack said quickly. "They don't carry diseases or anything. And we have leech killer inside."

She bit her lip, looking over her shoulder again. "We do?"

He nodded. "Salt. Leeches are pretty much all water. All you have to do is sprinkle them with a tiny bit of salt, and they kind of shrivel up and die."

"What? How do you even know that?"

"Alligator hunting with Dad and Paw-Paw. Gators are always covered with leeches. We, hmm, salt the hides before we skin them. Kills the leeches every time."

Jack kept his voice casual, trying to pretend that leeches were just your normal, run-of-the-mill nuisance and not creepy bloodsuckers that could give you nightmares. In truth, they creeped him out, too.

"I've got this," he told Olivia. "Don't worry, okay? I'll be back in a flash."

Jack ran to get the salt from the cabin. He poured a little into his hand, then sprinkled the four leeches that clung to Olivia's right shoulder.

They immediately rolled up into tiny balls, surrendering their sucker grips and dropping off onto the porch.

"See?" Jack asked, pointing to the small, squirming balls.

Olivia shuddered. "Can you step on them?"

"Well, I mean, they're pretty much dead."

"Great. Now, kill them again," Olivia said. "Pretend they're zombies. Just keep killing them."

"That's cold," Jack said, suppressing a grin. "Leeches have to make a living, too, you know."

"Not on me, they don't." She shook her head. "Okay. So here's the deal. I don't care anymore. About *anything*. You just need to check me out and make sure there aren't more."

Olivia dropped her blanket to the porch floor.

For a second, Jack thought he might fall over.

Pulling himself together, he counted five more leeches on her back, plus two on her butt. He salted them quickly and stomped on them as they fell to the deck.

Clearing his throat, he asked her to turn around. He found two more on the flat of her stomach as she stood with her eyes closed, her hands clasped in front of her.

"So this might feel a little weird. Tickly, or almost like a burn," he said. "Just stay still, okay?"

"Do I look like I'm moving?" Olivia asked, her voice tense, her eyes still closed.

Jack got to work. The leeches fell off one by one, and Jack mushed them with his foot like before.

"So now I'm going to check your hairline and behind your ears. That's as far as they would have gotten. Just . . . ah . . . hold up your hair for me? It'll take just a second."

Olivia pulled her long black hair into a ponytail, twisting it into a knot on her head. Jack did a quick check, then nodded.

"Okay. You're good."

He picked up Olivia's blanket and awkwardly set it on her shoulders. She grabbed the loose ends and pulled it tight around her.

"Are you sure?" she asked, turning to look at him.

"Yeah. They're all gone."

She shook her head. "I can't stand this anymore, Jack. I'm sorry, but I can't. I just . . . I *hate* it. I don't care what we have to do, but we have to get out of this place, okay? We *have* to!"

"Well, sure, of course, I understand. It's natural that—"

She interrupted him. Her eyes were wide, her voice stretched thin like a wire.

"I just want to go home. I want my shower and my bed and clean sheets and my pajamas. I want my apartment. And my dad. And my friends. So can you just get us out of here, Jack?" she said, her voice rising even higher. "Because I would really, really, really appreciate it. Okay?"

She burst into tears, slumping against him as she sobbed. Jack curled his arms around her, patting her on the back, giving her a comforting hug. If Olivia fell apart, it would be easy for him to fall apart too.

"It's okay," he said. "I get it. Leeches are gross. Trust me, I'm not looking forward to checking myself. But they're dead, okay? Like, really, really dead. And hey," he said, suddenly remembering something. "I have a surprise for you."

Olivia stepped back, her reddened face streaked with tears.

"Like what? A plane out of here?"

"I wish. But there *is* an outdoor shower down by the cistern. You can clean up."

"Seriously?" Olivia wiped her cheeks with the back of her hand.

"Yeah. I mean, the water won't be super warm or anything," Jack said. "But it's open air, and the shower's in the sun, so it should be okay. You can dry off with the blanket. I'll wait up here."

"Do you mind coming down with me? Maybe turn your back and hold the blanket? I'm not feeling so great . . . you know, after being gnawed on by leeches. I'm pretty nauseous, actually."

"What, and waste those delicious beans?" Jack joked. "But sure, follow me."

Jack took Olivia's hand and led her down the steps to the shower.

"Just let me check it out first."

He turned a rusty red metal spigot, letting the murky water that had sat in the pipes run until it was clear. The pressure was good. Testing it with his hands, he found it surprisingly warm.

"Okay, it's ready. Sorry, there's no soap."

Olivia managed a wan smile. "What, you don't know how to make any?"

Jack smiled back at her. "Not yet." Turning his back, he held out his hand for the blanket.

Olivia handed it to him and stepped under the shower.

Jack pulled the blanket around his shoulders, looking up at the sky as Olivia doused herself in the warm water. A red-tailed hawk chased by blackbirds crossed the near horizon toward where the pond and dock lay. The blackbirds' angry squawks drifted across the calm blue sky. Somewhere, an unseen cardinal called, and another called back. Jack wondered where the birds were, trying to distract himself from Olivia showering six feet away from him.

His mind was still reeling from the leech hunt on the porch. That tiny butterfly tattoo, way south of her navel?

Yes. Olivia FitzGerald may actually be perfect. Seriously. Perfect.

It seemed like a long time before Jack heard the water turn off.

"I'm done," Olivia said.

Jack took the blanket from his shoulders and, without turning around, held it out to her.

"Okay," she said. "That was something."

"Feel better?"

"A little."

"Well, then, today's your lucky day," Jack said like a game show host. "Because I'm not out of surprises yet."

"Really?" Olivia asked. "You can look now, by the way."

Jack cautiously turned around, relieved to see that Olivia had wrapped the blanket around herself again. Even with her hair wet, draped in that ratty blanket, she looked beautiful.

Jack cleared his throat again. "So, you want to take a walk?"

"How far?" Olivia asked suspiciously.

CHAPTER 16

TWO HOURS LATER, their clothes were finally dry. Olivia and Jack sat on the rickety wooden chairs they'd dragged down to the dock on the pond. The sun blazed overhead in a bright blue sky.

It was warm but not too hot, and Jack was thinking about a swim. Olivia, on the other hand, was never going in the water again. Well, in swamp water.

"If you don't touch bottom, you're fine," Jack told her. "That's where the leeches live."

"I'm fine right where I am," she said. "But you be sure to have fun!"

She'd used the outhouse, grudgingly, while Jack kept watch outside the door. But she'd been considerably more excited about the prospect of fishing. Grilled fish topped lukewarm Walmart beans any day.

Jack left her on the dock to root around under old logs with a sharp stick he'd found, searching for grubs or earthworms. After digging up a handful, he returned, dumping his finds, squirming on the dock. He picked out a small earthworm and skillfully threaded it on the hook.

As soon as he dropped the bait in the water, the bobber disappeared. He pulled and, within seconds, a hand-sized crappie was flopping on the dock. Within five minutes, Jack had caught two more, plus a decent-sized bream.

He pointed to the green, white, and black speckled crappie. "The Cajuns call that fish the *sac-à-lait*—bag of milk. Paw-Paw says that's because it's the sweetest tasting fish in the bayou."

"That's crazy."

"Here," he said to Olivia, baiting the hook with a tiny white grub and handing her the pole. "You should catch one."

"Are you sure?" she asked dubiously. "I don't want to screw anything up. What if I break the pole or something?"

"It's fine," Jack said. "Go ahead. You should get a feel for it."

He pointed to a small cypress stump rising out of the water to the right of the dock. "Go for the edge of that. There should be fish hanging out around it."

Olivia, who'd watched Jack carefully, sent the bait flying into perfect position.

"Nice," Jack said. "Wait, you're not a ringer, are you?"

Before Olivia could answer, the bobber disappeared with a loud *thwuck*. She instinctively pulled, and suddenly, the pole bent double, the line sizzling through the water.

"Holy shit!" Jack yelled. "That's a monster!"

Olivia found herself yelling, too. "It's trying to pull me in!"

The fish made a frantic run for the dock, then abruptly turned away and dove deeper. The pole, bending fiercely, was beginning to slip from Olivia's hand when Jack, standing behind her, reached frantically around and grabbed it just above her hand. The two of them held on in an awkward dance as the fish tugged and thrashed beneath the black tannin waters.

"Okay, okay," said Jack. "Don't horse it. We could break the line or straighten the hook. Let it tire out and come belly up to the dock."

Long minutes passed before the fish finally broke the surface, swimming in slow circles, its gills laboring.

"A catfish!" yelled Jack. "Look at it. It's at least five or six pounds. Plus, it's delicious when cooked right."

Olivia squinted down at the huge fish. "Really? Because it looks ... gross. That head, so weird."

In a few more minutes, the fish played itself out, rolling on its white belly to the surface. Jack got down on his stomach and reached into the water, nudging the catfish right side up. He grabbed it across the back, isolating its sharp front fins between two fingers of each hand so that the cat couldn't stick him. The fins were mildly poisonous and extremely painful if they penetrated the skin.

"It's a flathead cat—a *goujon* to the Cajuns," Jack said as he hoisted the fish to the dock. "Paw-Paw caught a forty-five pounder once, but they get even bigger—fifty, sixty pounds out here. But this one's a thing of beauty. Nice work."

"Beginner's luck," Olivia told him. "But it was strangely kind of fun."

Jack nodded. "Tell me about it. I live to fish. I can't remember *not* fishing. I think my dad and Paw-Paw started taking me when I was two."

Olivia nodded.

She looked down at the dock, an awkward silence falling. "Sorry I haven't asked more about your family at all. I'm not trying to be rude or anything. It's just—"

"Don't worry about it," Jack interrupted. "Seriously. It's not like we haven't had other things to worry about. Come on, let's get this catfish on the fire. Then, if you want, I can tell you all about the Landrys."

He grinned. "More than you probably want to know."

"Okay," Olivia said, smiling back at him. "How are you going to cook it, anyway?"

"A spit of some kind? I'll have to wing it."

"What about the smaller fish?"

"We'll save them for later. Here, I have an idea."

Jack unlaced his right sneaker and tied off a loop on one end of the lace using a simple overhand knot. Then, he threaded the lace through the gills of the still breathing fish, running the free end through the loop on the outside, pulling it tight.

"A stringer," he declared, lifting the fish on his shoelace and lowering them gently into the water. They began to fin slowly, pulling the stringer taut. He tied it to a bent rusty nail conveniently sticking out of the end of the dock. "It'll keep them alive for another meal."

"Smart," said Olivia.

He gave a little bow.

"Me Swamp Boy!" Jack said, grinning as he curled up his right arm in an exaggerated way to show off his muscles.

Olivia tried to suppress a smile but failed. "You're so lame, Jack Landry," she said. "Don't get carried away."

Carrying the catfish over to a grassy patch of ground, he dispatched it by driving the long blade of his knife through its brain. "Sorry, big guy," he told the fish. "But it's not like you'd want to be cooked alive."

He quickly gutted it, wishing he had a place to stow the guts. They'd make good fish bait, or even crawfish bait. Instead, he tossed them into nearby bushes. Some animal would eat them tonight. Nothing got wasted out here.

Jack carried the fish to the camp, washed it thoroughly in the sink, and then sprinkled some of the salt and the seafood seasoning they'd found into the cavity. He left it there and went outside to look for firewood.

On a hunch, he searched the covered area beneath the porch and found that someone had left a small cache of crudely cut oak. He'd still have to scrounge kindling in the woods to start the fire, and cut and whittle a thumb-thick branch to use as a spit. But the oak was a huge help.

Sooner than he'd expected, Jack was kneeling before the red-hot coals of a smoky oak fire, slowly turning the catfish on a spit made from a thin oak branch sharpened at each end that he had driven through the fish's mouth clear out its tail. The spit sat on two, slingshot shaped Ys that he'd whittled from willow branches and driven into the ground at opposite sides of the fire.

The roasting fish smelled even better than he'd expected. "This might actually be good," he told Olivia, who'd moved her chair from the dock to the shade of a tree by the fire.

She took another sip from her glass of water. Jack had brought down the pie plates, eating utensils, and box of salt. It was as close to a picnic as they were going to get.

"It smells good," she said. "Honestly, I didn't have high hopes."

He grinned. "Don't get too excited until we taste it."

"Which will be . . . when, exactly?"

"I'm not sure," he admitted. "But we definitely don't want catfish sushi. Maybe ten, fifteen minutes?"

She nodded. "So, tell me more about the famous Landrys while we wait."

Jack sat back on his heels. "I don't know," he said. "We're pretty typical . . . well, typical for down here. We hunt, we fish, we eat good, go to Mass on Sundays. Well, most Sundays. Well, my mom, anyway. The rest of us go sometimes. My dad does the payroll for the big sugar mill on our side of the swamp. Plus, he has the farm. We grow a little sugarcane and veggies and stuff, and we have a couple of pigs and a few head of beef cattle. Some chickens and ducks. It's more of a hobby than anything. We only have twenty acres. Dad grew up on a farm like ours, and he likes the life. We all help out. I mean, our parents kind of expect it. My younger brothers—that would be Jake Junior and Jerry—and I aren't allowed to sit inside and screw around on the internet all day. My parents are kind of strict that way."

He stopped to give the fish another turn.

"My mom's a librarian at our bayou elementary school. She put herself through college—a small state school, not LSU. She and my dad are both from families of seven kids, but my mom's the only one on either side to get a college degree."

Olivia nodded. "So you must have a ton of cousins?" Jack smiled. "Thousands."

"But how many, really?"

"Thirty-one, last time I counted."

Olivia turned her water glass back and forth in her hand. "I have one. Don't get me wrong, he is a fine cousin, but . . ." She shook her head. "How did your parents meet?"

"A dance. My mom's senior year in college, she and her friends started going to this dance hall down at a place called Chack Bay."

"I'm sorry, did you say *dance hall*?" Olivia interrupted, her voice incredulous. "How old are your parents, anyway?"

"Hey, that's what they call it! It's like another world down there. A lot of the old people still speak French instead of English. All the bands play Cajun French music. The dance hall scene is huge. Anyway, my dad was friends with the guys in the band, so sometimes he got invited up to play the washboard."

Olivia shook her head in confusion. "Did you say a washboard? Like a real washboard? To wash stuff with? How is that a musical instrument?"

"It's a big deal around here," Jack explained. "The Cajuns call it the *frottoir*. It requires real skill and practice to play on stage. In Paw-Paw's day, the musicians used it to keep time on actual washboards because they didn't have drums or they didn't have money to buy drums. Now, they make them specially as musical instruments. Anyway, Dad was on stage when my mom came up to put in a request. I think it was one of those love-at-first-sight things. Or at least that's what Dad is always saying."

"Did your mom think so, too?"

He nodded. "Pretty much. They're still crazy in love. Like . . . sometimes, I still catch them making out on the couch."

"Yikes," Olivia said.

"Believe me, I know. Anyway, they danced all night and got engaged maybe six or seven weeks later, and then they were married before the year was over."

Olivia sat back in her chair. "That's sweet," she said. "Really."

"I guess," Jack admitted. "What about your parents?"

Olivia shrugged. "They met in college. They were at Harvard together. I don't really know that much about it. My father never talks about it, and my mom . . . I was little when she got sick."

Jack looked down at the fire. "Sorry," he said.

"Me, too." She gave him a perfunctory smile. "I don't really know her. When her illness became really bad and it became impossible to care for her adequately at home, Dad found this amazing place where she could get state-of-the-art treatment. The best doctors in the world. The latest drugs. Sure, I visited her all the time and still do, but she wasn't around to do mom things with. It sounds bad, but sometimes it feels like I don't even have a mom."

"But, I mean, she *loves* you, right?" Jack asked awkwardly.

Olivia paused.

"Yes, I'm sure she does. It's just . . . she's never been there for me, you know? It's just been me and my dad. Which is why he's so into trips like this, I think. He's the one who lost my mom. I never really had her to begin with."

Jack turned the catfish on the spit one more time, then looked up at Olivia. "I'm sorry," he said. "I had no idea."

She smiled again, her eyes just a little too bright. "It's fine. How could you know? It's just . . . what if my dad isn't okay? Who's going to take care of my mom? I can't even take care of myself. I mean, I lost it over some *leeches*. How pathetic is that?"

Jack stood and walked over to Olivia, kneeling in front of her. She was biting back tears, her hands clenched around her water glass.

"It's not pathetic," he said. "It's okay to be scared about things you don't understand, scared about the future. I'm scared all the time."

"Really? You don't seem the type," Olivia said.

"Well, I'm actually kind of a worrier. And I don't have nearly as much on my shoulders as you do."

She nodded. "I wouldn't have thought that of you. You usually seem so upbeat."

Olivia paused. "Like, you seem to actually think we might be rescued. But I mean . . . is anyone actually looking for us, Jack? Why haven't we seen any planes or anything? Shouldn't there be search parties?"

"*Someone* will come," Jack said firmly, willing himself to believe the words, too. "Everyone's got to be looking for us. The cops, my family. Jeff Robichaux must be going crazy. And everyone in New York knows your dad. They've gotta be pulling out all the stops."

"I hope so," she said.

"I *know* so. And, hey, look."

He turned, pointing toward the spit, where the fire had grown smoky. "I think lunch is ready."

He headed for the fire, lifting the spit and taking in the cooking aromas. It actually smelled great.

"This might really be edible," he said.

With Olivia's help and the bent fork, Jack peeled the skin away from the steaming catfish and scooped portions onto the tin pie plates. The fish flaked off the bone like Jack had planned it that way.

Olivia sat back down, and Jack pulled his chair up next to her. She stabbed a piece of the catfish and took a tentative bite. She closed her eyes.

"Oh, my God," she said. "This is a miracle."

Jack took a bite. Olivia was right.

"Admit it," he said. "I'm good."

She grinned at him, taking another bite. "I'll withhold comment for a later date."

CHAPTER 17

"TAKE A LOOK at this guy."

In the daytime, with dry weather and no rush, the treacherous log bridge back to the clearing hadn't been quite so treacherous.

As they reached the other side, Jack pointed out a shiny, blue-black snake, maybe three feet long, that crawled languidly across the trail in front of them.

He stepped in its path, blocking it with his sneaker. Instead of bolting, the snake stopped, looking up at them like it was curious.

"Check it out." He stooped and gently grabbed the snake behind the head, lifting it to show Olivia its underbelly.

"A mud snake," he said. "Harmless, totally gentle. And look at the coloration."

The underbelly of the snake was a checkerboard of blacks and fire-engine red.

"It's like someone painted it," Olivia said, keeping her distance.

Jack gently lowered the snake to the ground.

"People tell weird stories about the mud snake. Like it bites its tail and rolls itself into a hoop and then comes after people, trying to bite them. I have no idea where they come from. The old Cajuns had some weird superstitions."

"You think?" Olivia asked, grinning.

They kept hiking, stopping only long enough to gaze at Jack's upside-down snapping turtle, still fitfully batting the air with its webbed feet.

"I feel bad for it," said Olivia.

"So do I," Jack replied. "I'd rather order takeout but, you know, I haven't run across any restaurants. Survival is tough business."

Olivia nodded. "Yeah, I get it. I just don't like it."

Before long, with temperatures rising and no breeze to cool them, they reached the dreaded palmetto brake, covered in sweat. The warmth of the day had brought out the deer flies.

"*Ow!*" Olivia said, swatting one away from her leg and examining the large welt. "Why do these hurt so much?"

"Yeah, they never quit. Those green heads are the worst. They're like vampires. That day when you saved me from the bog, I thought they were going to sting me to death. Here, just follow me and keep moving. I'll try to find the path I made earlier." He looked around, searching for broken palmetto fronds.

"There," he said, catching sight of one. "This way."

They found the path and bulldozed their way through, Jack muttering under his breath when fronds wouldn't bend to his will. They emerged drenched sweatier than ever and picked up the trail again. In another ten minutes of walking, their clearing appeared, but something was different.

"Damn," Jack said, stopping in his tracks. "That's incredible."

The large cypress to which they'd tethered their makeshift tent was still standing, but a giant branch—at least a third of the tree—lay in a splintered mess on the ground.

"Lightning from our storm," said Jack, pointing to a jagged, charred scar two-thirds of the way up on the tree trunk. "It's a good thing we weren't here. We would have been right under it."

"So . . . where's the lean-to?" Olivia asked. "And the life jackets?"

Jack shook his head. "Buried under the rubble, I guess. Come on, let's see what we can salvage."

An exhausting half-hour later, they'd recovered two of the orange life vests, the emergency kit, about half the silver space blanket, and four tent ropes. The rest, including the water bottles and Jack's death star, lay crushed or stuck under the massive branch.

The water bottles were the biggest loss. That and the death star. But the space blanket gave Jack an idea.

"Time to advertise," he told Olivia.

She raised her eyebrows at him.

"We'll make a rescue sign," Jack explained.

With Olivia's help, he spread the shiny space blanket out in the clearing, using the Swiss Army knife to carve out three-foot-high letters that spelled HELP, and a similarly sized arrow pointing toward the camp. Hacking thin bamboo reeds into pointed stakes, he used the hammer he'd brought with him to anchor the letters to the ground so they wouldn't blow away.

"What do you think?" he asked.

"Brilliant," Olivia said.

"It's like a billboard, right? I mean, it can't hurt." He paused, running his hands through his hair as if thinking.

"What now?" Olivia asked.

"Let's go back to the bamboo brake," said Jack. "I'd like to whittle us another spear. And a death star. We can't have too many weapons, right?"

"No kidding," Olivia said. "Remember the *panther*?"

"Ah, I suspect he's long gone," Jack replied. "And it's not like a bamboo spear would have even done anything against it."

"I dunno. You could poke it in the eye. When my father and I were in Africa, we visited a tribe where the young men, to prove their manhood, were required to kill a lion with a spear."

"No!"

"That's what they said."

"Hmm. Better them than me."

"Why Swamp Boy, I'm shocked. I was thinking that would be the kind of challenge you'd welcome. You, hunter of alligators."

"Yeah, right. Anyway, I'm thinking they have real spears—not lightweight bamboo lookalikes. And gators have a weakness in their jaws. Lions? I can't think of one. As for that panther, I think it was as afraid of us as we were of him."

"Really? I got the impression that he was heading my way with dinner in mind."

"Maybe. But he let a fake dog run him off."

"That is true. But he might not be fooled again."

"Well, we won't be seeing him again, I'm sure."

"I'm not so sure. But the more weapons, the better."

Jack smiled. "I like your attitude."

At the bamboo brake, he whittled out a new spear while Olivia helped him knot the rope around his new death star. He gave her a quick lesson on throwing it before they headed back to camp.

Olivia was surprisingly good at it. When he said so, she replied, "I'm sure it's my lacrosse training. I told you I was good. Our team's been Manhattan city champions three years in a row. It's a big deal."

"I don't know anything about lacrosse," Jack confessed. "Although I saw it on ESPN2 once. I liked the helmet thing."

"It's rougher than it looks," Olivia said. "Native Americans used it to settle scores. People didn't get killed, but it could get violent."

"Down here, people don't get soccer, let alone lacrosse. It's all pretty much baseball, basketball, and football. *Especially football.* People worship football. It's like religion."

"Wait, you told me you're on your school's swim team. So you're, like, a freak because you swim?"

Jack grinned. "Pretty much."

They walked back toward camp, carrying everything between them. The palmetto brake was easier to navigate this time through. Ten minutes later, they came upon the hapless snapping turtle. Jack walked over and stooped beside it.

"You probably don't want to watch this," he said to Olivia.

"Believe me," Olivia said. "I have no intention of watching."

She turned away as Jack brought out the tools he brought with him for this very purpose, removing the hammer from a loop in his khakis and the screwdriver from his back pocket. He walked over to the snapper and bent down. "Sorry, old guy," he whispered. "Nothing personal."

He'd thought this over carefully. Placing the screwdriver blade against a spot of the turtle's under shell where he thought the heart would be, he drove it swiftly through with the hammer.

He hit the spot.

Blood spewed out like a tiny oil well. The turtle shuddered, its legs clawing wildly at the air, and then suddenly went still.

Snappers were infamous for their primitive reflex actions, even after they were supposed to be dead. Jack had once watched Paw-Paw Landry dress out a big alligator snapper, then throw its heart into a bucket with the guts to be disposed of later.

The heart kept beating for hours.

Jack cautiously prodded the turtle's withdrawn head with the screwdriver blade. The snapper chomped down on it. Putting a foot on the shell to hold it still, Jack pulled until the head was exposed. Taking out the knife, he decapitated the turtle, tossing the head into nearby bushes.

Grabbing a piece of rope, he lashed it around the turtle's tail and hung it up on a nearby branch to bleed it properly. It would make the meat tastier.

"Okay, done," he called out to Olivia. "I need about twenty minutes to let it bleed out, and then we can go. I'll finish at the camp."

Olivia turned to see the headless snapper hanging from the branch.

"That's sickening," she said, shuddering.

Jack shook his head. He didn't disagree. It's simply what he had to do.

Survival sucks, he thought.

CHAPTER 18

DARKNESS CAME QUICKLY, ushering in a surprisingly warm night. Stars littered the sky above the pond where Jack and Olivia had fished earlier.

They sat in the wooden chairs by a crackling fire. The aroma of boiling turtle filled the air, strong but not unpleasant. Or so Jack thought. The smoke from the fire drifted around them on a small breeze, enough to keep the mosquitos at bay.

Crickets chirped from darkening trees nearby, and somewhere in the marshy distance, a bullfrog croaked, its deep voice floating across the water.

"You know French, right?" Jack asked, hearing the bullfrog. "So a frog is *un grenouille* in proper French. But in Cajun French, it's *ouaouaron*—wohn-wahron—because that's how it sounds."

"Cute," said Olivia. "How's *your* French?"

"Okay. Not as good as yours, I'm sure. Your dad said you were fluent."

Olivia cocked an eyebrow. *"Vous êtes un garçon drôle."*

"Nice accent," Jack said. "And, yes, I guess I am a funny boy."

"Too easy. Okay. *Vous êtes le plus ancien des trois frères.*"

"I'm the oldest of the three brothers in my family," Jack said promptly.

She narrowed her eyes. *"Nous sommes perdus dans cette étrange désert."*

Jack thought for a second. "We're lost in a foreign place?"

"Ha! I got you!" she said triumphantly. "A strange wilderness!"

"Okay, fine," Jack said, holding up his hands in surrender. "You're amazing. They must love you in France."

Olivia smiled, leaning back in her chair. "I suppose. *Et merci beaucoup*. How's the turtle coming?"

"Ten more minutes," Jack said. "The beans should be ready then, too. Assuming this works."

He walked over to the fire where he had created a sort of cradle with logs, balancing the turtle shell on top to use as a pot.

It was tricky; the shell had to be close enough to the flames to cook the turtle meat but not so close that it burned through.

He'd separated the edible turtle parts from the viscera, setting those aside to be used as bait later. Washing the shell thoroughly, he'd put the meat back into it, filled it about a third of the way with water, and poured in a healthy dose of salt and crab boil. He was winging the cooking time. When it came to turtle meat, he was guessing overcooked was better than under.

Of course, overcooking could turn it to rubber.

Even though the turtle had probably weighed fifteen pounds alive, Jack had only been able to get two or three pounds of meat. He was heating up a can of the beans for Olivia. She just couldn't bring herself to try the turtle. The fish on the stringer he'd hoped to save for dinner were gone, along with Jack's shoelace. Jack was still kicking himself for tying the stringer to the dock. He'd made it easy for a gator, turtle, or gar to steal his meal. Everything out here was hungry.

They did, though, have some good luck. On the way back from the clearing, Olivia had somehow managed to spy the penlight Jack had dropped on the night of the storm. It had stuck in a spray of now dry mud. Miraculously, it still worked.

It was a huge convenience; not only could they build the cook fire out by the pond instead of next to the cabin, but they could find their way back in the dark without messing around with the kerosene lamps.

Speaking of the penlight, Jack checked his watch again, deciding that the turtle should be ready. Now he just had to tamp down the fire enough so the turtle could cool without putting it out entirely.

Picking up the chipped coffee mug he'd brought out earlier, Jack walked over to the dock and scooped up a cup of pond water, dumping it on the fire. It took several trips later, but it did the job.

He'd opened Olivia's can of beans with his knife, bending back the top to make a handle of sorts. Taking off his long-sleeve shirt, he used it as an oven mitt to snatch the steaming can from its place at the edge of the fire. Pouring half the can into one of the tin pie plates, he handed it to Olivia, along with the fork.

"Careful, it might be hot."

Olivia took the plate. "You know, I never thought that I'd literally be drooling over a plate of beans."

"Never say never," Jack said.

He took the spoon and bent over his turtle pot, fishing around in the broth for chunks of meat, managing to scoop two steaming chunks of turtle and a bit of broth onto the plate.

He warily took a bite. "Definitely not my mom's turtle sauce piquant. But not too bad. Kind of . . . chewy."

The broth itself was good, although anything heavily salted and spiced with crab boil probably would be.

They ate in silence, both having seconds. Jack figured he might as well finish the turtle meat; there was no way to refrigerate leftovers.

Olivia got through a little more than half the can of beans before she was full. They could save the rest of those; they'd still be good in the morning.

Cold beans for breakfast sounded gross now, but he knew that, by morning, they'd be appealing. He leaned back in his chair, resting his plate on the ground.

"I can't believe I'm actually full."

Olivia nodded. "I know, right?"

Jack pointed to the low sky beyond the dock. "Look, full moon," he said. "If we had a boat, we could go for a nighttime paddle."

"It's gorgeous," said Olivia. "It looks massive."

"Totally amazing. I'm still surprised they don't have a pirogue stashed here. It doesn't make sense unless whoever owns the camp drags one back and forth when they come. This is perfect pirogue territory. If we had one, we could catch a mess of frogs, find some other places to fish . . . maybe sneak up on some sleeping ducks with the penlight, deeper in the marsh. Now *those* would be good. I could wring their necks in a flash, no problem. We do it at the farm with chickens all the time."

Olivia wrinkled her nose. "Seems pretty savage."

"If you do it fast, it's painless," he said. "I mean, it's not like I don't feel for them. But you've got to eat."

Jack shrugged. "Even vegetables are alive when you pick them. All life depends on death."

"I guess, technically," Olivia said. "But at least a carrot doesn't scream or bleed."

Jack laughed. "True. I suppose it's all about what you're used to. My grandpa's old enough to remember when there weren't supermarkets or even grocery stores nearby. If you wanted chicken or pork, you raised chickens and pigs and slaughtered them. Messy but necessary. In the spring, there's still a thing called *cochon de lait*. A pig roast. Whole families come together to kill a pig and feast just like in the old days. It's still a big deal, especially in the western Cajun bayous."

"What are they like?" Olivia asked.

"I don't know," Jack admitted. "I haven't been to one. I will one day. I really want to travel. You're lucky that you get to."

"Well, you have to aim further than a pig festival next door. I wouldn't call that travel."

Jack arched his eyebrows. "Come on, now. Don't make me feel worse. I still have time, uh . . ." He trailed off.

Olivia stared into the fire. "You're right. I'm sorry. I guess I don't think about it much. It's like what you said, it's kind of what you're used to. I can't remember *not* traveling."

When Jack didn't respond, Olivia wondered if she'd hurt his feelings.

She spoke up. "Anyway, Swamp Boy, you clearly have an adventurous spirit, so I'm sure you'll be traveling one day, and you must put Maine at the top of your list. You'd love it there. There's some part of it that will remind you of this place. A lot of it is totally different. We have mountains and beaches and the sea. But there are marshes and these enormous bogs. And so much of it is wild, like this swamp. My family has a place there, a cottage up by Acadia National Park. We've been going there every summer ever since I can remember."

Jack nodded, mesmerized by her description. "Sounds incredible," he said. "I'd love to see it. My parents have been talking about buying a fishing camp down in the saltwater by the Gulf for years. I don't think it's ever going to happen, though. It's a money thing. With my brothers going to college in a few years, and everything, even the little shacks on stilts have gotten so expensive. I think they've decided they can't afford it."

"Your brothers?" Olivia turned, studying him full on. "What about you?"

"Me?" Jack grinned. "I'm not college material. Seriously. School bores the hell out of me. Well, most of it. I like English. Some history. And biology, I guess. But the rest of it?" He shook his head. "Torture."

"Please," Olivia said. "Everyone thinks school is boring. That's no excuse." She tilted her head, looking him up and down. "What's your real reason?"

For some reason, Jack felt himself blush. "Hey, college isn't everything. Ever heard of Steve Jobs? Bill Gates? Besides, after working for Mr. Robichaux, I don't know, I'm pretty sure I could start my own company . . . you know, personalized tours, heavy on the ecology, but with the Cajun touristy stuff people like."

He shrugged. "I could bring in Cajun bands, storytellers, things that Mr. Robichaux doesn't offer. I think I could make it work."

"Sure, for now," Olivia agreed. "But what about ten years from now? Don't you think you'll wonder if you could've done something else?"

"Maybe. But Mr. Robichaux's making a killing off his company. In the off-season, he flies all over the world. Fishing, hunting . . . I could live that life. Who wouldn't want to?"

"You could live that life *and* go to college first," Olivia pointed out. "Just saying."

"I guess," Jack said. "But here's what I don't understand. Like, I've looked at the LSU catalog. I think I'd be perfect for marine biology. But there's no way. I mean, the first two years are all stuff like calculus and organic chemistry. I barely got a C-minus in second-year algebra. And that was only because my teacher liked me. I'd get up to Baton Rouge and flunk out and then what? Besides, it's not like I *need* organic chemistry to understand the life cycle of the white shrimp or the nesting habits of the great egret. I already know those things. There's something wrong with the whole system."

Jack looked up, catching Olivia staring at him.

"Okay, hold on. It's not like you *have to* be a marine biologist," she said. "What about writing? My dad practically drooled over your essay. And he's not a drooler. You could be an English major, take some writing courses. And then . . . who knows? Become a writer."

"Doesn't sound very practical."

"What, are you secretly an old man or something? We're too young to be practical."

She gave him a little shove on the shoulder. "Don't you want to go just to *go*? See something different? Have fun? Meet new people?"

"Sounds like an expensive way to meet people," Jack said, grinning. "Especially when I've already got lots and lots of friends."

Olivia pushed her hair back, looking suddenly annoyed. "What?

Good-ole-boy hunting pals who talk about their guns and boats and alligator hunts? God forbid you'd want to meet someone new. Or different."

She folded her arms in front of herself, glaring at him.

Jack stared at her, returning her annoyance.

"For the record, my friends might be more interesting than you think they are. And how do you not get that it's different for me?" he asked, irritation creeping into his voice. "Your entire life has been like one big college application. Compared to you, I *am* just a swamp rat."

He spread his hands wide, encompassing the surrounding bayou. "*This* is my home, okay? This is what I *know*. I love it. I *am* a serious student of this ecosystem. There are few places like it in the whole world. I, uh—"

Olivia stopped him. "Well, that might be true, but you haven't seen the places that might compare in the rest of the world. And you should! College could be a good place to start. Most schools offer all these far-flung trips on the cheap. You could see the Everglades. You could see the Congo, the Amazon, who knows. Wouldn't you want to do that?"

Jack nodded. "Okay, maybe. But here's the thing. Even if I didn't flunk out, I *still* wouldn't fit in at college. I can't think I would have much in common with the average college student. You know, people trying to become teachers or engineers or lawyers or doctors. What would we talk about? Besides, people might think my swamp obsession is weird."

Olivia managed a smile. "Well, it *is* a little weird. But, oh, c'mon. This is about fear and, what, you think you're the only one who's afraid? Both of my parents went to Harvard. My dad has always talked about me going there, too, like it's some sort of done deal. But who knows? Even with prep school and the grades and test scores and everything else I do, what if it's still not enough?"

"Get serious," Jack said. "Like you actually need to worry about getting in. Your dad could always just donate a new library or something."

Olivia frowned. "Okay, that's not fair. If I get in, I want it to be because of me, not my dad. But then what?" she asked, her voice suddenly losing its edge. "Just *going* there isn't enough. I have to live up to my dad. Carry on the *FitzGerald legacy*, whatever that means."

She paused for a second, looking at Jack. "What if *I'm* not up for it?"

Jack opened his mouth to reassure her, then closed it. Olivia was right. He didn't know anything about her life except that maybe it wasn't as carefree as he'd imagined.

"Whatever," Olivia continued. "My point is that you're not the only one who's scared, okay? Just don't let it stop you from doing something that you ought to do. You could go to college and still have your swamp-tour company. The two aren't mutually exclusive."

A long moment of silence passed between them.

Finally, Jack nodded. A friendly note returned to his voice. He found himself grinning. "Okay. I get what you're saying. I'm not saying I agree, but I'll think about it. I *am* going to travel one day, however. When I hear about the places you've been, it really gives me the bug to go."

Olivia smiled. "Well, that's great. And if you ever want to see your first mountain, you're always welcome at our place in Maine."

Jack found himself mildly flustered at this statement. *Is she serious?*

"Is that an invitation?"

"I don't say things I don't mean," Olivia replied, shrugging. "I just hope you like mushroom collecting because my dad's obsessed with it. You'll spend a lot of time walking the woods after it rains and you will be forced to retire to the kitchen to watch him cook them. Well, mushrooms and his boat. We try to get out on the boat a couple of times a week in the summer."

"That part sounds like fun. You mean, like a sailboat? Motorboat?

Rowboat? What are we talking about here?"

"More like a lobster boat. I don't even know how to describe it. But it's not too big. Maybe, like . . . forty feet?"

Jack had to struggle to keep his mouth from popping open.

"Forty feet? That's big to me. Our fishing boat's an eighteen-footer."

"I just like it because you can sit up high and see everything. Sometimes Dad even lets me take the wheel."

"Lucky you," said Jack as he brushed at a bug flitting near his ear. "I have no idea what a lobster boat looks like. But I'm guessing it's the kind of boat with a name."

Olivia smiled. "Yes. But I'm not going to tell you what it is."

"What? Why?"

"It's *embarrassing*."

"Oh, come on. Now you've *got* to tell me."

"Ugh, okay, fine." Olivia rolled her eyes. "It's the *Miss Olivia*. There. Happy?"

Jack laughed out loud. "Yes, Miss Olivia," he said. "Extremely happy. Now I can't *wait* to see it."

Olivia shook her head in mock seriousness. "Well, try to control yourself, Swamp Boy. It's not that exciting. It's just a boat."

At that moment, she slapped her neck. "Ow, that one hurt. Are you getting bitten? I think the mosquitoes are coming out."

"Yeah, big-time," Jack replied. "Want to go in?"

Dousing the fading fire, they gathered their dirty dishes and the can with the leftover beans. Jack didn't bother switching on the penlight. The soft glow of moonlight clearly outlined the path back. They walked side-by-side in silence, past the outhouse and then the cistern, where Jack stopped, switched on the light, and rinsed the dishes.

"Good enough till morning," he said.

They were climbing the porch stairs, about to open the camp door, when they were stopped by a low rumbling noise, growing steadily louder.

They turned to look.

Standing at the bottom of the steps, looking up at them, was the panther. It seemed to have appeared out of nowhere.

Olivia grabbed at Jack's arm. "You said it was gone," she whispered.

"It was *supposed* to be," he whispered back. "They're usually super wary of people. I don't understand what it's doing."

"Isn't it obvious?" Olivia hissed. "It's *stalking* us. It was probably watching us the whole time we were out there!"

Jack shook his head. "If it were really stalking us, it could have attacked at any time. Taken us down on the trail."

"Not reassuring."

"It probably just smelled our food and came to check things out. If it wanted us, we'd be dead by now."

"How cheery," Olivia whispered again.

Jack's theorizing was cut short by that sound again, not a growl but more like a loud rumble that softened into a purr that filled up the quiet night. Jack had never heard anything like it.

As they watched, the panther stretched, settling onto its belly at the foot of the stairs. It looked up at them like some strange, gargantuan house cat, its eyes glowing in the moonlight.

"This is *too* weird," Jack whispered. "Really slowly, we're going to open the door, go inside, and lock it. Don't scream or run. We're talking slow-motion movie here, okay?"

"Okay," said Olivia. "Is it just going to sit there all night?"

"I don't know," he whispered. "But look at it. It doesn't seem threatening. Maybe it just likes us."

"Oh, good, the two-hundred-pound *panther* likes us. Why don't you go there and pet the kitty?"

He arched his eyebrows. "Is that a dare?"

Olivia narrowed her eyes at him. "Do *not* be stupid, Jack Landry," she said.

"Just kidding. Where I come from, the mommas drown all the dumb ones."

Olivia couldn't suppress a guffaw. "That is *so* wrong. Do *not* make me laugh! Not with that *thing* down there!"

"Right, sorry. I know. I'm bad."

"You're awful. Terrible. Horrible."

But Olivia was unable to suppress a grin.

"Come on," Jack said softly. "Let's go . . . slowly."

They backed carefully toward the door, keeping their eyes on the cat. Olivia found the handle, wincing at the slight clanking sound it made as it turned. As she nudged the door open, Jack bumped into her, knocking the tin pie plates that she'd been carrying and sending them clattering to the wooden porch floor.

The panther rose, stiffening into a crouch. Jack wondered how fast it could take the steps. *Pretty fast!*

"It's okay," Jack said in a whisper that came out louder than he intended. "Just leave everything where it fell. Inside . . . quick!"

Olivia was already beginning to shut the door as Jack squeezed through.

She closed it with a bang, turning the flimsy brass latch that hung below the doorknob by only one of three screws that was supposed to hold it.

"Shit," Olivia said, peering anxiously at the door.

"It'll be fine."

"Really? We're basically being held prisoner by a jungle cat."

"Swamp cat, technically," Jack replied.

He shook his head. "I really don't think it's here to hurt us."

Still, there wasn't any point in taking chances. Switching on the penlight, he jiggled the door handle. The wooden latch would be useless against the panther's full weight.

Jack shined the light around the room, pausing at the old table.

The legs were unsteady, but the top was made of heavy oak.

"That," he said, pointing. "We can move it against the door. Turn it up on its side and use it as a barricade."

"I thought you said there wasn't anything to worry about?"

"It's just a precaution. Better safe than sorry, as they say."

"Fine. Well, then we're drawing the curtains, too. I don't want that thing watching us."

"A peeping tomcat," Jack said.

She socked Jack on the arm.

"Ow!" he said.

"Well, remind me to laugh when I'm not actively terrified for my life."

"Okay, okay. That hurt."

"Sorry."

Jack walked to the window and looked out, relieved that the panther had left his perch at the bottom of the steps, but a little spooked by the fact that he couldn't see it. He pulled the curtains closed, blocking out the moonlight. He flicked the penlight around to get his bearings.

"Should we light the kerosene lamps?" he asked Olivia.

She shook her head. "They smell weird. Plus, I'd be worried about the cabin burning down. I just want to wash my face and go to bed."

Jack hadn't given much thought to sleeping arrangements. He shined the flashlight at the bunk beds across the room.

"So, which do you want?" he asked. "Top or bottom?"

Olivia didn't hesitate. "Top . . . with you. You can sleep on the outside."

Jack nodded.

And then it hit him.

"Wait, am I supposed to be panther bait?" he said.

Even in the dim glow of the penlight, he could see Olivia's smile.

"I think you *really are* college material, Swamp Boy."

CHAPTER 19

THE WIND CAME up during the evening. Gusts riffled through the trees surrounding the cabin, buffeting the windows.

Something skittered across the porch.

Jack, who couldn't sleep anyway, rose quietly and slipped down the wooden ladder of the bunk bed. He tiptoed to the outline of the big window and cracked the curtains, looking outside. A small branch had lodged itself in the railing, shaking in the wind like some strange, trapped animal. That explained the skittering noise. At least it wasn't the panther.

The moon was no longer visible, but pale stars twinkled everywhere, lighting up the sky.

Jack turned and climbed back up the ladder, easing himself into the bunk next to Olivia, who slept facing the wall.

As he settled in, he felt Olivia's hand reaching for his. She pulled his arm around her.

Jack moved closer, a strange wave of protectiveness sweeping over him.

"Are we about to be eaten?" Olivia asked, her voice drowsy.

"Coast is clear," Jack whispered.

"You think it's gone?"

"I don't know. It's not on the porch, at least."

"I was dreaming about my dad," Olivia said quietly, still facing the wall.

"A good or bad dream?"

"I don't know. We were on the boat in Maine. It was foggy, but you could tell the sun was trying to break through. There was this stretch of light—almost like a tunnel—ahead of us. I was at the wheel. Dad kept trying to get me to steer into it." She sighed. "It seemed so real."

Jack considered it for a second. "That's not a bad dream. A little obvious."

"Obvious?"

"Light at the end of the tunnel," he said, smiling. "Maybe we're about to be rescued."

"Or maybe my subconscious just sucks at metaphors," she said.

"I was dreaming about pancakes," Jack told her. "Pancakes and coffee."

"What kind of pancakes?"

"Blueberry."

Olivia pulled his arm closer around her. "I love blueberry pancakes. There's this place in Maine, near our cottage... Chester's. They keep a table for us; we're there so often. They make blueberry pie, too. It's incredible."

"Isn't Maine, like, the blueberry state or something? My mom makes ours from a mix. It's hard to get fresh blueberries down here. Actually, I don't think I've ever tasted one."

"That," Olivia declared, "is tragic. Now you definitely have to come to Maine." She absently fiddled with the back of his hand.

"I'd kill for pancakes right now," she said. "Or scrambled eggs. Anything besides beans."

"I hear you," Jack said. Then he laughed, louder than he intended.

"What's so funny?" Olivia asked, half-turning to look at him.

"It's nothing. I was just thinking about the most disgusting thing I've ever had for breakfast."

"What?"

He shook his head. "I can't even tell you. You'd be grossed out."

"Well, now you *have* to tell me."

Jack smiled. "Squirrel brains."

"No!"

"Squirrel brains and scrambled eggs, actually."

"*No!*"

"Yes."

"Ugh. *Why?*"

"Lots of people eat them in the South. Well, probably not as many people as there used to be, I guess. It's Paw-Paw's thing. During squirrel season, he fries up the meat for dinner, but he saves the brains for breakfast, scrambling them with a skillet full of eggs. A little salt, a little pepper, a dash of Tabasco . . ."

"You're kidding, right?"

"Nope. My mom won't even go in the kitchen when he's cooking them. Honestly, though, they're not bad. Kind of sweet."

Olivia rolled the rest of the way over, her face just inches from Jack's.

"I don't think I can ever kiss you again."

Jack's heart skipped a beat. His mouth felt suddenly dry. "When did you kiss me before?" he asked.

"Mouth-to-mouth," she reminded him. "You were Prince Charming . . . uh, I mean, the Swamp Prince. You know, saving my life."

"That doesn't count. You barfed shortly thereafter, remember? That doesn't give a guy great confidence. But we could try again."

When Olivia didn't immediately answer, Jack figured he had simply put his foot in his mouth once more. *What was I thinking?*

He was about to try to turn it into a joke when Olivia surprised him.

"I haven't brushed my teeth in forever," she said. "It might not be that much fun."

"Like I have?"

"Right."

"Plus, I'm out of practice," he admitted. "I haven't kissed anyone in forever."

"Me either."

Jack rolled over, looking intently into her eyes. "Hard to believe.

Surely, back in New York, you have a boyfriend?"

"How do you know it's not a girlfriend?"

"Well, whatever. You know what I mean."

"I don't have a boyfriend. Or a girlfriend. Well, the way *you* mean it. Why, do you have a girlfriend?"

"No. Unattached. Free agent. In tenth grade I, uh, had a, uh . . . oh, actually that was nothing."

"Jack?" Olivia whispered. "Do me a favor, okay?"

"What?"

"Stop rambling. Shut up and kiss me."

They closed their eyes and their kiss was tentative at first but it slowly deepened. Jack reached up, pulling her close to him on the narrow bunk. She pressed against him. His hands tenderly caressed her face. Her hands encircled the back of his neck.

Jack forgot to breathe. He forgot everything but the warmth of Olivia's body, the softness of her lips against his.

Olivia found herself surrendering to a place she couldn't have imagined. The kiss might have gone on and on and on, a kiss that might have led down other tender roads, until a loud rattling from the window startled them both.

Olivia pulled away. "Okay. That was nothing, right?"

"Should I look?"

"Sorry. Do you mind?"

Jack slid regretfully out of bed, climbing down the ladder again. He was about to crack the curtain open when he heard the sound of paws skittering on the porch.

Olivia sat up in the darkness. "What was *that*?"

"No idea," Jack said. He fingered the curtain, slowly pulling it aside.

The panther stood at eye level, its paws on the window, staring straight at him. In its mouth was a rabbit, its hind legs still quivering.

Jack whisked the curtain closed, trying not to panic.

"Jack?" Olivia asked. "What's going on?"

Jack tiptoed back to the bunk bed, easing himself up the ladder. "It's back," he told her softly. "At the window. I need the penlight."

"For *what*?" Olivia asked. "You're not going *out* there, are you?"

"Duh, no. But we need to scare it away again. I'm thinking we light the hurricane lamps and start banging on the pots. Open that curtain and see if the light and noise make it run."

"And if it doesn't?"

He shrugged. "You have a better idea?"

"Um . . . lie here and see if it goes away?" she asked hopefully.

"We already tried that," he pointed out. "Plus, it's weird. He's got a rabbit in his mouth."

"A what?"

"A rabbit. I think it's still alive."

Olivia stared at him. "*Why*? Do you think it's sick, maybe has rabies or something?"

"I mean, it wasn't foaming at the mouth or anything. It seems more like it's curious. Anyway, the light's here somewhere. I definitely brought it up here with me."

Olivia looked down, finding it tucked in the fold of the sleeping bag. She handed it to Jack.

"Thanks," he said. "Here, help me out."

He climbed down the ladder, Olivia reluctantly following. Shining the flashlight around, he found the two kerosene lamps and the lighter on the kitchen counter. The pie plates were next to them.

Jack picked up the death star from the floor, then quickly lit the lanterns. "Okay, grab these," he told Olivia, handing her the pie plates and the star.

He picked up the lanterns. "I'm going to hold these up over my head. You pull back the curtain, then start banging on the plates. I'll swing the lanterns and do my barking thing. Hopefully it works again."

Olivia swallowed, nodding.

They moved into position. Jack whispered, "Now!"

Olivia jerked open the curtain. The cat was still staring in, the rabbit dangling from its jaws.

Flinching from the sudden light and the noise, the panther bounded from the window and somehow landed on the porch railing, balancing like a tightrope walker.

It stared at them for a second. And then, calmly jumping down from the railing, it dropped the rabbit on the porch in plain view. With one last look at the window, it bolted over the railing into the night.

Jack and Olivia stared at each other.

"What the hell?" said Olivia.

"I think it just gave us a present," Jack replied.

CHAPTER 20

ON THEIR FOURTH morning stranded in the swamp, the low drone of a plane in the distance startled Jack awake. Even through the fog of sleep, he could tell that it wasn't close enough to find them. The drone grew softer as the plane flew away from them. Soon, it was gone.

Jack sat up slowly, rubbing his eyes and looking around. He and Olivia had gone back to bed after the panther incident, realizing that it was three in the morning. They hadn't talked about the kiss—or repeated it.

Olivia had climbed in first, settled in against the wall with her back to Jack, pulled his arm around her, and whispered, "Good night."

Jack had relaxed against her, whispering, "You, too."

And that was it.

He'd expected the adrenaline rush of everything to keep him awake, but instead, he'd conked out almost immediately. Awake again, he turned to see Olivia still sleeping, pressed close to the wall. He swung his legs off the bed and climbed quietly down the ladder.

Tiptoeing to the window, he opened the curtain just a tiny bit, checking to see if the rabbit was still there. It wasn't.

Maybe the panther had taken it back, but he doubted it. The yard cats on his farm had left mice in front of their door before. A gift was a gift.

The swamp wasn't short on predators and scavengers. *Something* had come up on the porch and taken the rabbit away. Jack found himself riffing on Paw-Paw's sense of humor.

At least they still had the beans for breakfast. Unfortunately, they still had beans for breakfast.

Jack let the curtain drop, tiptoeing toward the door. He tried not to wake Olivia as he pulled the impromptu table barricade aside.

She stirred anyway, propping herself up on one elbow. "What's going on?"

"Nothing, thankfully," said Jack. "The panther's gone. So is the rabbit."

Olivia yawned. "Oh, well, I wasn't high on panther-chewed rabbit anyway."

She stretched. "God, I'm tired."

"You should go back to sleep," Jack said. "I was just going to look around. Maybe other gifts have appeared."

"Just don't go far."

"Scout's honor," he said.

Olivia nodded, turning back toward the wall. "Be careful."

"Always."

Outside, Jack glanced at his watch. It was almost nine-thirty. The sun was rising over the cypress and oak tops surrounding the cabin. There was a light breeze, just a hint of fall in the air. Jack had seen this weather before in October, during the start of hunting season—clear, cool days stretching on for two or three weeks without so much as a cloud in the sky.

Hopefully, they were done with storms for a while. On the other hand, Jack couldn't ever recall the weather being this fickle at this time of the year. And historically, October had seen its share of hurricanes ravage the Louisiana coast.

Out of sight of the camp, Jack relieved himself in some bushes, not bothering with the outhouse. But as he walked past it, he could have kicked himself for not bringing the death star.

A cottontail sat in the open, not thirty feet away, nibbling on a patch of grass.

Jack stopped and watched the rabbit for a good five minutes. When he finally walked forward, the rabbit spooked, leaping out of sight into some willow brush.

Jack headed for the cistern, turning on the spigot and drinking from his cupped hands while water spilled onto the ground between his feet. He splashed some water on his face, drying himself with his T-shirt sleeve. Then, he backtracked toward the pond. Halfway there, he paused. A dull banging noise seemed to waft on the breeze from the pond.

When he stopped to listen, there was only silence. *Must be the wind,* he thought, starting forward again. As he reached the dock, though, he stopped in shock.

A camo-colored aluminum boat, known as a johnboat hereabouts, with an outsized, camo-clad outboard motor, lay partly beached next to the dock. As the wind blew again, the boat's stern clunked against a wooden post.

That's what I heard! We're saved!

Jack sprinted forward. "Hello? Hey! Anybody here?" There was no reply.

On the dock, Jack called again, but there was still no answer.

Strange.

He stepped into the boat, putting his hand to the outboard motor. It was cold. Whoever's boat it was had arrived sometime in the night.

Jack looked around the boat more closely. It had a forward steering wheel and a small metal console. The keys that dangled in the ignition were attached to a floating key chain wrapped in camo tape.

Somebody doesn't want this boat to be spotted.

Still, knowing how loud outboards were, Jack was surprised that he hadn't heard the boat arrive last night. Either he'd been more exhausted than he'd thought he was, or they'd been running the motor dead slow.

Jack stepped back onto the dock. Footprints dotted the mucky bank nearby.

Someone in rubber boots had stepped off the boat into a muddy patch, taking three steps before disappearing in the grassy high ground. The tracks were clearly heading up the left bank of the pond.

Jack headed after them, calling out as he went.

"Hey, is anybody here? Hello?"

A gust of wind was his only answer.

He stopped for a second, wondering if he should go back to the cabin to get Olivia.

He decided to give it another five minutes. If he didn't find the boat's owners by then, he'd return for her and they'd continue the search together.

The trail soon narrowed under a canopy of dwarf oaks. Judging from the length of the grass, it wasn't used much after the first fifty yards or so. Jack kept thinking he was hitting dead ends, but they were just sharp bends disguised by brush.

He checked his watch again. Seven minutes had passed. *Just a little farther*, he thought.

The trail straightened, opening up a little. Trees and palmetto brakes mostly hid his view of the pond to his right, but he could see the wind was rising. Small whitecaps riffled the water.

Jack was about to turn back when he saw a patch of sunlight in the distance. *A clearing, maybe?* He'd go far enough to check it out, and then head back. He was right. The trail ended in a field, maybe two acres in all, bathed in sunlight. It was planted in neat rows of stalky plants, their broad green leaves waving in the breeze.

It took a few seconds to register. He was just mouthing the word *marijuana* when a man stepped out from the edge of the field, not twenty feet away.

He was a big, paunchy guy, maybe six-foot-five, dressed head to toe in camouflage gear, except for his blue ball cap, its red letters big enough for Jack to make out *Ole Miss*. He wore a pistol in a holster, cinched down low across his waist. A very, very large pistol. Like in a cowboy movie with bad guys.

"Well, howdy there," the man said, his accent vaguely reminding

Jack of some of his relatives on his mom's side who lived in Mississippi. "I reckon you're too young to be the law. I guess they're making pot rustlers younger and younger these days."

CHAPTER 21

THE MAN'S RIGHT hand drifted down nonchalantly to the handle of his gun.

Jack swallowed, trying to find his voice. "That's not . . . I mean, I'm not . . . I mean my name's Jack Landry. I was in a plane crash a few days ago. My girlfriend and I . . . I mean, my friend . . . survived, and we ended up here. We're holed up in a hunting camp nearby."

Jack pointed in the general direction of the shack. "I saw your boat and your tracks heading up the bank and—"

He trailed off.

"We just want to get back to our families. Really, sir, I didn't even know about this place until this very minute."

The man looked hard at Jack. He nodded.

"That's a real good story, but you don't look too beat up for somebody who just fell out of the sky."

He smiled. Jack noticed a row of extremely crooked teeth.

"Why don't you tell me more about your girlfriend, though? Is she perty? I ain't seen a woman for almost a month now. I get paid good money to look after a few patches around here, but this big swamp gets lonesome sometimes."

He sucked loudly at his teeth, fidgeting with his gun handle. "Why don't we go find this girlfriend of yours and talk it over?"

Jack felt his blood go cold.

Dummy. Shouldn't have mentioned Olivia.

He tried to think.

He could run. If he got clear, the larger man would never catch him. But Jack wasn't a great sprinter, just fast over long distances. And for all he knew, this guy was one of those gun nuts who practiced fast draw and would mow him down in the back the second he bolted. Besides, he didn't want him anywhere near Olivia.

"Sir, look," Jack said. "I don't care what you do or who you do it for. I don't rustle marijuana. I don't even smoke it. I'm a swamp-tour guide and our plane went down in that big storm a few days ago. I'm sure it's been on the news. I know people are looking for us, and when I saw your boat, I thought we'd been found. If you could just drop us someplace where we could be picked up, I promise, we wouldn't say anything about all of this. You have my word."

The man's smile widened. "Oh, really, Jack Landry? And just how much is that word of yours worth? Nah, I don't think that's the solution to our little problem here. The stuff you're lookin' at is worth a coupla million dollars, probably, and the fellas who own it are comin' soon to harvest it. I'm afraid I'll have to discuss your situation with them."

He stopped, taking off his cap to swat a deerfly buzzing his ear. "I ought to tell you, though," he continued, "these aren't particularly gentle people, if you get my drift. But, hell, who knows? Maybe your girlfriend will have something she can trade with 'em. Huh?"

For a second, all Jack could see was red. By the time he shook his head to clear it, the man was walking toward him, pistol drawn.

Jack's family didn't own handguns; Paw-Paw was against them, declaring them useless for hunting but dangerous to people in the wrong hands. But Jack knew this gun. He'd once had a chance to fire it. His boss, Jeff Robichaux, was a handgun collector and had shown Jack one that surely was identical—a long-barreled Colt .45 revolver. They'd gone out to a shooting range, where Jack squeezed off a dozen shots. It was a beast. It roared like a cannon and kicked like a mule. Mr. Robichaux swore it had been used by outlaws and lawmen back in the Wild West. In the right—or wrong—hands, it could kill from fifty yards.

Jack tried to stall.

"What, you want me to put up my hands, like in the movies?" he asked, still trying to talk his way out of the situation. "Sir, seriously, this isn't what it looks like. I'm a high school kid, like I told you. We crashed in the swamp. We're just trying to survive till we get found. That's all there is to it."

"Tell it to my bosses," the man said. "They'll be here soon enough. Now, let's go visit your girlfriend."

Jack glared. "And if I say no?"

The man shrugged. "I can either shoot you, or drag you kickin' and screamin'. Yer choice." He sucked his teeth again as he languidly twirled the gun in his hand. "It don't much matter to me."

The word *me* was still hanging in the air when something whizzed past Jack's head.

A flash later, the gun was flying in the air as the man fell backward to the ground, clutching his right arm and howling in pain.

The death star had slashed into his biceps, blood spraying his camo shirt. In desperation, he pulled it out and flung it aside as he tried to stanch the flow of blood.

Olivia was suddenly at Jack's side, screaming at him and punching him hard in the arm. "You big jerk! We had a deal, no wandering off, remember? Now grab the gun . . . get the gun!"

Jack, flustered, rushed forward while the man tried to get to his feet, cursing violently. Jack kicked him hard in the crotch, and he went down again, the wind knocked out of him.

Jack sped past, frantically scanning the ground for the pistol.

"Damn, where is it?" he shouted to Olivia.

"More to the right . . . try more to the right!" she yelled back.

Jack veered right, kicking at the ground cover until he felt his toe stab a hard object.

The gun handle!

Jack snatched the pistol up, cocked it, and fired a shot in the air.

Olivia flinched, startled. "What the hell are you doing?"

Jack lowered the pistol, aiming it at the man on the ground. "Sorry," he told Olivia. "That was for him. Just to get his attention."

He walked toward the man, who was now sitting up, clutching his arm with one hand and his crotch with the other. The death star lay on top of a crushed marijuana plant, a few yards away.

Jack pointed to it, turning to Olivia. " Let's not forget our little invention there," he said. "How did you think to bring it in the first place?"

"Well, Jack Landry, every time you wander off, trouble seems to follow. I thought it best to come armed."

"I like the way you think," Jack replied. "And I'm sorry about wandering off. Honestly, I was a second from turning around when Burl, here, waylaid me."

"Burl?"

"That's a joke," Jack replied. "A generic name for rednecks like this prick."

"Right."

"Anyway, I need to have a word with our friend."

"Just don't do anything stupid," said Olivia.

"What, like shoot him in the head?" Jack asked, his voice level. "No promises."

The man on the ground looked up at him, his eyes narrowing.

Jack stepped close enough for his shadow to fall across the man's body, making sure to stop out of grabbing range.

"Listen up," he said sharply. "Like I told you before, my name's Jack Landry. I'm a high school kid. We were in a *plane crash*. And now, we're going to take your boat and rescue ourselves. When we get some place where there's people, we're going to send the cops back after you."

The man glared up at him.

"And just so you know," Jack told him, "I know how to use this pistol. My grandpa spent a *lot* of time teaching me to shoot. I could take your ear off at fifty feet, no problem, but it won't be your ear I'll be aiming for."

So what if that's a lie. Jack sounded convincing.

He continued, "So don't get any ideas about trying to follow us. Now, we're going say goodbye."

The man looked down, spitting on the ground. He'd recovered his voice and some of his swagger. "Kid," he snarled, "you don't have a clue who you're dealin' with. You just need to give me back my gun and let me negotiate with my people or bad things are gonna happen to you."

He pointed straight at Olivia. "And her."

Jack cocked the pistol and fired again just to the right of the man.

He scooted backward on his hands, away from them. "Dammit, son, okay! Now I've said my piece. You better git, and fast, too."

"We're goin'," said Jack. "But one more thing. I'll have your holster. You don't need it now."

The man shook his head but unhitched the holster belt and tossed it at Jack's feet. Jack picked it up and, still holding the gun, cinched it up tight.

Burl spoke again. "Like I said, Jack Landry, you're gonna be terrible sorry for what you've done."

As he spoke, a distant drone began to fill the sky. A low-flying plane was approaching.

"Well, well, well," the man said, raising his voice to be heard over the plane. "Looks like my people are early. Too bad, boy. Y'all really *are* screwed now."

Seconds later, a small, green float plane, a two-seater on pontoons, roared low over the pot field, dipping its wings first left then right.

"That was the signal," the man said. "I'm s'posed to signal back if the coast is clear. If it's not, they'll come loaded for bear. It won't be fun."

Jack glanced at Olivia. There was fear on her face, but something else, as well—*anger.*

"Do you think he's telling the truth?" she asked Jack, staring up at the plane.

"Probably," Jack nodded. "Let's go."

"Maybe you *should* shoot him first," she said. "At least then he wouldn't be able to talk."

Jack was pretty sure she didn't mean it. Well, kind of sure.

"I'm not going to waste a bullet on this bastard," he said. "Let's just steal his boat and get the hell out of here. It's powered by a big-ass outboard. If we can get out of the pond before they land, they'll never catch us. I know how to hide a boat in the cypresses."

Olivia glared at the man on the ground. "You're just lucky he's got the gun," she said, anger dripping from her voice. "Wasting bullets doesn't bother me a bit."

Jack was impressed by Olivia's improv—*God, this girl's good!*—and didn't miss a beat. "I'd listen to her, podnah. She's a natural-born killer."

The man glared at Olivia as he massaged his bloody arm. But then, inexplicably, he smiled a crooked smile. "You know, now that I think about it, I actually might'a heard something about that plane crash you were talkin' about. Dang, it's just comin' back to me now. Weren't there four people, not two? I believe I heard that two were still missin'. One had been rescued and one was dead."

Olivia gave an involuntary flinch, stepping closer to the man. "What? Where'd you hear that? Who's dead?"

Jack placed a hand on her arm, reminding her not to get too close. Stooping down, he stared the man right in the eye. "Where did you hear that?"

"Sore spot, huh?" the man asked. He spit on the ground. "None of your bidness."

"Did you hear a name?" Olivia demanded. "Of the person who got rescued?"

The man's smile broadened. "Who cares?" he asked.

"Wait, you knew I was telling the truth?" Jack said, putting the pieces together. "You knew the whole time!"

The man glanced at him. "Nothin' personal, son. Just more bad luck." Jack moved in closer, cocking the gun again. The man eyed him warily. "Now, hold on!"

"Shut up!" Jack yelled at him. "And think of me tonight when your balls swell up, asshole. Come on, Olivia, let's go."

Olivia stood in shock.

"They found someone alive," she said, staring intently at Jack. "Did you hear him? They found someone *alive*."

"I know. But we don't have time to talk about it right now," Jack said. "Come on. We've got to *go*."

The man couldn't resist one more taunt. "Behind that plane, they're comin' with a whole squad of boats. They're gotta cut this field tonight and git it out. There's a storm brewin' in the Gulf. Even if you dodge them fellas in the plane, they'll be others lookin' for you. You need to give me back my gun and let me handle this for you. I'm sure I could get my people to cut you some slack."

Jack shook his head in derision.

"Geez, Burl, you're even dumber than you look, and that's hard to imagine. C'mon, Olivia, we're going."

Uncocking the Colt, Jack tucked it into the holster. Grabbing the death star, he nodded for Olivia to follow him. But as they started to leave, a low growling noise suddenly filled the air.

Jack and Olivia froze.

The panther sauntered through the field, walking slowly toward them. As it grew near, it stopped, settling down on its haunches. It stared at Jack and Olivia for a moment, then turned its attention to the man on the ground.

As they watched, it slowly licked its lips.

"Jesus Christ," the man whispered.

"Hey, buddy," Jack said, looking at the big cat and giving it an exaggerated wave.

He then trained his glare on the downed man.

"Be a good sport," he said, "and look after our kitty for us, will you?"

He turned to Olivia, dropping his voice.

"Let's back out slow from the clearing," he whispered. "And then run like hell."

Which is exactly what they did.

CHAPTER 22

THEY MADE THE dock in no time, Jack scooping up the cane pole and tossing it into the boat alongside the death star.

At the sound of the float plane's engine overhead, Olivia looked up. "They're coming back. Are we really going to run?"

"It's our best shot," he said. "Get in. I'll push us off the bank."

"What about the other boats? And the storm he talked about? We could run the other way, cross over the bridge, and try to push it in behind us."

"We could," Jack said as he struggled to push the bow of the boat off the bank. "But, personally, I don't want to stick around to meet that guy's bosses. Do you?"

Olivia sat, shaking her head. "Do you want me to hold the gun while you steer?"

"Well, actually, you should know how it basically works . . . you know . . . just in case."

He took the Colt out of the holster and handed it to her. She took it carefully with both hands, raising it up level.

"It's heavy."

"Yeah. Billy the Kid used to carry one like it."

"You're joking?"

"Not really."

He tersely recited the gun's outlaw pedigree.

"Geez," Olivia said as she stared at the weapon. "How do I shoot it?"

"Easy. It's a revolver. Just pull back the hammer, aim, and fire."

"That's it?"

"Yeah. But be prepared. As you heard, it's loud and has a nasty kick."

"Got it. Now, let's get the hell out of here."

Olivia handed the Colt back to Jack, who slipped it into the holster. She quickly moved to the stern and Jack was able to manhandle the boat off the bank. He hopped forward to the helm, rotating his ball cap backward and motioning for Olivia to do the same. He turned the key and the outboard, smoking and sputtering for the first nerve-wracking thirty seconds before roaring to life.

Jack waved Olivia into the metal bench seat next to him as he eased the boat into reverse and guided it past the dock, turning the bow away from the wind. "Hold on!" he yelled as he shifted into forward and pushed down on the throttle as far as it would go.

The bow pitched up for an unsettling moment, and then the boat literally leapt out of the water before leveling off onto a plane.

"Jesus, this thing is like a rocket!" Jack yelled above the growling of the outboard.

"Which way?" Olivia yelled back.

"Straight across, I guess. He came in this way, so we should be able to get out."

The boat sped along, flying atop the foot-high whitecaps whipped up by a steady tailwind. Jack had driven fast boats before, but nothing like this. Built from heavy-duty aluminum and maybe eighteen feet long, this boat was way overpowered for its size, clearly meant for outrunning cops or game wardens.

Even with both hands on the wheel, it was all Jack could do to keep it on a straight line.

Two minutes later, he saw the pond's exit, a narrow chute lined on both sides by pickets of cypresses. It curved slightly left.

"Hold on," he yelled. "I'm not slowing down."

As Jack navigated the turn, the boat slid right, its starboard side scraping loudly against a protruding log.

For a split second, he thought they might spin out—or flip. As he struggled to regain the center of the channel, Olivia clutched at his arm.

The boat righted itself, and they sped forward through the short chute. A hundred yards away lay the mouth of a bay, a lot bigger than the pond they'd just crossed.

As they sped into open water, they spied the float plane descending and heading right for them.

Jack did some quick calculations. The pond was probably too small for the plane to make a safe landing or takeoff. Based on their glide path, they were going to land in the bay. The boats that the man had mentioned earlier must be coming to portage them through the chute.

Jack scanned the water left and right, wondering if there was a quick way off the bay, a bayou or man-made canal they could slip into. The only thing he saw was an open expanse of water with a tree line maybe a mile straight ahead . . . that and the ever-descending plane.

"Are they going to smash us?" Olivia yelled over the motor.

"Not without smashing themselves," Jack called back. "They can't be that stupid!"

But the plane continued straight toward them, a quarter mile away and closing fast.

If they were trying to scare him, they were succeeding.

But Jack had one advantage; in a turn, the boat was a lot more agile than the plane.

"Hold on!" he yelled again.

Jack cut the wheel hard right, unsure how deep the water was, but determined to get out of the plane's trajectory.

Just as quickly, the plane banked toward them.

Christ! They really are trying to smash us.

Jack swung back hard the other way, steering in an erratic zigzag motion.

The plane banked again as Jack heard the pilot gun the engine; the right wing pitched down toward the water as it came at them again.

This time, Jack steered hard left and watched in horror as the plane roared by much closer than he'd expected, its wing slicing through the air like a giant blade.

Olivia screamed.

Jack, mesmerized, couldn't help looking back. He saw the plane right itself as the pilot suddenly cut back the engine.

It was going to land.

The pilot, whoever he was, knew what he was doing.

Jack wondered why they hadn't gunned the plane for another go-around when he had his answer; he saw the outline of at least two, maybe three boats entering the bay at the tree line in the far distance.

"Oh, shit," he said aloud, pointing.

Olivia peered forward. "That doesn't look good!" she called back.

Jack fought back a wave of panic.

If their boats were anything like this one, he couldn't outrun them. Even if he did manage to make it through, the plane could take off again and serve as a spotter. They could call in other boats or even shoot them from the air.

Olivia had been right. They should have taken their chances on foot.

Unless . . . maybe they still could.

"We're going back!" he yelled to Olivia.

"Going *back*? What do you mean?"

"We'll take the plane out, then head back through the pond. Get over the footbridge, try to kick it in behind us like you said, and hide out in the swamp."

"Are you kidding me?" she yelled. "Do I even want to know how you're planning to take out a plane?"

He gave her a reckless grin, his eyes wild.

"Sneak attack!" he yelled.

Olivia closed her eyes for a second. "Just make sure you kill *them* and not *us*, okay?"

"It's a deal. You ready?"

"No," Olivia called back.

Jack's manic grin widened. "Brace yourself!"

He made a U-turn, heading directly for the plane. They were just in time to see it touch down, its pontoons throwing up twin rooster tails of water behind them. Jack was rapidly gaining on it.

As he sped up from behind, the pilot did just what Jack hoped—he took the plane in a slow turn right, trying to see behind him.

"Get down flat!" Jack yelled at Olivia. She dove forward onto the metal deck between the helm and bow.

Jack saw his target—the back of the left pontoon—and aimed the boat toward it, leaning forward as though that might make it go faster.

As they neared, he caught the look of wild surprise on the face of the man in the passenger seat. He was just beginning to pry the door open, clearly about to step out onto the pontoon.

There was something in his right hand, a rifle, maybe, or a shotgun. Jack felt like the world had slowed. He could see the man mouthing words as he scrambled back into the cockpit, yanking the door shut behind him.

The pilot gunned the engine in desperation. But it was too late. The heavy bow of the camo boat slammed into the pontoon with an ugly scream of metal on metal.

Jack flung himself down, throwing one arm protectively around Olivia as he struggled with his free hand to keep hold of the wheel.

The tail of the plane zoomed just over his head; three inches lower and it would've scalped him.

The boat heaved up on its left gunnels as it flew past, the prop whining as it briefly left the water.

Jack thought for a moment that they were going over. He screamed in unison with Olivia.

A second later, the boat righted itself. Jack bolted up, yanking back the throttle. The boat heaved to a stop, throwing a large wake in front of it. Jack glanced back at the plane.

Success. The bow had done its damage, literally cleaving off the last two feet of the pontoon like it'd been hacked away with a giant hatchet. It was already taking on water. Jack could see the plane, spun ninety degrees by the collision, beginning to list left, even as it tailed away from them as the pilot continued to jam down the throttle.

The plane was picking up speed, but not enough for the pilot to get it off the water. If he slowed, the plane would sink.

"What's happening?" Olivia asked, sitting up and shading her eyes as she stared at the plane.

"I crushed the pontoon. They can't take off, but I'm not sure what the hell they're doing."

A second later, Jack realized that the plane was speeding toward the chute that led into the pond.

"Damn! They're going to try to beach it on the marsh at the entrance. If they do, we'll never get by. The guy in the passenger seat has a gun. The pilot probably does, too."

"What do we do?" Olivia asked.

"I don't know," Jack said, staring.

"Wrong answer!"

"Let me think!"

As they neared the bank, the pilot cut the engine. The plane lurched to a stop on a marshy point with a perfect view of the chute. Both doors immediately flung open.

Jack saw the gleam of the long gun's barrel as a man emerged on the passenger side, trying to steady himself on the pontoon.

"Okay," Jack said. "Time to go."

"*Where?*"

Jack heard the blast of a shotgun just as he throttled down the engine.

"That gun doesn't even have the range," he called to Olivia. "He's just trying to scare us!"

"Mission accomplished!" Olivia yelled back.

Another gun fired three shots in quick succession.

Jack looked right and saw the thrip of bullets zinging against the water.

Damn!

It wasn't a shotgun—it was a large caliber rifle. The plane was at least a hundred yards away.

"Get down!" he shouted to Olivia.

But she'd already flung herself to the deck again.

Jack hit the throttle and the camo boat roared away, Jack steering erratically as he tried to dodge any incoming bullets. Long seconds passed before he heard the next round of shots; by that time, the plane was a fading object in a rearview mirror.

He looked ahead instead. He'd been wrong; there were *four* boats.

Three looked like extra-large crew boats—the kind that ferried workers and supplies to the oil field installations scattered throughout the swamp and the Gulf of Mexico to the south. They had big enough cargo holds for smuggling marijuana.

The fourth had broken away from the pack and was coming right at them. From its speed and low profile, Jack guessed it was a bass boat. Kitted out with the right sort of engines, some of those things could run seventy miles an hour on flat water, maybe even faster.

But Jack suddenly saw an advantage. Bass boats were built for flat water. And this wasn't flat. The wind had picked up since they'd left the dock. Two-foot whitecaps now frothed the surface. The bass boat was fighting to maintain speed and control as it plowed headlong into the mounting waves, throwing up fountains of white spray as it flung itself out of the water atop some wave peaks.

Jack was running on a following sea. The broad, hulking, heavy camo boat could plow right through these waves without slowing.

If he could get past the bass boat without getting shot, they could easily outrun the slow-moving crew boats.

Looking ahead, Jack saw the bass boat was bouncing wildly

across the white-capping waves. *Not a stable shooting platform,* he thought.

"You want to practice your pistol shooting?" he called to Olivia. "I have an idea!"

"What kind of idea?"

Jack unholstered the Colt and handed it to Olivia.

Jack's grin was back. "Ever played chicken?"

She stared at him. "No, and I'm not sure I want to."

"Stay low for now. When we get close to their boat, raise up and fire a shot. Aim high. We don't really want to shoot anyone. They just need to know we can."

"Okay, tell me again how I shoot this?"

"Just pull back the hammer and squeeze—not yank—the trigger."

Olivia nodded. "Squeeze not yank. I think I have that." She nodded uneasily. "Are you sure about this?"

"Nope!" he called out. "But get ready!"

With the following sea and the stiffening wind, the camo boat sped like a surface-running torpedo at the bass boat. Jack guessed their speed at well better than sixty knots. As they got closer, Jack could clearly see three men—one at the wheel, one in a seat beside the driver, and another kneeling on the flat bow that normally served as a fishing platform. With his right hand, the bowman was holding on to a length of rope lashed to a stanchion. He was clearly struggling, pitching back and forth as the boat lurched wildly through the waves, trying to use the rope to steady himself.

In his left hand, he held a rifle.

As the boats hurdled toward each other, the driver of the bass boat throttled down, probably aware of the fact that the gunman up front couldn't aim with the boat lurching from wave to wave. Slowing didn't help much. The boat was still pitching wildly as the bowman struggled to stand.

The bass boat was a sitting duck. Jack corrected course, aiming directly for their bow.

"Stand up," Jack shouted to Olivia as their boat sped forward. "Let them see the pistol! When I tell you, pull back the hammer and squeeze off a shot. Remember to aim high!"

"What if I accidentally shoot someone?"

"Plead self-defense. I'll testify for you at the trial!"

"That's really funny," Olivia said grimly.

The gunman on the deck was still having trouble getting into a firing position, and the crew was so preoccupied with helping him that they hadn't caught on to Jack's plan.

By the time they glanced up, the camo boat was forty yards away, bearing down on them at full throttle. Olivia stood, legs spread, gun steadied with two hands, aiming right at them.

She looked like she'd been doing this kind of thing forever.

"Now!" Jack yelled.

At the last second, Olivia jerked the gun skyward, firing. The shot boomed across the frothy lake, amplified by the wind.

It worked.

The driver hit the throttle in full panic and cut the wheel hard right. The bass boat lurched upward. Jack cut the wheel hard the opposite way, just in time to avoid a collision.

He saw the gunman toppling off the bow as the bass boat tried to speed off.

The wake of the camo boat sloshed over the bass boat's side, knocking a second crewman into the water.

"Yes!" Jack yelled, pumping his fist in the air.

Olivia lowered the gun, rubbing her ear with her other hand. "Damn, that was loud!" Olivia called out. "I think I'm deaf!"

Jack pointed toward the crew boats. "Great job, Annie Oakley. Now we've just got to get past these other guys. But they're slow. They'll never catch us."

"How are we supposed to get around them?"

"See where they're clustered? I'm guessing there's a channel that runs mid-bay. I'm imagining each boat has a GPS with a depth finder.

Those boats draw, like, three or four feet of water. They can't leave the channel without getting stuck. We'll just do an end around and head for the bank where it's shallow. They won't be able to follow us."

"What if they have guns?"

"I'm one-hundred-percent sure they have guns. But we'll stay out of range. Or try to. Our boat's small, and we'll be moving fast. Not an ideal target."

"Good to know . . . I guess."

"Hold on," Jack called back. "We're heading toward the bank."

Jack cut hard for the cypress-shrouded shoreline, struggling to keep his nerves under control. His strategy was riskier than he'd let on. Prop-sucking mudflats or prop-eating stumps could easily strand them.

If that happened, they'd either have to abandon the boat for the swamp or become sitting ducks for anyone with a high-powered rifle. Either option could kill them.

Olivia glanced back, tapped Jack on the arm, and pointed. The bass boat had righted itself. They were back in the chase. "I thought we ditched them?"

Jack looked back. "I saw their engine. It's just a one-forty horse. With three people in the boat, they'll never catch us."

"I really, *really* hope that's true," Olivia replied. "I'm getting a little tired of starring in this swamp western."

Her words were cut short by an amplified voice booming on the wind.

They looked left and saw that the crew boats, still ahead of them, had come to a stop in a cluster, their bows turned toward the bank.

Jack was right. They were stuck in the channel. Meanwhile, his maneuvers toward the bank had already put a good seventy-five yards between their boat and theirs.

"Stop," the voice boomed as it waffled on the wind. "We got no intention of hurting you."

Jack and Olivia peered toward the sound, shading their eyes.

"Look," Olivia said, pointing. "The guy on the bow has a megaphone."

"What a moron," said Jack as he steered the skiff in a line that rapidly increased distance between them and the flotilla. "Does he think we're stupid?"

He nudged Olivia. "Show them your gun."

"I'll show them more than that."

Olivia raised the pistol, pointing it in their direction. Smiling sweetly at the men, she flicked them off with her other hand.

Jack laughed. "There's your answer, assholes!"

Suddenly, another man appeared on the deck of one of the boats with a rifle. As he shouldered it and aimed it toward them, Jack began to steer erratically again, cutting ever more sharply toward the bank. At the speed they were running, he was sure they were out of range, but he yelled to Olivia, "Down again!"

Then, the thin crack of automatic rifle fire. Jack flinched but kept his eye on the shooter. He watched as an array of bullets splashed harmlessly in the water a good twenty yards behind them.

"We're free!" he yelled to Olivia as he steered the skiff back toward the deep water of the channel.

"What about the bass boat?"

Jack looked back. It was barely in sight and clearly rapidly falling behind.

Maybe they'd even give up soon.

"We made it . . . whew!" he said to Olivia.

"Any idea where we are?"

"No," said Jack. "But maybe we'll run across something I recognize. There could be other camps, too. There are clusters of them all over the Atchafalaya. A lot of them have generators and propane tanks, maybe even food. Maybe even people with cell phones."

"If you find one of those," Olivia said, "I'll kiss you for as long as you want to be kissed."

"Seriously?"

"I wouldn't lie about something so important."

Jack grinned. "Something to definitely live for," he said.

As they sped on, Olivia handed Jack the pistol.

"You better secure this," she said.

Jack tucked it back into the holster.

Ten minutes later, the camo boat had crossed the wide bay and entered what was clearly a natural bayou. Jack could tell from the frequent curves. Man-dredged canals were always beelines.

Jack had a sense, more of a gut feeling than anything else, that he might be entering familiar territory. He scanned the banks for some sign—an odd tree, a misshapen stump, a clearing in a thicket on the bank, anything that might seem familiar. So far, nothing.

As they raced through another curve, the motor began to sputter.

"Crap," he said, glancing back at the outboard.

The sputtering continued for another ten seconds or so. And, abruptly, the motor died.

"No, dammit!" Jack muttered to himself. "No, no, *no!*"

"What is it?" Olivia asked in alarm.

Jack switched off the ignition key and turned it on again.

The outboard sputtered and coughed some more before dying again.

Jack glanced down, for the first time noticing the gas gauge tucked down at the bottom of an instrument panel.

The needle sat buried below the letter E.

"We're out of gas," Jack said, shaking his head in disbelief. "We're out of freaking gas."

"Are you serious?" Olivia scrambled forward, staring down at the instrument panel.

"Maybe there's a spare tank," Jack said. "Let me check aft."

He moved toward the engine, lifting the rear hatch. There was a spare tank—as empty as the main one.

"Unbelievable," he said, scouring the banks around them. "Un-freaking-believable. Burl wasn't just a crook—but an incompetent crook!"

The left bank of the bayou was all swamp and marsh, the right bounded by a natural levee that indicated a ridge.

"If I thought the bass boat had given up, I'd say we stick with the boat. The wind's still behind us. It would at least push us along, and we'd have a chance of running into another boat. But if they're still coming, they can't be more than five minutes behind. We can't stay here."

"So, what do you want to do?"

Jack shook his head. "We scuttle the boat and swim to shore."

"Seriously?"

"You got a better plan?"

"No, but I can't believe this. Surely there's another way?"

"I wish there were. But we can't be caught by these people. This isn't a game. They will likely kill us. Or worse."

"That's a cheery thought. You're freaking me out, Jack."

"I'm sorry. But we're wasting time. You need to go."

"Right. But how are you going to sink the boat?"

"There's a drain plug here at the back. I'm going to pull it and shoot a couple of holes in the bottom with the pistol. The motor's heavy. It should drag it down fast."

Jack drew the Colt from the holster. He used it to point toward the bank.

"See that stump there? There's a cut in the bank. That should be an easy place to get up on the levee. I'll be there in a minute. Take off your shoes and try to hold them above your head if you can. At least you'll have dry feet that way."

Olivia pulled off her sneakers, not bothering to untie them. "Well, there goes your kiss," she said, jumping overboard.

Holding her shoes above her head, she began dogpaddling one-handed toward the cut on the bank. "Did I tell you how much I hate being wet again?" she said as she pulled away.

"I know. I'm sorry. I'm going to hate it, too."

Jack bent and pulled the rubber drain plug on the back of the boat.

Water began to rush in.

He hopped forward, jumping up on to the bench seat near the steering wheel to keep his feet dry. Pulling off his shoes, he used his remaining lace to lash them together. He lowered the gun and pumped two slugs through the bottom of the boat, the shots echoing loudly across the swamp.

Water spewed like mini fire hydrants from both holes as the boat began to list aft.

Jack put the lace of his shoes in his mouth and eased his feet over the gunnels. Then, holding the pistol aloft, he slipped into the warm, dark water, kicking hard as he awkwardly tried to keep both his shoes and the gun dry.

By the time he made the bank to join Olivia, who was waiting to give him a hand, he'd given up on his shoes. But the gun had stayed dry.

He had two bullets left.

As Olivia helped pull him up the cut, Jack glanced back and saw the camo boat yawed up at a forty-five-degree angle, the head of the motor halfway submerged.

By the time they reached the top of the levee, the front of the boat was even higher as the heavy outboard dragged the boat downward. It had just slipped from the surface when they heard the drone of an approaching boat—not more than a curve or two behind them.

Jack scanned the levee, trying not to panic. A thicket of palmettos lined the backside of a nearby clearing.

"There," he said in a loud whisper to Olivia. "Behind those!"

They scrambled across the clearing, ducking into the thicket as the noise from the approaching boat grew louder. Jack pushed aside two palmetto fronds that were blocking his view of the bayou, freezing in horror; the fishing pole and death star, which he'd forgotten about in the boat, were bobbing on the surface, being pushed across to the opposite side of the bayou by the wind.

If anyone noticed them, they'd be a dead giveaway.

Too late now.

Seconds later, the bass boat came roaring past. A man stood on the deck with a rifle, scanning the water ahead of him.

Jack let the palmetto fronds slip back together, praying he hadn't been seen. "Get ready to run," he whispered to Olivia.

Tensing, he waited for the boat to slow, a sure sign they'd spotted the floating objects. But somehow, miraculously, they didn't. Jack parted the palmettos again, watching as the bass boat's wake pushed the fishing pole and the death star to the cover of the swampy bank.

He thought about diving in, swimming the bayou to retrieve them. But what if the bass boat came back? It was too risky.

Long minutes passed.

The drone of the engine gave way to the silence of the swamp. The only sound was the breeze ruffling the treetops.

Jack looked at Olivia, hoping to conceal the uncertainty in his eyes.

"I guess they didn't give up," he said. "Bummer."

Olivia plopped to the ground in a seated position, still clutching her sneakers.

"They'll be back, you know," she said.

"They'll never find us," Jack replied.

Olivia nodded. She stood up to look around, wiping mud from her knee. She eased her feet into her sneakers.

"What if nobody else finds us, either?"

CHAPTER 23

"HERE, TRY ONE of these," Jack said.

"And what is it again that I'm about to put in my mouth?"

"Muscadines. Remember, I told you about them before? Swamp grapes. They make really good jams and jellies. The skins are really tough, so you basically have to bite a hole in a corner and then suck out the pulp."

He demonstrated.

"Damn," he said as he tasted the first one. "These might literally be the best thing I've ever tasted."

He tried to smile. "Well, I mean, when I was lost and hungry."

Olivia tried one, too, then grabbed a handful from the pile that Jack had made on his long-sleeved shirt stretched out on the ground. "Interesting," she said as she popped a second into her mouth.

"I hope 'interesting' means good because this is dinner, too."

He could fold the leftover muscadines into his shirt and carry them with him.

But where exactly are we going?

The thought made him more than a little anxious. They'd have to figure out some sort of shelter before it got dark. A lean-to of palmetto fronds might be the best they could do.

What if running was a mistake?

Jack tried to push the thought away. Second-guessing decisions now would only drive him crazy.

Finding the vine loaded with purple muscadines climbing its way up a small oak had been their one piece of good luck since leaving the levee. Jack had shimmied to the top and harvested a couple pounds of the ripest ones, dropping them a handful at a time to the cushion of his spread-out shirt.

Before that, they'd walked for an hour on a finger of ridge that snaked away from the levee through the swamp. The path had led them through endless, deep woods. The day was still warm and breezy, but the sun was gone, hidden behind bank after bank of the passing gray clouds that loomed over the treetops. The air felt damp, like it might rain.

The adrenalin had faded, giving way to reality. All they had, besides the clothes on their backs and the Colt .45, was the emergency kit knife and the butane lighter. Luckily, Jack had tucked both in his pocket that morning.

He had no idea if the lighter even worked, given their latest impromptu swim. He'd try it later, after it had a chance to dry out.

He could see depression creeping into Olivia's face. He didn't blame her because he was down, too. He just couldn't show it.

He thought about the rescue sign they'd made back at the first clearing. It would be pretty useless now that they'd fled who knows how many miles from its location. But surely it would be enough to keep people looking for them.

Jack squeezed another muscadine into his mouth, trying and failing to think of anything else positive, when Olivia nudged him.

"Feel that?" "What?"

"Rain."

Jack looked up through the breaks in the heavy tree cover and saw mist against the pale light of a bone gray sky.

"We should get going . . . scout for shelter."

"The guy back in the field said a storm was coming," said Olivia, seated with her back against the muscadine oak.

"He was probably just trying to spook us into staying. Anyway, I thought he meant it was at least a day or two out. That's why those guys were rushing to grab their crop."

Olivia shrugged. "You're probably right. It doesn't really matter." She closed her eyes. "I'm tired, Jack, really tired. Honestly, I don't even care what happens anymore. Sorry."

Jack leaned in, letting his shoulder press against hers. "Hey," he said. "Just because we haven't found anything yet doesn't mean we're not going to. There are camps all over this swamp. We could run into someone. *Anything* could happen. But not if we just sit here."

Olivia tilted her head against his shoulder. "Not your best pep talk."

Jack didn't want to tell her it was because he was faking it.

The mist was thickening. Jack could feel sprinkles on his bare arms. He gritted his teeth and said a silent prayer. *"Seriously, God. Give us break, would you?"*

He turned to Olivia and said, "C'mon, I'll bundle up the muscadines and we'll go. Just give it another couple of hours and see where we are then, okay?"

He stood, holding out his hand for Olivia. She didn't take it right away. When she finally did, she looked up him. "Do you think it makes me a terrible person that I'm hoping Joe is the one who died?" Her voice trembled. "Because, honestly, I don't think I can take another step if my dad didn't survive."

She pulled herself up, wiping tears away with her palms.

Jack folded her into his arms. "You're not a terrible person. It's just . . . it's a terrible situation, okay? You're human. Of course you want your dad to be alive. I would feel the same if I were you."

She nodded against his shoulder. "I guess."

"And if he *is* alive," Jack said, "he's going to be pretty pissed if we give up now."

She gave him a faint smile. "Right. Let's go."

They walked, mostly in silence, the drizzle intermittent. Jack skillfully steered them around the occasional bog and over random logs and other obstacles. They spotted game—a fleeting rabbit, a nutria wandering across their path, a pair of wood ducks that they flushed from a tree.

Jack could've easily shot the nutria, but with only two bullets and the muscadines procured for supper, he decided to save his ammo—either for defense or to signal to possible rescuers.

Besides, an echoing shot right now could attract unwanted attention. Who knew where the bass boat could be right now?

Not to mention he would have to skin and somehow roast the nutria. He had skinned exactly one nutria in his life and the revolting smell it gave off convinced him to never skin another. Furthermore, the Cajuns, who had turned crawfish and alligator into tasty treats for the world, declared nutria unwelcome in their pots.

His main worry, besides the rain, was that they were going to hit a dead end, that the narrow ridge would just peter out into swamp, and they'd either have to wade ahead through leech-filled water and see if the ridge picked up later or else return to the levee. So it was a relief when, rounding a bend, the ridge broadened out at a small clearing circled by moss-draped live oaks larger than any they had seen before.

For the first time, they faced a choice about which direction to go.

Something that looked like a deer trail veered left of the clearing, sloping toward a thicket of willows and tupelo gum. Straight ahead was a classic oak ridge, the trees taller and the understory, where the trees shaded out the light, less dense.

"Okay," said Jack, motioning for them to stop. "See these big trees? They show we're on higher ground than what we've been walking through."

"Which means . . . what?" Olivia asked.

"Maybe nothing. But there's not a lot of high ground around here. That's why so many people build their camps on top of the natural levees. They were built up gradually by hundreds of years of floods. In lots of places in the swamp, they're the only high ground around."

"So, there could be camps here?"

"Or there could be nothing. But it's worth exploring. We'll go right and stay away from that animal trail. I'm guessing that will land us back into the low ground."

"I'm following you," said Olivia.

Jack glanced at his watch, almost four. They had about two-and-half-hours left of daylight. If they didn't miraculously stumble into a camp or another hunting shack, they'd need to pick a campsite by five, at the latest, so they'd have a chance of building some sort of shelter before dark. Even if it was just a palmetto lean-to.

A half hour later, the rain began in earnest, not hard but steady. The thick oak canopy would act like a leaky umbrella for a while until the leaves, saturated, could absorb no more water. They needed to speed up their search or risk being soaked. Their clothes from their impromptu swim were mostly dry now. Jack quickened the pace.

What's with this freaky weather? Jack thought.

Minutes later, he stood before a mammoth live oak that seemed to loom up out of the woods and dwarf anything else around it. Besides its sprawling branches, some of which dipped almost to the ground, the tree's singular feature was a large, blackened hollow at its base.

"Look at this," he said, pointing out the opening. "This had to be done by fire—probably lightning—a long time ago. I think we've found our camp."

Even though rain was pelting harder in the treetops, Olivia looked dubious.

"What if there's something else in there?"

"What, like a panther?" said Jack.

"Not funny. But, no, I was thinking more like snakes or spiders. Creepy-crawlies."

"I'll go in first and check it out. No matter what, it's got to be better than standing out in the rain. Or sleeping in it."

Olivia motioned toward the opening. "Be my guest."

Jack stepped inside, marveling at how big it was. He could stand without ducking. Sure, it was a little dark and musty. But there was a window of sorts—a gargantuan, hollowed-out branch, maybe thirty feet in length, that jutted out about four feet above the base and acted as a kind of oversized ventilation shaft. *Or a chimney,* Jack thought. It was so large that he could poke his head and shoulders into it and look up. It was clearly open at the top, no doubt from the same fire that had carved out this odd chimney.

The floor beneath him was also solid, covered with a bit of leaf litter. He nudged around with his right foot, trying to spook out any hiding insects. He flushed two small spiders and smashed both with his right shoe, pulverizing any evidence.

Olivia picked up on the scuffling noise. "What was that?"

"Nothing. You should come in, check it out. It's dry. And no bugs."

Olivia stepped tentatively inside and looked around, giving her eyes time to adjust to the dimmer light before saying anything.

"Okay. This isn't so bad. I mean, it smells a little, but . . . " She trailed off.

"Let me get some Spanish moss, spread it on the floor. It'll be easier on our backs when we bed down."

Olivia nodded. "I guess. Our shack seems pretty great right now, huh? Kind of like the Plaza."

"Is that a hotel?"

"Yeah, a famous one in Manhattan."

"You stayed there?"

"No, but when I was younger, my father would take me and friends there each Christmas for a visit. They'd do up the lobby big-time."

"I see. Well, we could pretend this is the swamp equivalent."

"Hmm. That would take more imagination than I have right now."

"Right. I should get to work."

Jack had no problem plucking three large armloads of gray moss from the oak's branches. Soon enough, they were settled into the hollow, seated on a thick moss layer with their backs against the wall opposite the opening.

He'd put his shirt with muscadines between him and Olivia and the revolver on the ground to his left.

"Home sweet home," Jack said.

"Maybe," Olivia said. "Are we at all concerned about the fact that we don't have a door?"

Jack stared at the opening.

"Damn, I didn't even think about that."

"What about those palmetto thingies?" asked Olivia. "You have your knife, right? Can we cut some and kind of smush them into the opening?"

"That might actually work. I saw a stand of palmettos not too far away. I'll go grab some now before the rain gets worse."

"Ugh, I forgot about the rain. Don't bother. You'll just get all wet."

"I'm already wet," Jack pointed out. "And a door will stop anything from wandering in *and* keep out the rain."

Olivia started to stand. "Then I'll go with you."

"No, it's okay. I'll do it. We only have one knife, anyway."

"Then I can help you carry them," Olivia said. "Come on already."

Jack followed her out of the opening, leading her to the stand of palmettos. He had to admit it was easier with Olivia's help. Jack cut six large fronds, leaving foot-long stems on each, and Olivia scooped them up two by two and dashed back to the opening.

"Thanks. Here, inside."

He'd already thought about how to secure them. Sharpening the stem ends of the first two fronds, he pushed them side by side into the spongy ground just outside the hollow. They more than filled the opening. Then he sliced long furrows in the fronds of the rest and wove them, clumsily, into a self-supporting lattice.

"We have a door," he declared.

"Impressive," said Olivia.

"But wait," Jack said. "I can go one better. How about a fire?"

"What, in the tree?" Olivia asked, looking around. "Won't that smoke us out?"

Jack pointed to the open shaft. "It's a natural chimney," he said. "You can already feel a draft in here. It'll whisk the smoke right out."

Olivia remained dubious. "It's not like we have anything to cook.

And it's not cold. Well, not yet, anyway."

"But it'll give us light. And keep any curious critters at bay."

Olivia nodded. "Ah, that's an interesting point. We don't need any furry or slithering intruders."

"Right. I'll keep it small," Jack said. "Wait here a sec. I'm going to grab some dead moss to use as kindling before everything gets soaked. That stuff burns hot and fast."

He eased through their makeshift door and returned a few minutes later carrying an armload of dead, dry moss and small sticks and logs. He rearranged the palmetto door back in place and placed his wood pile in proximity to the air shaft.

"Hmm, the lighter. Let's hope it still works."

He dug it out of his still-damp khakis pocket, struck it, and was secretly amazed that it flared immediately. Pretty soon, a small fire illuminated the oak hollow, the smoke rising easily up the natural chute.

"Okay," said Jack, "Supper. I'm sorry that all we're serving in this fine place are muscadines."

Olivia raised her eyebrows. "Have I mentioned that I'd kill for the roasted beet-and-goat-cheese salad at Cavatappo right now?"

"Is that, like, your favorite restaurant?"

"One of them. It's in our 'hood. My dad and I eat there all the time."

"Nice. I was thinking about those pancakes you were talking about up in Maine," said Jack. "Or, actually, I take that back. I need to *stop* thinking of those pancakes."

He unfolded the shirt holding the leftover muscadines. They ate hungrily in silence for a few minutes, savoring every bite. Especially the juice, after a day without water. They worked their way down into the pile until there were only ten left.

"Now or breakfast?" said Olivia.

"We should save them, I guess. We'll be happy we did in the morning."

Olivia sighed. "Makes sense."

Jack rose to tend his fire, carefully adding another small log.

"It's not going to burn all night, is it?" asked Olivia.

"It could if you want. I'd have to make another wood run."

"No, it's fine. Don't go back out. We can just talk until it burns out and go to sleep. Or try to, I guess."

"Good plan."

Jack settled back against the tree trunk next to her.

Outside, the rain had grown louder. The palmetto door was bowing in and out as wind gusts buffeted the woods and shook water from the trees. The fire stirred fitfully in the draft created by the chute.

There was no way the door would hold up to a big blow. But that was out of their control.

Olivia stretched and yawned. "Bored?" asked Jack.

"Tired."

To his surprise, she shifted, settling her head in his lap and stretching her legs out in front of her.

"How about a bedtime story?" she asked.

"You tell me one," he said. "You've been to Africa, right? Tell me about that."

"Like the time we had a deadly black mamba crawling on the dining room table in our lodge?"

"Seriously?"

"Yeah. But I'll save that one for later. Snakes get you too excited."

Jack laughed. "What about the Amazon, then?"

"Ah, the diarrhea cruise," Olivia said, allowing herself a curt smile. "Those were the best of times."

"Hah! I was thinking about something more uplifting," said Jack, unable to suppress a laugh.

Olivia yawned again. "Are you sure? It's a funny story. Well, in a dark sort of way."

Jack stared at her intently. "You *do* look exhausted. Try to get some sleep, and we'll save story time for another day. I'll keep watch for a while."

Olivia looked up at him inquiringly. "We're not expecting anyone—or anything—are we?"

"Are you kidding? I think we're the only ones unlucky enough to be out here tonight. I'm just not quite ready for sleep."

"Okay," Olivia said. "But wake me up if you need me."

"I will," he promised.

Olivia closed her eyes, reaching for Jack's hand before folding her own across her chest.

Jack couldn't help but stare.

Even after days in the swamp and all they had endured, she was still stunningly beautiful.

Of course, her beauty had been apparent from the moment he first saw her. But he hadn't known then about her wit and wry sense of humor, her devotion to her family, her courage when it mattered.

Looking down at her in the flickering firelight, he thought about how much he *liked* her, wondering if, maybe, he even loved her.

Now that would really be dumb, he thought.

Her head on his lap, Olivia's breathing slowed into the soft rhythm of sleep. Jack stared down at her, remembering how many lies he'd told her today. They'd been forced to flee to a place even farther off the beaten track. He doubted anyone was coming to rescue them. They would have to save each other.

CHAPTER 24

A ROAR STARTLED Jack awake.

For one exhausted second, he wondered if the noise was coming from a train. *A train out here?*

He opened his eyes, turning instinctively toward the fire, which had gone out. He was still sitting upright, Olivia's head in his lap. He'd never been in a space so black.

Disoriented, he wondered if the darkness itself was a dream. Then, suddenly, a blast of wind slapped him wide awake. The roar grew louder as trees began to shudder and groan.

There was a loud *thwuck*. The rain began to slash at him sideways, stinging his face and arms.

A muted explosion—*thunder?*—swallowed the enveloping roar. A streak of light flashed through the hollow.

His flimsy palmetto door had vanished.

Another blast of water pummeled through the opening like a wet piston, drenching them both.

Olivia, startling awake, screamed just as Jack yelled out over the din, "Tornado! Grab on to me. Grab on!"

They managed to find each other in wet, chaotic blackness, and Jack, having gotten his bearings in the flash of light, rolled them toward a nook in the hollow farthest from the opening.

Another blast of water, another steak of lightning, another violent shuddering of the tree, and then an unmistakable splintering sound.

"What's happening?" Olivia yelled.

"I don't know!" Jack screamed back. "The tree . . . it . . ."

Before he could finish, their world suddenly tilted. They rolled through the impenetrable dark, desperately trying to hold on to one another.

They failed, tumbling apart like flung dice.

A violent gust blasted the hollow, so intense that it pinned Jack to the wall or floor—he couldn't tell which—and seemed to suck the very breath out of him. For a minute, he thought his ears might burst.

Recovering his voice, he cried out for Olivia. To his relief, she yelled back. She sounded close, but not near enough that Jack could touch her.

"Keep talking," he yelled. "I'll find you."

"Here," said Olivia. "Here!"

As Jack crawled toward the sound, the roar reached a crescendo and the tree rocked so violently that it knocked him off all fours and sent him rolling. When he stopped, he was on his back in what felt like a puddle of water.

Jack heard Olivia's muffled screams, and then, like a snuffed candle, the roar was gone.

Her voice went with it. The roar had swallowed everything.

All that was left was black, still silence.

"Jesus," Jack said, scrambling to his knees. "That was crazy. Right? Olivia? You there?"

No answer.

On the verge of panic, he was about to call out again when he felt a hand on his shoulder. His involuntary shriek ripped apart the silence.

"Sorry," Olivia said, her voice strangely calm. "It's me. I'm right behind you. Don't ask me how I got here."

"You scared the hell out of me," Jack said. He squinted in the darkness, trying to make her out. "I thought you were . . . dead."

"What happened?" Olivia asked.

"I think the tree came down," Jack said. "Here, wait."

He dug the lighter out of his pocket and struck it. The gray walls were different.

"Where's the opening?"

"The opening?"

"It's gone," Jack said, whirling around in a circle, the lighter held in front of him.

"That's impossible," Olivia whispered.

Confusion turned to shock as Jack realized what had happened.

"The tree must've come up by the roots, falling with the opening facing down. We're standing on it."

"So, then, how do we get out?"

Jack lowered the lighter. "Good question."

"Wait, are we *trapped* in here?"

"I don't know," he said. "Let me just think for a sec."

Jack shuddered. He was mildly claustrophobic—well, more than mildly. The closed-in spaces of the swamp didn't bother him. But the few times he'd ridden in elevators, he was never happier than when the doors opened.

The knot of panic tightened in Jack's stomach. He'd give his left arm for real light or a hatchet. Actually, maybe a chain saw.

"Let me just look around."

A sudden gust of wind blew out the lighter, plunging them back into darkness.

"For the record, I *hate* this," Olivia said.

"I'm with you," Jack said. He flicked the lighter again and again. On the fourth try, it flared.

"Thank God," he said under his breath.

He turned to Olivia, "Okay, so that's good, right? Something blew my lighter out. Which means . . ."

He walked forward, holding the lighter in front of him.

Another soft breeze swirled the flame.

"The chimney! That's it!"

He pointed to an opening about chest high up the wall. With

the tree fallen over, the chute was now parallel to the blown-over trunk. Its exit would be the forest floor. A glimmer of hope surged through Jack.

"What about it?" Olivia asked.

"It's our way out. We just have to crawl through it. And then, hopefully, it's wide enough at the end for us to slip out."

"Hopefully?" Olivia asked. "You're not sure?"

"How would I know? I haven't been up there. But, I mean, it *looked* big. And it sucked the smoke out like crazy. And we're getting good ventilation. That counts for something."

Jack wondered if he should confess his claustrophobia, then thought better of it.

"I'll go first," Jack said. "I can check it out. If it looks okay, I'll crawl back and help you out."

"And if it doesn't look okay?"

"I still have my knife. I can whittle us out."

Olivia blurted a brittle laugh. "Whittle us out? With a pocketknife?" she said, a little wildly. "How many days will that take? Get real, Swamp Boy."

Jack gazed at Olivia in the flickering glow of the butane lighter. He hoped she didn't see the worry in his eyes.

"Okay, fine," he said. "But there's only one way to find out. I'll go first." Olivia didn't seem convinced.

"Okay, say you get out. But then what? Listen to it out there, Jack. The tornado might be gone, but it's storming like crazy. Are we supposed to walk through the swamp in the middle of a hurricane? We don't even know where we're going."

Jack nodded. He hadn't paid much attention to the racket of the storm, but Olivia was right; it *was* howling out there. Better to stay put until morning. The chimney meant fresh air, so they weren't going to suffocate. They could try to escape after the storm had passed. Maybe someone would even come along and hear their cries and . . .

Nah, Jack thought. *Pure fantasy.*

It made sense to test the opening now. Olivia still looked dubious. "Fine," she finally said. "But can I keep the lighter? It's just . . . the dark makes me feel trapped."

"Sure," said Jack, handing it to her. "I'll be quick, I promise."

Olivia managed a wan smile. "Right, quick, and with good news, okay?"

Easing himself into the shaft, Jack began to crawl ever so slowly, and then stopped. It was *so* tight, so dark. It smelled of smoke from the fire. What if he got halfway to the opening and got stuck, couldn't back out?

They'd both die.

Jack felt a lump in his throat. Sweat drenched his face.

"I can't do this. There's got to be another way."

He found himself backing out.

Olivia was kneeling near the opening, still holding the lighter.

"Well?" she said.

Jack stared at her a long time before speaking.

He looked away. "I dunno. I can't. I can't do it. I can't crawl through there. It's like a tomb. I'm, um, sorry."

He told her about his elevator fears.

Olivia shook her head. "Okay, but you fit, yes?"

"Yeah, like a worm in a straw."

"Fine, I'm going."

"What?"

"I'm going. Do you have a better idea?"

"No."

"Did I tell you I used to be claustrophobic, too? So I get it."

"No, you didn't. But you aren't now?"

"A little, maybe. But I took a SCUBA course . . . well, my dad insisted. The instructor had been a Navy SEAL. He put me through all kinds of survival scenarios. He said diving is easy until you get into trouble. Then you die if you don't know what to do. He called one of his little tests, 'The Do or Die.' I had to sit on the bottom of a twenty-foot diving pool with a blacked-out mask. He told me other divers were coming for me, to simulate getting caught in a tidal surge. 'Hold on to your regulator at all costs.' The waiting was crazy. I'd never had so much adrenalin flowing through my body. I didn't know you could sweat under water. They grabbed me and turned me end over end. Then they yanked off all my equipment except my weight belt. I had to fight like hell to keep my regulator in my mouth."

Jack looked at her, shaking his head. "Holy shit. And you passed?"

"I did . . . not that I would want to do it again. The diving instructor was truly a masochist, but I have to give him credit—it was a confidence builder."

"Damn. I don't think I could've done that. I would've freaked out."

"Who knows," said Olivia. "So, I'll go. I'll try to find the way out. And anyway, I'm skinnier than you."

Jack nodded.

"I'm embarrassed," he said.

"About what?"

"Wimping out."

Olivia gave him a smile, putting a warm hand on his cheek. She looked at him intently. "Stifle it, Swamp Boy. C'mon, you got me out of a wrecked plane, you swam the equivalent of a marathon to get me to high ground. You killed my leeches and scared off a panther. You still have money in the bank, as Terrence FitzGerald would say. Now, here, you take the lighter. I'm going."

And with that, Olivia disappeared into the darkened shaft of the tree.

Long minutes passed—how many, Jack didn't know. He'd lost track of time. He'd blown out the lighter and kneeled in the dark, waiting by the shaft's entrance. *No use wasting the fuel.*

He could still hear the storm raging outside.

Morbid thoughts crowded his head. *What if she gets stuck? Well, then, we're screwed. They'll find our bones someday. Maybe.*

Running from the marijuana bandits, he now realized, had been a huge mistake. Well, not huge. Probably fatal.

Jack went to Mass when his momma made him go. He wasn't particularly religious. But he crossed himself and whispered a small prayer. "Get us out of here, God, if you don't mind. Please. I promise to make Mass more often. Okay? I mean it."

Suddenly, Jack felt a strong gust burst from the shaft, the first in a while.

And then Olivia's voice, muffled but understandable, tumbling through the blackness. "I'm out! I'm out! It's crazy blowing, like a hurricane, and raining like hell. And there's a strange light in the sky. But we're not trapped!"

Jack flicked on the lighter to illuminate the entrance to the shaft and peered in. He realized he didn't need it. The shadowy outline of Olivia's head was visible at the opening.

Jack called out, "How far do you think it is to you?"

"Uh, I dunno. Not so far. Maybe thirty feet, a little more. It's not so bad. Yeah, a little tight in places, but I never felt stuck. The trick is to keep moving. Squirm like a worm."

Jack realized he still wasn't crazy about making the claustrophobic journey and, given what Olivia had reported about the conditions outside, wondered if they ought to just hole up in the tree until the storm abated. He was about to suggest that to Olivia, wondering how she would feel about making a return trip, when he noticed something shocking.

Water!

Rivulets were pouring into the tree cavity. The floor wasn't level and, where it canted downward, a foot of water had already accumulated. The muscadines they had so carefully saved were floating on the mucky flood. There went breakfast.

The water stirred in menacing little whirlpools. It was coming up quick. Jack now knew one thing for certain—*crawl out or drown.*

CHAPTER 25

JACK TWIRLED THE lighter around in the air, making one last frantic sweep of their temporary shelter.

The revolver!

It leaned in its holster up against the tree wall just out of the swirling water's reach. He snatched it up and strapped it on so that it hung across his backsides. It was a bitch to lug the thing around, but it had served them well so far. If it hung him up on the crawl out, he would just ditch the whole thing.

He doused the lighter and stuffed it into his khaki pockets. At the entrance of the shaft, he took a deep breath to calm himself. *You can do this.*

He then realized he *had* to do it—half his sneakers and the cuffs of his pants were already under water. It was pouring in. A knot of panic welled up in his chest.

Olivia called to him, a note of impatience in her voice.

"You coming?"

"Yes, right, on my way," Jack replied, trying to sound more confident than he felt.

Jack pulled himself up and eased into the shaft. Olivia was still staring in, illuminated, Jack guessed, by the strange light she'd noted earlier. The light was something of a small comfort.

Jack began worming his way forward, using his knees, elbows, and feet to push ahead. It was slow going. Had he ever sweated so much?

Olivia kept calling out to him. "You're doing great. Just keep moving. You've got this, Jack."

Easy for her to say. She's out.

Every inch required him to choke back panic. Strangely, it was the breeze from the opening that kept him steady. The breeze and the dim light. And Olivia's calming voice above the roar of the storm.

Maybe two-thirds of the way, he lost progress; something snagged the back collar of his T-shirt. No way to reach behind him. He squirmed harder and harder, trying to wrench free.

He couldn't, and tried again.

"Olivia, uh, I'm stuck. Something's got me."

"Stuck? On what?"

"I don't know, like a branch, a snag, I guess. It's caught my shirt."

"Crazy. I didn't feel anything when I came through."

"Well, like you said, you're skinnier."

"Can you keep pushing?"

"I've *been* pushing. I can't break free."

Then a silence.

Jack hadn't told Olivia about the rising water. The shaft canted up slightly, and Jack could feel the water now all the way up to his knees.

He had, what, maybe ten minutes? Maybe less. He told Olivia.

"I know," she said. "It's coming up like crazy out here. I just didn't want to spook you."

"Ah, how considerate."

"Don't be a smart ass. Hold on, I'm coming to get you."

"What do you mean? How?"

I'm gonna come down toward you face-first and hook my feet over the rim of the opening. You'll grab my hands and pull free."

"And what if I pull you in instead?"

"You won't."

"But what if I do and you can't back out?"

"Well, then we'll die in this miserable place together. You ready?"

"No. But c'mon. The water's up to my ass."

Olivia eased into the shaft, arms and hands extended, hooking her feet over the entrance. Her move blocked out the light, and the sudden darkness startled Jack, back on the verge of panic.

"Where are you?" he cried out.

"Here," she said, her voice sounding closer. "Right here. Extend your hands. All the way. You should be able to grab mine."

Jack complied. His fingertips barely brushed hers.

"I can't grab on," he said. "You're not down far enough."

"I can't come any farther. I have to keep my feet curled over the edge. You've got to come to me."

"I can't."

"You can."

"I can't. I've tried."

Silence.

Then Olivia's voice, crackling with anger. "Jack, I need you to listen to me. Just worm your sorry ass another few inches and grab my hands. Now! Or maybe you *really are* a wimp."

At that moment, Coach Galjour's voice entered Jack's head. *Landry, for God's sake, what the hell is wrong with you? Do what she says!*

Jack felt primal anger well up as he mustered every ounce of energy to make another push for the inches he needed to reach Olivia.

"Dammit, let me go!" he screamed, as if the tree might hear him. He wormed and writhed forward, struggling as he'd never before.

He felt something tear and, after a moment of sheer terror, felt Olivia's hands.

Of course, if the holster snagged, he'd still be stuck.

"Got you!" she said. "Now, c'mon, I'm going to back out with you, nice and slow."

It was an awkward dance, but soon Jack and Olivia were seated side by side on the trunk of the overturned tree, where they'd climbed to get out of the rising water. Jack was amazed the Colt had made it through the tight opening.

Maybe some good luck, finally?

He reached for Olivia, taking her in his arms. She didn't resist.

"Thank you," he whispered. "If not for you . . . well."

He hoped she wouldn't notice the tears on his cheek.

Olivia gently pulled away and looked deeply into his eyes.

"Jack. Shh, shh, shh. It's okay. We're in this together. Just hold me."

They held on tightly to each other, until a loud rumble of thunder brought them back to their predicament.

"I guess that psycho wasn't lying about the storm," said Olivia. "What now?"

Good question.

They might have been out of the tree, but they weren't out of danger.

Jack looked down at his watch—five o'clock. Daybreak of their fifth day in the swamp was more than an hour away.

Glancing up, Jack saw the unusual glow in the sky, like the clouds had somehow become backlit. Maybe it was the phenomenon known as heat lightning. Or something stranger.

But it cast enough light that, when he stood and looked around him, he was able to see something shocking. He *would've* drowned in the shaft because a quickening tide of dark water had already turned their giant tree trunk into an island. An island that clearly would soon be submerged.

Can this actually be a hurricane?

October storms that welled up in the Gulf before roaring ashore weren't unheard of. Hurricane Betsy in 1965 had been one of them. Jack remembered Paw-Paw Landry recounting how kids had gone to school in the morning, only to be told at lunchtime that they needed to hurry home. A cat-4 hurricane was only hours away from slamming the coast.

But if it is a hurricane . . .

The Great Atchafalaya formed part of a vast spillway system connected to the Mississippi River. In times of extreme flood threats, like the approach of a hurricane or tropical storm, operators could open massive gates and dump huge volumes of water into the Atchafalaya Basin to relieve pressure on the river levees that protected New Orleans and other vulnerable areas.

It had happened in Katrina. Water in the Great Atchafalaya had risen on galloping crosscurrents as high as nine feet in some areas, flooding hundreds of camps. Luckily, no one had tried to ride out the storm in a camp in the swamp, so nobody had drowned.

"Jesus," he said to Olivia, after he explained his theory to her.

"We might have another half hour on this tree, and that's it. Maybe not even that long."

"So what's the plan?" she asked.

"I don't know."

Jack looked out at the swirling water. "We could try to swim to a cypress. Climb up high in the branches and wait it out."

"And if we get another tornado?"

He shook his head. "Well, we'd know what it feels like to fly. For a few seconds, at least."

"Seems like a lousy way to die."

"At least it would be quick."

"Right. But no more death talk, okay?" said Olivia. "Surely there's a way?"

Jack had no immediate answer. Scanning the water brought more bad tidings. The fulminating flood had loosened logs, stumps, and branches from all over. They were eddying around the oak in a sort of weird, meandering parade. More ominously, some were stacking up against the trunk itself, which was now less than two feet above the swirling tide.

It would be bad enough to be swept from the trunk by the water. It could be fatal to be knocked off by debris pushed by a heavy current. They would be crushed before they drowned.

Time was running out. Swimming seemed like their only option.

Jack pivoted, looking for a way out. Suddenly, the trunk was jarred by a large *thunk*. He turned toward the sound; something big, dark, and curved like a giant turtle shell had struck the tree near its upturned roots and was now sliding down the current toward them.

It took a minute for him to realize it was the broad bottom of an overturned wooden boat with a sharply raised keel defining its center.

"Look!" he called out to Olivia, pointing. "There!"

"What is it?" she asked, pushing herself up.

"A capsized boat. It's our way out!"

CHAPTER 26

WITH OLIVIA FOLLOWING his lead, Jack launched himself from the trunk, throwing his right arm across the boat's upturned bottom and grabbing the raised keel. The boat rolled toward him. For a second, Jack thought he might lose his grip and slide off.

But he didn't. The bottom was broad enough so that only his feet were in the water.

He couldn't figure out the sharp pain in his stomach until he patted it, realizing he'd forgotten that he'd readjusted the holster to keep the pistol in front of him for fear of losing it. He was lying on top of it. He lifted himself up on his elbows, unstrapped the holster, and balanced it on the keel.

When Jack looked back in the dimness, he saw that Olivia was barely clinging to the stern.

"My hands slipped!" she yelled. "I don't think I can hold—"

And before she could finish, she was gone. Jack yelled out to her. "I'm coming!"

Then a quick thought, *Lose the shoes.* He yanked off his sneakers and plopped them near the keel.

He pushed himself off the boat, the pistol be damned. He knew enough about the weapon to know that it would still fire so long as the cartridges stayed watertight.

He fought the current looking for Olivia. At the moment, when an agonizing scream welled up in his head saying he had lost her, she surfaced in front of him, spitting water and coughing violently.

"Are you okay?" Jack yelled, grabbing on to her.

She coughed again, more violently this time.

"Swamp water," she said, pointing to her throat. "I think I'm going to be sick."

"No time for that. We need to catch up with the boat."

They swam awkwardly, Jack pulling her along and reaching the stern first. He latched on with one hand, trying to slow the hull so that Olivia could latch on.

"Grab here," he shouted, pointing with his free hand to the raised keel.

Olivia followed his instructions, grabbing on with both hands, and then violently vomited a stream of water.

"Ugh ... sorry," she said.

"Impressive. That would've definitely won an Olympic barfing contest. Here, c'mon up on the boat."

Olivia tightened her grip on the keel as Jack pushed her up from behind. He almost laughed out loud at his ludicrous thought. Whatever fantasies he may have had about touching Olivia's cute butt, they did not involve surviving a hurricane.

Sure that she was secure, he swam forward, slowly inching up on the hull, trying not to destabilize the boat and pitch Olivia back into the drink.

Jack eased his way back to his original spot, knowing he'd reached it when his hand brushed the revolver. His sneakers were still there, too.

Two miracles, he thought.

"Feeling any better?" he called out to Olivia.

"Some. Funny what a little vomiting can do for a girl. Any idea what we're floating toward?" she asked.

"Not exactly. But I'm thinking the general direction has to be south. If they're dumping water from the river, there's no place for it to go except the Gulf."

"Great. So, we're going to be washed out to sea?"

"Not if I can help it. And anyway, it's a long way from here." Jack wished he felt as confident as he sounded.

Another rumble of far-away thunder echoed through the

swamp, followed by a howling blast of wind that shattered the lull they'd been floating through. It began to rain again, a slashing, sideways rain that stung Jack's cheek and exposed hands.

He looked toward Olivia. He could barely see her. It was like driving through an automated car wash.

"Not the kind of shower I was hoping for!" he heard Olivia yelling over the din.

Jack felt helpless. When he and his family had ridden out Katrina, on the edge of the storm, the wind and rain had come in bands, with lulls in between them. They'd already been through one lull. *When's the next one going to come?* It couldn't be too soon.

Another rumble of thunder cascaded over the treetops, so loud that Jack wondered if something had exploded above them.

Streaks of lightning began to fill the sky, filtered by clouds so close and dense that Jack, glancing up, thought were coming down to smother them. He'd never seen weather like this.

The overturned boat was picking up speed, propelled ever faster by the wind and the quickening flood. He scanned the water ahead for obstacles. Ramming into a tree at this speed would be dangerous. An even worse visions raced through Jack's head of each being knocked from the boat by low-lying tree limbs and plunged into the roiled, dark, debris-filled water, separated from each other.

At the risk of unbalancing the boat, Jack began inching toward Olivia, reaching back to pat the revolver. He had no idea if the gun would still fire, but it was somehow comforting just knowing that he had it. The endless flicker of lightning was actually a plus, illuminating her outline. Her head was down in the crook of her arm.

He reached her, putting a hand gently on her shoulder.

She stirred. "What is it?"

"Take my hand. And whatever happens, don't let go. We have to stick together. And stay on the boat at all costs. It's the only way we're getting out of here."

She nodded. Their hands entwined, hers cold to Jack's touch.

Good thing the water and rain were warm. They'd be battling hypothermia, too.

In the time it had taken to reposition themselves, the raging wind had slackened. Now, it was more of a moan than the howl of a thousand wolves. The rain had slowed with the wind.

Another lull? Jack prayed that it was. In the eerie calm, Olivia spoke.

"Jack?" she asked quietly, looking up. "If I don't make it, will you tell my dad I love him?"

"Hey," Jack said, his voice catching. "Stop that. You're going to tell him yourself, okay?"

"Yeah, but—"

Olivia trailed off.

Jack clutched her hand tighter.

The strange lightning continued to illuminate their way. They floated on and on through an endless grove of tall, backlit cypresses, the upturned boat steered by an unseen and uncaring hand. Squalls came and went, rain and wind battering them at random, in between lapses of relative calm. During one calm moment, Jack looked skyward and thought he'd glimpsed the moon through the trees. It couldn't be possible, though.

Dark, unseen things bumped up against the boat now and then, causing them both to flinch and squeeze each other's hands more tightly, none hard enough to knock them off yet, though they kept Jack nervously scanning the water, looking for possible exits if they had to swim.

The thought was terrifying. During the lulls, Jack had nothing to do but catalog his own exhaustion, calculating how little he'd drank, eaten, or slept since the morning before.

Adrenalin had propelled him this far, but he wondered what kind of reserves, if any, he had left. He wondered how long he would last in the water.

The boat had twirled around again, putting him in the forward position. He glanced up, but it wasn't what he saw that alarmed him; it was something that he heard. He peered in the direction of the sound.

A deer, its antlers high above the water, swam toward them, its front hooves noisily cleaving the surface as it snorted in distress. When it saw them, it would spook and veer away, or would it?

But as the deer came closer, barely a hundred feet from them, its eyes locked on the upturned boat.

A *frisson* of fear suddenly gripped Jack. The deer might have been swimming for hours. It was looking for anything or any place to keep itself from drowning.

If it tried to mount the boat, it would be a disaster. Its sharp hooves could cleave the boat, and them, to pieces.

Jack nudged Olivia. "I need your voice."

"What?" she said, looking up.

"There," he pointed. "We have company."

Olivia's eyes followed Jack's finger. "Are you serious? Is it coming our way?"

"Looks like it. Start yelling."

They started to scream, Jack pounding with his left hand on the bottom of the boat. Instead of veering away, the deer turned directly toward them, swimming faster.

"No!" Jack screamed. "Come on! Get out of here!"

"It's going to ram us!" Olivia yelled.

The deer was less than twenty feet away now. Jack knew they had only one chance.

"Hold on," he said as calmly as he could. Letting go of Olivia's hand, he pulled the Colt from its nearby holster.

If the gun didn't fire, or if he missed, they were screwed.

"Don't look," Jack said as he cocked the gun, gripped it with two hands, and leveled it at the approaching animal.

"Do we have to kill it?" she asked, staring at the gun.

"I wish we didn't."

"Oh, God." Olivia ducked her head deep into the crook of her left arm.

Jack continued to yell.

When the deer was six feet away, wild-eyed, swimming madly at them, Jack fired, shocked, actually, that the Colt went off.

He'd also changed his mind and his aim; he couldn't bring himself to kill the deer.

Jack watched mesmerized as the bullet took off about six inches of the deer's right antler.

But the boom of the gun and the shock of the bullet did the trick; the buck veered sharply up current, and the boat slid safely by.

Jack watched the deer vanish into the gray wash of the storm. He said a silent prayer for its survival.

"Is it gone?" Olivia asked, looking up.

"Yeah," replied Jack, staring down at his hands. "But I didn't have to kill it. I spooked it away."

"Thank goodness."

"For sure. A big buck can weigh three-hundred pounds. It's not like he wanted to hurt us, but a frightened animal will do what it has to do to survive. It wouldn't have been pretty."

"Right. Survival sucks, doesn't it?"

Jack had no answer for that. He tucked the heavy pistol back into the holster. One shot left.

They joined hands again, drifting on in dreary, edgy silence. Another squall descended to pound them with driving wind and stinging rain. Jack dosed on and off, startled to attention when a wild gust spun the boat around or a particular bright strip of lightning sizzled in the sky. He couldn't figure out what he wanted to do most—sleep, eat, or drink. Getting dry ranked up there, too.

At one point, Jack felt an unfamiliar motion, waking him from a doze. It took him a second to recognize the sensation; the boat was rocking, as if entering a series of waves, but not from a passing boat.

The mystery solved itself. They were sliding from the cover of the swamp on a quickening current of white water, heading toward an open channel being rocked with massive waves. A logjam, like some gargantuan beaver dam, blocked about two thirds of the exit of the channel, pushing the water into a narrow chute where the waves welled up even higher. They couldn't be more than a few minutes away from floating into it.

He nudged Olivia, who was slow to stir.

"What?" she said, exhausted.

"More trouble," said Jack, pointing. "Look over there."

CHAPTER 27

OLIVIA PEERED AHEAD. "What *is* that?"

"A dam, basically. That's gotta be the mouth of a bayou or canal. All the dreck that's floated up on the flood is getting trapped there."

"And that's where we're going?"

"And fast, too. But we *can't* go there. If we get pushed into the logs, we'll be crushed."

"What the hell?"

"Hold on. I need a better look."

Jack rose slowly from his stomach, first to his knees. Pushing up with his hands, he stood as the skiff continued its unsteady slide toward the dam. He'd never ridden a surfboard but imagined it had to be something like this. Struggling to keep his balance, he stood with his feet apart, arms extended like airplane wings.

The waves welled up bigger. As the boat rode up a crest, Jack saw the only possible escape; they'd have to steer themselves around the logjam into the chute, even though the waves heaped up like rapids on a whitewater river.

"Here," he said to Olivia, pulling the pistol from the holster. "Hold this. I'm going to try to swim us out of this."

"How?"

"I'm going over the side. I'll kick like hell, trying to push us toward that bank," he said, pointing. "With any luck, we'll thread the needle into the chute."

"Should I help?"

"Yeah, for now, be my eyes. But if we start getting too close to the log pile, you'll have to jump off and help push. We *can't* get sucked into that thing."

Olivia nodded. "Jesus. Okay."

Jack slipped into the water, flattening his palms against the side of the skiff. He began kicking as violently as he'd ever kicked at any swim meet. The boat began to pick up speed.

A minute later, Jack felt a slow fire burning through his suddenly heavy and fatigued legs. He battled past it, straining to kick harder, his feet breaking the water behind with deep, chugging sounds.

"How are we doing?" he yelled to Olivia.

"I dunno!" she called back. "It's going to be close."

Jack bore down even more, his face barely above the water, sucking in breaths like a racing swimmer, oblivious to anything but his kicking.

Olivia's sharp cry broke his oblivion. "Jack . . . Jack!"

"What?" he called out.

"There's a light!" Olivia yelled, pointing. "Past the logjam, there's a light on the water!"

Jack stopped kicking, trying to push the boat away from him so he could see where Olivia was pointing. At first, he saw nothing. He wondered if she'd seen a flash of lightning.

"Where?" he shouted, exasperated.

But then, there it was—a spotlight that at first blinked on and off and then swept the water in the distance.

"Oh, my God!" Jack cried out. "You're right . . . somebody's there!"

"What if it's bad guys?"

"Who cares right now? We've got to get out of here!"

"Oh, shit," Olivia said, pointing frantically. "The logs! We're getting sucked in too fast!"

Jack moved quickly hand over hand to the front of the boat, looking over and cursing under his breath. Olivia was right.

He fought back a ripple of panic. *Maybe if I push the prow in the direction of the current, I can speed us toward the chute.*

He began to kick frantically. The prow turned and Jack, now between the logjam and the boat, could clearly gauge their chances.

He needed help.

"Olivia," he yelled. "Get over the side! If we both kick, we might have a chance."

"What about the gun?"

"Leave it near the keel. Just come on! If we lose it, we lose it!"

A second later, Olivia was in the water, kicking hard beside him.

"I have a bad feeling about this," she said, staring past Jack at the churning logjam.

"Just kick!" Jack said. "Give it another minute. We're safer with the boat than without it."

A wave, the largest so far, welled up from behind. Instead of rocking the boat, it seemed to gently lift it and push it forward, gaining them distance. Suddenly, their angle looked better.

Jack glanced at Olivia as they continued kicking. "One more big push and then back on the boat. We're gonna make this."

"Promise?" she said, gasping for breath.

"Oh, yeah. This is it. Come on, kick . . . harder! And watch what I do."

They kicked violently in unison as Jack silently counted to ten and then yelled, "Now! Back on . . . go, go, go!"

In a desperate flailing of hands, elbows, and knees, they scrambled back on board just as the boat was picked up by another wave. As Jack regained the center, his hand brushed against the revolver, another small miracle. Forget the holster. He swiped it up and tucked it into the rear waistband of his soggy khakis.

Looking ahead, he saw the first light of dawn edging into the sky, illuminating their path. The chute in front of them raged. Ominous as it was, it beat being pulverized in the logjam.

"Hold on!" he yelled to Olivia. "We're going in."

Then the mysterious light swept the water again, clearly moving their way.

It has to be mounted on a boat, Jack thought. *Is someone looking for us?*

Their impromptu raft dove hard into the trough of the frothing whitewater chute. Jack felt Olivia's hands clutch for his arm. A wave crashed over them, almost sweeping them away.

And then the skiff was rising again, swinging around sideways to the current. Another wave sloshed over them, less violent this time. Jack sucked in a deep breath, wondering how many more strikes they could take before being washed overboard.

As they ascended another crest, a sharp light jabbed into his eyes and just as quickly disappeared as the bobbing boat slid back down a trough.

"A spotlight!" yelled Jack. "Did you see it?"

"I had my eyes closed! All the spray!"

Looking forward, he saw the spot sweeping the tree line on what was clearly a bayou bank beyond the chute. Even over the drone of the wind, he heard the unmistakable deep growl of a diesel engine.

Battling the bouncing of the waves, Jack struggled to his knees, hoping for a better look. When that didn't work, he rose unsteadily to his feet.

Maybe a hundred yards away, the darkened outline of a boat rose from the mist. It was making a slow turn away from them, its spotlight painting a path of retreat.

"No!" he screamed. "*No*! You can't leave us here!"

Fighting off a sudden wave of helplessness, Jack clenched his fists in rage, only to realize that he had a chance.

He swiped the gun from out behind him, cocked the Colt, and aimed it for the sky, praying it would fire one last time. The gun thundered, jolting his hand and reverberating over the slackening din of the storm. And then Jack pitched violently forward as the upturned boat struck something below the water.

Suddenly, he was tumbling toward the churning white maw, twisting in horror to see Olivia tumbling after him.

A scream was still forming on her lips when Jack hit the surface, flat on his back. Olivia came down on top of him, turning her shoulder at the last minute to protect herself, slamming her full weight into his gut.

Jack's lungs sucked desperately for air but found none. His head plunged under the water, and then struck something hard. He felt the boat cascade atop them, driving them down deeper.

Woozy and breathless, Jack found himself aloft in a wet, dark place, unable to do anything but reach up with his arms. He could feel himself beginning to sink on a slackening current.

Somewhere far away, he heard a whining, pitched noise that grew louder and louder.

Maybe a boat engine?

But it didn't matter. The sound couldn't save him. Jack sank lower and lower.

Something brushed against his outstretched right hand, and then was gone. A second later, it returned. Something grabbed him by the arm. And then Jack was rising, rising quickly. As he rose, he opened his eyes. The world was dark and blurry, save for a distant light.

Jack closed his eyes and opened them again, and the light was nearer. His lungs burned, his mind fogged. He felt himself starting to lose consciousness. He was floating toward the light, being tugged upward, and then he saw it—Olivia's face coming close to his.

Jack reached for her, but she was gone.

There was nothing but silence and blackness all around him . . . until something clutched the collar of his shirt, pulling him upward. He felt himself rising again.

And then the blackness returned, and he felt nothing.

CHAPTER 28

"IS THAT REALLY you, Paw-Paw?"

"C'est moi."

Jack blinked into the gloomy light. "Am I dead?"

"No. We tought you might be when we pulled you out dat bayou. You was whiter den the belly of a catfish. But you gonna be okay."

His throat was killing him, probably from all that screaming. His head was a mess. It wasn't just pain but a strange fuzziness.

"Where am I?" he asked, trying to remember what had happened.

"A crewboat. We're headin' to a storm shelter on de west side of Lost Lake."

"Whose boat?"

"You know Mr. Babin who lives on de bayou up from us? His. He leant it to us so we could keep lookin' after de sheriff give up 'cause de storm was comin' and he didn't want nobody caught out in it."

The storm. Right.

"A hurricane?"

"Tropical Storm Irene. Still a perty doggone good blow. Seventy mile-an-hour winds and we got a surge of nine feet already and she's still comin' up."

Jack, who'd been lying flat on a cot under a canvas awning, propped himself up on one elbow, looking at his grandfather. His mop of white hair was sticking up everywhere. He bore three or four days of chin stubble. There were bags under his eyes, but he was smiling.

"Where's Olivia?" Jack asked, a stab of worry suddenly knotting his stomach. He sat up straighter, fighting a wave of nausea. "Is she okay? She is, right? Oh, my God, she has to be."

His grandfather put a reassuring hand on Jack's shoulder.

"It's okay, son. She made it and she'll be fine. She's down below wit' your daddy and your podnah, Spencer Gautreaux, who worked wit' you on dat ambulance deal. He volunteered to come wit' us to look for y'all. We got her out of dem wet clothes and into a blanket and give her some water and a Thermos of soup. Well, gumbo, actually."

A funny thought formed in Jack's mind. *Finally, Olivia is eating some Cajun food.* He managed a wan smile. "Jesus." Jack slumped forward with relief. "Thank God. You have no idea what we've been through, Paw-Paw."

"I know some of it. That li'l gal's somethin'. Tougher than she looks, and she tells a perty doggone good story. She said you were sumpin', too. She's been axin' for you, but you been out now for about two hours."

Jack shook his head. "I don't remember much of what happened after I fell into the water."

"You hit your head bad on a log or stump. Spencer stitched you up and give you a shot of somethin' to numb you."

Jack put his hand on his forehead, feeling the bandage for the first time. "Geez."

His grandfather continued, "Lucky Olivia was dere. She de one who got you to de top. We wouldn'a made it in time."

"I kinda guessed that."

"She tole us she wouldn't be alive wit'out you."

"Well, we stuck together. But you taught me well. You and Dad."

"That's 'cause you a good student. It ain't like I wadn't worried. But I figgered if anybody could make it, you could."

Jack gave him a ghost of a smile. "There were times when I didn't think we were going to."

"You never quit, dat's what mattered. And y'all got quite a few beer-drinking stories to tell. Stories are important."

"Does Momma know we're alive? And my brothers?"

"Dey do now. The captain got on de radio to de shelter and dey managed to get a landline call through. I tink I could hear your momma holler all the way across dis swamp. Dey all gonna get to de hospital before we do, I reckon."

"Okay," Jack said. "Wait, why am I going to the hospital?"

"Both of you goin'. Spencer says you probably got a concussion on top of that bad cut and you both dehydrated. Anyway, best that you get checked out."

Jack nodded. *Makes sense.* "So how did you find us?" he asked his grandfather. "Why were you there?"

"Well, a plane spotted dose signs y'all made and radioed us. So, we knew somebody had made it out dat plane and had set up some kinda camp. We got to dat huntin' camp and knew you'd been dere. Then we run into dat fella y'all put a whuppin' on. He was in a world of hurt. He finally tole us what happened after Spencer volunteered to shoot him up with Novocain. And Gilbert Gautreaux threatened to shoot him wit' a gun."

"Gilbert? Spencer's brother? The deputy sheriff? I thought you said the sheriff had called off the search?"

"He did but Gilbert said if his li'l bro was goin' on dat wild-goose chase in the middle of a storm wit' dem crazy Landrys, he wadn't gonna sit at home. It's a doggone good ting you made such good friends, Jack."

Jack shook his head. "That's crazy."

"Shuh, dat ain't nuttin'. Gilbert, him, got the whole story outta dat fella. He tole Gilbert dem guys who were comin' to cut dat marijuana had hauled ass and lef' him behine. I guess they figgered y'all would get some place and call de police. Gilbert radioed dat in and dey sent a squad of helicopters and rounded up de whole mess 'em. Dey all coolin' deir sorry butts in de parish jail."

"Seriously?"

"Oh, yeah. But there's one ting dat ugly fella said that I wadn't shore about. Somethin' about a big ole black wildcat y'all sicced on him? He said dat ting bit him on da butt bad, but den let him go. I guess dat fella didn't taste good. He looked kinda rough to me."

"Our pet panther," Jack said, managing a chuckle and shaking his head in disbelief. "I'll tell you the whole story later."

"Cain't wait to hear it. I also heard dat y'all put a hurtin' on an airplane. We saw it about half sunk when we got to the bay leadin' to the camp. Wadn't nobody in it. Dem fellas had hauled butt, too. I'da liked to seen dat. Rammin' an airplane wit' a johnboat. I could see how dat could be fun. You might be crazier than me."

Jack laughed. "Ow," he said, wincing. "Don't make me laugh. It hurts."

Paw-Paw smiled. "Anyway, that's how we knew what direction y'all had gone. Dat fella said y'all had took his boat and there was only one way out. But we was lookin' for a camo boat, not for some Huck Finns ridin' on some upside-down skiff."

Jack nodded. "We ran out of gas while we were being chased. We had to sink the boat so they didn't know where we jumped off. But that's another story, too."

"I cain't wait to hear dat one. But you need to go see Olivia. She's down dere fidgety as a cat in a tow sack. She's got stuff she wants to tell you."

Jack's wet clothes were gone, replaced by a green blanket instead. He sat up, swinging his feet from the cot to the floor. The motion made him dizzy, and he paused to massage his forehead. All of a sudden, it hit him, and he looked at his grandfather.

"Oh, God! What about Olivia's dad?" he asked. "Was he found? Is he alive? We heard that only one—"

Paw-Paw cut him off. "I cain't say, Jack, 'cause Olivia wants to tell you herself. Go see her now. It's down dat li'l ladder. Be careful. It's tricky. I awmost broke my neck goin' down dat ting."

Jack stood, steadying himself for a minute on his grandfather's arm. He climbed down the small spiral ladder, into the well-lit cargo compartment of the crew boat. The thrum of the diesel was muted by heavy metal walls.

He saw his dad, Jake, and his friend, Spencer, in one corner and was about to wave to them when Olivia, draped in a blanket identical to his, ran toward him. Before he knew it, she was in his arms.

"Oh, my God, Jack," Olivia said, leaning against him. "That creepy man . . . he told the truth. They found my dad and Joe, and it was my father who made it. It's not good. He's in a coma, but he's alive. But poor Joe . . . he's dead, Jack. His family. His wife, his kids. I can't imagine. It seems so unfair."

Olivia buried her face in Jack's chest, sobbing.

Jack pulled her closer. "I'm so sorry, Olivia. Jesus, yes, Joe's poor family. But your dad . . . it's great news that he made it. Do we know anything else?"

She pulled back and looked at Jack, tears in her eyes. "I don't know much more except that he's alive and in a local hospital. Your dad says I can see him tonight. He was conscious for a while when they brought him in, and he refused to be evacuated until we were found. I can't even . . . I can't . . ."

She broke down again.

This time, Jack couldn't hold back his own tears. He couldn't find his voice through his own sobs. It was the strangest mixture of sadness and relief he'd ever felt.

More arms enfolded them and, after a few minutes, Jack could finally speak.

"Hey, Dad, hey Spencer," he said, clearing his throat. "Sorry. It's—"

"Sorry for what?" his dad said. "Whatever you're feeling, you've earned it. Y'all both have. We're all sad for Joe and his family and everybody—I mean everybody we know and lots of people we don't—is praying for Olivia's daddy."

Jack nodded.

"You got a hard head, bro," Spencer said, punching Jack playfully on the shoulder. "It's a good thing, too. You took a hit."

"Hey, Spencer," said Jack, wiping away a streak of tears. "Thanks for coming. I owe you big-time."

"Not really. I know you'd do the same for me. But maybe you can take me to that secret duck-hunting spot you've been bragging about. Or just get your momma to invite me over for gumbo."

"Consider it done," said Jack, smiling weakly.

"C'mon, Spencer," Jack's dad said. "Let's give them some time alone. We'll be up top with Paw-Paw, if y'all need anything. We should be at the landing in about twenty minutes. There's an ambulance waiting to take y'all to the hospital, assuming the roads are clear. The storm's finally moving out."

When they had gone, Olivia stepped from his arms, still holding his hands in hers. She wiped the last of her tears away with the edge of her blanket.

"Your family's great, Jack. Your dad couldn't've been nicer to me. And your grandfather is something else. He reminds me of you."

"Yeah. I've heard that before," Jack said.

Olivia tried to smile. "I can't wait to meet everyone else."

"I'm sure they'll all be at the hospital waiting for us."

They lapsed into silence, gazing intently at each other until Olivia finally spoke. "I can't believe we're here... well... here alive. If you hadn't stood up and fired that gun, your dad said they were turning around. They never would have seen us."

"Thank God for the Colt," said Jack. "And for you for not giving up on me. Paw-Paw said it was you who pulled me to the surface."

"I have never been so terrified, actually. The first time I grabbed you, you slipped away. I thought I'd lost you. I didn't think I had the energy to try again, but I knew if I didn't, well, I couldn't bear the thought."

Jack pulled her close. "I know. I owe you everything. Everything."

"No," she replied. "It's not like that. It's because we stuck together, helped each other when it counted. That's why we're here."

She paused. "Of course, when we're finally actually out of here, I'm *never* going even near this swamp again."

Jack pulled away, nodding in sympathy. "I can understand that," he said, "but, who knows, maybe one day you'll change your mind. And as Paw-Paw just told me, we have enough beer-drinking stories for a lifetime."

Olivia managed a weak laugh. "Ugh, beer. Not my thing. I'm strictly a scotch sort of girl. Didn't I tell you that?"

Jack shook his head, managing a smile. "Seriously? I think the stuff tastes like lighter fluid myself. Not that I've drunk a lot of it. Well, hardly any."

"Now, now. I get the scotch thing from my father, and I realize it's a bit of an acquired taste. But you've got to stick to the good stuff. 'No drinking bilge water.' That's Terrence's number-one rule."

"I see."

"You have to try single malt. Just wait until you come to Maine. I know where my father hides the key to his secret stash."

Jack tried to process this.

Is she actually inviting me to Maine instead of theoretically inviting me? To secretly drink from her dad's stash?

Jack Cane Landry encircled Olivia FitzGerald in his arms and when, instead of resisting, she pulled him closer, he whispered, "What, are you *trying* to get me in trouble?"

She pulled gently away and smiled.

"Maybe I am," she said.

CHAPTER 29

A YEAR LATER...

"So, let me get this straight," Jack said. "We're actually getting on that thing?"

"It's not *that* crowded," Olivia said. "I've seen it worse."

"Not possible," Jack said, shoving his hands nervously into his jacket pockets.

"Come on," Olivia said, laughing. "Follow me. It'll be fine. And I promise, no alligators. Although, there might be other things."

It was Columbus Day weekend and Jack, standing with Olivia on the East 96th Street platform of the 6 subway line, had been in New York City for three days now. The train was just pulling in.

Jack peered into cars as they rattled by, slowing for a stop. He'd never seen so many people jammed in so tight before. Anywhere. Ever.

He was staying with Olivia and her Aunt Georgina, Terrence FitzGerald's sister, in a guest room of the family's Fifth Avenue apartment. He could see Central Park from his window, which was just... unbelievable.

Although not more unbelievable than the art that lined the walls, the floor-to-ceiling windows, the grand piano, the sculptures in the foyer, or the part-time cook and full-time housekeeper.

They were so obviously fond of Olivia, and so aware of their survival story, that they treated them both like rock stars.

Jack didn't know what to say except, "thank you," and "you shouldn't have," and "that would be great, thanks."

He would always add, "Olivia was the real hero."

The only thing the apartment was missing was Terrence

FitzGerald, who had died three months after the crash in a hospital in New York. Jack had booked a plane ticket for his funeral, but a blizzard blew in and canceled all the flights into the city for three days. He'd been heartbroken that he couldn't be by Olivia's side.

Now, a year after the crash, she'd invited him to join her at a memorial celebrating her father's life. FitzGerald had been a member of the legendary Explorers Club. It's where he was being honored posthumously for his Amazon expeditions and his generosity to the organization.

Jack had been blown away after Googling the Explorers Club. The members were people like Admiral Peary, the first person to sail to the North Pole, and Sir Edmund Hillary, the first man to climb Mount Everest. Not to mention astronauts who'd walked on the moon.

The Explorer's Club event was a dinner. He and Olivia were headed to lunch with friends who couldn't make the evening ceremony. They were going to her dad's favorite Thai restaurant, near his Times Square office where he'd conducted his Broadway play business.

It wasn't Olivia's favorite restaurant, but the fact that it had been her father's was all that mattered.

Grabbing him by the hand, Olivia led Jack onto the subway, miraculously finding a space at the metal rail just inside and left of the door. Jack had fretted he might be claustrophobic on the subway, but . . . well . . . so long as he was with Olivia, he felt fine.

"Hold on," she said, pulling him close. "It's only four stops to 59th Street. We can get the N to Times Square."

Jack grinned at her. "Is the next train going to be as bad as this one?"

Olivia smiled back. "Are you kidding? Far worse."

"Something to look forward to," Jack said as a recorded voice instructed them to, "Stand clear of the closing doors, please."

"You'll get used to it," Olivia said. "I promise."

Jack wondered about that. He looked around as the train lurched to a start. The whole world was in this subway car, people of every age and color and style of dress. It seemed like a galaxy away from Black Bayou, Louisiana. Jack wondered what Paw-Paw would make of it all.

"I'm glad you came, Jack," Olivia said, smiling over at him. "It means a lot to me."

"Of course. I wouldn't have missed it for anything. I still can't really believe it. I'm just so sorry."

"He put up a good fight," she said, her smile faltering just the tiniest bit. "And I'm glad I had the time with him that I had. He was only conscious for four days of that time, but it was something, at least. And it was *him*."

Jack tilted his forehead against hers for a second. "How are you holding up?"

"Better now that my aunt's here full time. I was in a funk for months. Well, you know some of that. That was my disappearing period. I'm sorry we lost touch for that time, but I was in a bad place and just needed the alone time, I guess. It's better now. I'm okay most days, others not so great. But my father would want me to carry on. That's what he told me in the hospital. That's what we FitzGeralds do, you know. We carry on."

"That sounds like your dad," Jack said. "Or, you know what? Actually, it sounds like you."

"I still cry a lot," Olivia admitted. "Like, pretty much constantly on some days."

Jack nodded. "Paw-Paw says grief is a big rock in the road and there's no way around it. You just have to go over it, which takes time. My grandma died when I was little. Paw-Paw's still sad, but he says it's easier now, because he only remembers the good things. And remembering the good things . . . it's like a kind of happiness."

She nodded. "Maybe. I don't know if I *can* get over it. Or want to."

"Hey, I've seen what you can do when your back's against the wall. And my back, too. You're my hero, you know."

Olivia smiled again, a real smile this time. "It feels so long ago, doesn't it? Like a lifetime. Or several thousand lifetimes."

"I agree. My family sends their love, by the way. I don't even know how many candles my mom's lit for you and your dad and mom. How is your mom, anyway?"

"Okay. I'm still not sure she's gotten her head around the fact that my father's really gone."

"Maybe that's for the good?"

Olivia shrugged. "Maybe. But, hey, do you mind if we don't talk about this now? I mean, I'm glad we *can* talk about it, but today, I just want to concentrate on my father being honored, and I need to be in a good space for the event."

"Of course," Jack said, pulling her close with the next sway of the train car.

※

After their rescue, Olivia had remained in Louisiana for a week, staying with Jack's family until her father was deemed stable enough to be transferred by jet to New York. Jack had found himself momentarily fretting over these arrangements; how would a person who lived in what Jack could only imagine was a lavish apartment above Central Park adjust to life in a neat but modest farmhouse on the bayou shared by five people—six when Paw-Paw walked down from his little guesthouse on the Landry crawfish pond to have meals with the family.

The answer was that the Landry family enfolded Olivia into their home like a big, soft blanket, giving her room when she needed it and comfort when she wanted it. One morning, when Jack overheard Olivia exchanging French phrases with his mother in the kitchen, both laughing easily about something that had been misunderstood, he felt a surge of relief and happiness that he hadn't expected. He realized he needn't have worried.

One day, his mom called him aside and said a thing he hadn't expected.

"Jack, *cher*, we all have come to love Olivia. She's a seriously good and interesting and beautiful person. I can see how you might love her, too . . . be in love with her. No one could blame you."

She then took Jack into her arms and whispered, "Just be mindful of your heart and remember that, though she may even love you as well, she comes from a place far from the place you come from. And I don't mean just distance. Just be careful. Heartbreak is no fun."

Jack had told his mom not to worry. But—

On the fourth day after their rescue, a reporter for the local newspaper showed up at the Landry farmhouse. Jack only agreed to talk with her after Olivia said it was okay. She politely declined the interview, explaining it was still too raw for her.

The story created a sensation at Jack's school, and for a few days, he got a fleeting glimpse of celebrity. He didn't like it, and to his relief, the commotion died down after a couple of weeks. A few of the girls in his class talked to him more than they used to, and some of the guys still occasionally joked about his and Olivia's sleeping arrangements in the swamp. Jack tried to brush it all off.

But, still, the comments bugged him. People had no idea what it had been like out there. And he wasn't going to say more than he already had. The story belonged to him and Olivia; Jack felt strangely protective of it.

And anyway, who would understand?

They'd come back with bumps, scrapes, bug bites, dehydration, Jack with a mild concussion. On the outside, they'd healed. But a lot of days, on the inside, it felt like nothing had really changed. And sometimes it felt like *everything* had.

Jack had begun to rethink a lot of things. Maybe everything.

He and Olivia had stayed in contact, well, mostly in contact, except for those weeks when, as she had since explained, her grief became too awful to share and she had gone completely silent. Jack's mom had counseled patience, and Jack knew in his head that his mother was giving him good advice. But that's not what his heart felt, and as the weeks dragged on, he despaired of ever hearing from her again.

But then Olivia surprised him, as she had often done in the past, reemerging with a text that said, "I miss you. Call me tomorrow." Jack did and they had kept in touch, mostly texting, sometimes emailing, the occasional long phone call. Jack was relieved but tried not to make too much of things—or at least, he pretended not to make too much of things. For he knew that no matter what they'd gone through together in the swamp, things were bound to be different in the real world.

His mom had guessed his heart. Jack had fallen completely and utterly in love with Olivia. He knew it was stupid yet inevitable. There were thousands of miles separating them. They led completely different lives and were going in different directions.

But for the accident of being tossed together in the swamp, he would never have gotten to know her this way. *I don't have a chance with her,* his mind repeated over and over.

Still . . . his heart said.

As the subway lurched from stop to stop, Olivia's body warm against his, Jack couldn't help hoping his mind was wrong.

"Come on, there's a car downstairs."

Jack, who'd been instructed to pack for three days, was closing the zipper on his suitcase when Olivia poked her head through the door, knocking at the same time. It was five in the morning.

"And the car is taking us . . . ?"

She smiled mysteriously. "Road trip," she told him chirpily, leading the way downstairs and out into the chilly quiet of Fifth Avenue. A driver in a dark suit and black hat pulled open the rear door of a black Mercedes SUV.

"Feel free to sleep," Olivia told him, sliding into the seat next to him. "Here, I brought pillows." She reached behind her, handing one to him before tucking the other against the door next to her.

"Are you sure?" Jack asked.

"I'll wake you up when it gets exciting," she promised.

Jack buckled his seat belt. Stretching out his legs, he leaned back against the seat and fell asleep almost instantly.

By the time Olivia nudged him awake, a bright fall sun was shining through the tinted windows of the SUV.

"See the sign?" she asked.

Jack peered out the window.

Maine.

"Seriously?" he asked, turning to look at her.

She grinned. "I told you I'd get you up here. Besides, I wanted you to see the cottage. My aunt thinks it might be time to sell it. Terrence left it to me, but it's a lot to take care of, and there are so many memories."

She trailed off. "I haven't really decided yet. I haven't even been back here since the summer before we traveled to the swamp. I was kind of waiting for you."

"Really? Why?"

Olivia shrugged. "I don't know. There's something comforting about you."

Jack let that sink in. "Well, that's good to know."

She nudged him in the side again. "I think it's the Cajun accent."

"I don't have an accent," Jack protested.

"Don't worry," Olivia told him, grinning. "It's adorable."

They drove on through Maine, speeding along a freeway lined in tall evergreens, seeing the occasional moose-crossing sign, although, disappointing to Jack, no actual moose.

His mind trailed back to the Explorers Club. The event had been different than Jack envisioned—less formal. It was more of a group of friends getting together to tell stories about Terrence FitzGerald. Jack had laughed out loud at some of them. Olivia's speech at the end had been incredible—funny, moving, and real. She hadn't even seemed nervous, but when she'd slipped back into her chair afterward, she'd grabbed his hand and whispered, "I thought I was going to faint."

"You were amazing," Jack had told her. "And I would've caught you."

The car left the freeway for a rural road that ran past farmsteads, purpling blueberry fields, and an occasional shockingly beautiful view of the sea. After about twenty minutes, they came to a narrow rocky lane marked by a modest wooden sign that said *FitzGerald.*

A mile later, the cottage appeared. It sat in a clearing, hemmed in on either side by spruce and hemlock, a red-shingled structure with soaring windows, a green metal roof, an open deck on one side, and a cavernous screen porch on the other.

Jack laughed.

Olivia's *cottage* was way bigger than Jack's actual house.

"Wait until you see the view," Olivia told him.

From the wide windows, a pebbled beach framed a sweeping cove with a rocky, fir-clad island in the center. A long pier jutted out at one end of the beach. Under the clear, blue fall sky and early afternoon sun, it was breathtaking.

"Our boat's usually just off the end of the pier," Olivia explained, "but it's in dry dock right now. Still, you get the idea."

"The *Miss Olivia*, right? I'm sorry I missed her," said Jack.

"Well, next time you'll have to come in high summer. Even if we sell this place, I think I'd buy something small nearby. I can't see not coming to Maine."

"That would be great . . . next summer, I mean. This is beyond incredible. Do you even have neighbors?"

"Maybe a mile away. We have four-hundred acres. The entire cove is our oceanfront. Wanna take a walk? There's a trail that runs down by the water. Afterwards we can make a fire in the great room. Or, actually, *you* can make a fire. My aunt and her friend should be here by dinnertime."

"Yeah, I'd love that," he said.

Jack was surprised. Even after Olivia had revealed the surprise in the car, he didn't actually expect that they would have the place to themselves.

On the walk, Jack let the sea breeze and evergreen aroma wash over him. He breathed in the cool, pristine October air. He could not stop gaping at the ever-changing views. He closed his eyes and tried to picture what it would be like here in full summer. He could see why Olivia loved it. It was just as wild and beautiful and mysterious as the Great Atchafalaya, but in a radically different way.

Back inside, he knelt before the massive stone fireplace, smiling at how organized everything was—a wooden basket of kindling, neatly stacked oak logs of appropriate size, and an elongated propane fire starter.

Soon, he and Olivia were sitting before a roaring fire.

As if by magic, Mary, the caretaker, appeared, carrying a tray of hot chocolate and fresh-baked chocolate chip cookies.

To Jack, it seemed like something out of a movie.

She welcomed Jack with a smile, telling him and Olivia that a roast chicken and Olivia's favorite vegetarian casserole were already in the oven.

"I thought I smelled something good," said Jack.

Mary smiled appreciatively and headed back toward the kitchen.

Olivia grinned at him, handing him a cookie. "Are you ready for my second surprise?"

"Sure," Jack mumbled, not wishing to speak with food in his mouth.

"So . . . I'm not actually at Harvard. I know I told you I was going to go, but I decided to take a gap year."

"Seriously?" Jack asked, swallowing a bite of the cookie. "Why?"

"I don't really know. After everything that happened, I just didn't want to go somewhere so soon that reminded me so much of my father. Does that sound weird?"

He shook his head. "No, I get it. But what are you going to do instead?"

"Well, I've been waiting to tell you in person. Work, volunteer, maybe. Don't worry, Harvard's saving a spot for me next year."

"I think it's a great idea," Jack said. "So, where are you going to volunteer?"

Olivia leaned back against the couch, watching him carefully.

"You want to guess?"

"Hmm, Paris?"

"No."

"Please tell me you're not disappearing into Africa."

"No."

"The Amazon?"

"Too far away."

"Fine, I give up."

"Part of the year I'll be in Louisiana, post-Katrina recovery stuff."

"What!"

Jack was surprised how loud the word came out.

He stared at her intently. "Seriously? I thought you were never going back to the swamp?"

"Me, too," Olivia said, grinning. "But you know how my dad is. In the hospital, when he was awake, he told me how much he loved it down there. He was planning on going back, right away, once he got better."

"Really?"

"He wanted to help. He said that, after Katrina, the bayou and its people needed all the friends it could get. Including us. He was clearly taken with the place."

Jack shook his head, trying to wrap his mind around Olivia's words. "So, what exactly are you going to do?"

"I don't know yet. I was actually going to ask you for ideas."

A small thump came from the fireplace. Jack looked over to see that the logs had separated. The fire was getting smoky.

"One sec," he said, pointing. "We have a lot to talk about, but let me fix that first."

It took a few minutes to get the fire roaring again. When he sat back on the couch next to Olivia, he knew what he was going to say.

"Okay, I'll think of some volunteering ideas. But here's the thing. You're not the only one with news."

"Really?" Olivia asked. "What's yours?"

"So, there's this state school above New Orleans," Jack told her, his voice nervous. "Maybe five-thousand students at most. It's not fancy or anything, but it has a good creative writing program, and I applied and got in. Not this fall, obviously. I'll start in January," he added. "But I'm doing it. I'm going to college."

"What!" Olivia exclaimed, her cheeks reddening. She broke into an incredibly fetching smile, threw her arms around Jack, and kissed him on the cheek.

"Jack, that's seriously incredible! I'm so proud of you!"

Jack pulled her close, breathing her in.

"You're kind of the reason I'm going," Jack said. "I mean, I still want my own swamp-tour company someday. But like you said, doing one thing doesn't mean you can't do the other."

Olivia pulled away, looking at him. "You're going to do amazing. I know it. You're already a really good writer."

"Maybe," he said. "I just want to get through the first semester."

"Are you going to commute? Or live on campus?"

"On campus. All the freshmen have to. But it's only sixty miles from the farm. I'll be able to make it home on most weekends."

"No, you won't," Olivia told him. "At least not every weekend."

Jack drew back, puzzled. "What are you saying? Why not?" he asked.

"Because no matter which program I choose, I'll be living in New Orleans. It's the base for almost all the Katrina volunteer groups down there. So, you'll have to come to see *me* now and then. I'll have an apartment of some kind. Probably with some roommates. But still."

Jack stared at her.

"I mean, if you want to," Olivia added quickly, pushing her hair back. "Obviously, you don't, like, *have* to, if you . . ."

Jack smiled so wide it almost hurt. He pulled her close, cutting her off. "Have I mentioned how much I love you?" he asked.

A second later, he realized what he'd said.

"I mean . . . oh, wait. Did I really say that? Oh, God, I uh, I mean . . ."

Jack could feel his face turning boiled-crawfish red.

Olivia didn't respond. Instead, she stood abruptly, pulling him up by the hand. "Come on," she said. "I'll show you your room upstairs."

He couldn't speak. Humiliation poured through him in red-hot waves.

What have I done?

"You could probably use a nap, right?" Olivia said. "We woke up so early. And I mean, we have a couple of hours before my aunt and her friend get here."

"Sure," Jack managed to say, unable to meet her gaze, his voice deflated. "Uh, so, what are you going to do?"

Olivia smiled coyly. "I'm coming with you."

Jack turned toward her. He was blushing again, but for another reason.

"Coming with me?"

He blurted it out like an excited child, thoroughly confused.

"Yes, if that's okay with you. Besides, I have something I want to show you."

"Really? Like, a surprise?"

"Well, I don't know. It's a butterfly, but maybe you've seen one like it before."

"A butterfly?"

Jack canvassed his mind for a butterfly he might have seen with Olivia. And then it hit him. The day of the leeches, the butterfly in that delicate spot.

Jack's mouth hung open, beyond speechless.

Olivia stepped into his arms, drew him near, and kissed him tenderly on his cheek. "Look," she said, smiling. "I don't know what college will bring, Jack, but I do know one thing. You will always be in my heart, and I hope I will be in yours. We shared something that no one understands but us."

Olivia paused, then said, "Terrence used to say, 'People who love each other look after each other' and I could never really quite understand exactly what he meant by that. Until now. That's why we're here, why we survived. We looked after each other in the swamp when it really mattered. And I think we could both use some looking after now, right?"

Jack could only nod, his amazement growing.

She pulled him closer, whispering mischievously, "I was pretty sure you would remember my butterfly, Jack Landry, so I thought I'd let you see it up close again. Because it's entirely possible that, well, should I say it? I love you, too."

ACKNOWLEDGMENTS

TO EARLY READERS of this work, notably Terry Tannen and Elizabeth Seay, and Douglas Robertson, formerly of Bay Academy in Daphne, Alabama, and his terrific students in the Southern Mystique class for their candid and helpful feedback. And to my great friend Paige Buckner for her assist in that regard. And finally, to Bizu Horwitz, whose insights compelled some helpful revisions and clarifications.